D1201429

# *Greatest*
# *Short*
# *Stories*

VOLUME II

—

AMERICAN

P. F. COLLIER & SON CORPORATION

PUBLISHERS          NEW YORK

PRINTED IN THE UNITED STATES OF AMERICA

Copyright, 1915,
BY P. F. COLLIER & SON

Copyright, 1940,
BY P. F. COLLIER & SON CORPORATION

TL


The use of the copyrighted stories and copyrighted translations
in this collection has been authorized by the authors
or their representatives. The translations made
especially for this collection are covered by the general copyright.

PRINTED IN THE UNITED STATES OF AMERICA

# CONTENTS

PAGE

1. AN EXPERIMENT IN MISERY . . . . . . 5
   *Stephen Crane*

2. THE BRIGADE COMMANDER . . . . . . 23
   *J. W. De Forest*

3. THE DENVER EXPRESS . . . . . . . 69
   *A. A. Hayes*

4. THE AMBITIOUS GUEST . . . . . . . 109
   *Nathaniel Hawthorne*

5. MY TERMINAL MORAINE . . . . . . . 125
   *Frank R. Stockton*

6. THE GOLD BUG . . . . . . . . . 183
   *Edgar Allan Poe*

7. THE DAMNED THING . . . . . . . . 241
   *Ambrose Bierce*

8. THE LUCK OF ROARING CAMP . . . . . 257
   *Bret Harte*

9. MARJORIE DAW . . . . . . . . . 277
   *Thomas Bailey Aldrich*

10. THEY BROUGHT THEIR WOMEN . . . . 311
    *Edna Ferber*

11. BIG BLONDE . . . . . . . . . . 345
    *Dorothy Parker*

1

# CONTENTS

# AN EXPERIMENT IN MISERY

## BY STEPHEN CRANE

# AN EXPERIMENT IN MISERY

## BY STEPHEN CRANE

IT WAS late at night, and a fine rain was swirling softly down, causing the pavements to glisten with hue of steel and blue and yellow in the rays of the innumerable lights. A youth was trudging slowly, without enthusiasm, with his hands buried deep in his trousers' pockets, toward the downtown places where beds can be hired for coppers. He was clothed in an aged and tattered suit, and his derby was a marvel of dust-covered crown and torn rim. He was going forth to eat as the wanderer may eat, and sleep as the homeless sleep. By the time he had reached City Hall Park he was so completely plastered with yells of "bum" and "hobo," and with various unholy epithets that small boys had applied to him at intervals, that he was in a state of the most profound dejection. The sifting rain saturated the old velvet collar of his overcoat, and as the wet cloth pressed against his neck, he felt that there no longer could be pleasure in life. He looked about him searching for an outcast of highest degree that they too might share miseries, but the lights threw a quivering glare over

From "Men, Women and Boats," copyright, 1898, 1902, 1906, by Alfred A. Knopf, Inc.

rows and circles of deserted benches that glistened damply, showing patches of wet sod behind them. It seemed that their usual freights had fled on this night to better things. There were only squads of well-dressed Brooklyn people who swarmed towards the bridge.

The young man loitered about for a time and then went shuffling off down Park Row. In the sudden descent in style of the dress of the crowd he felt relief, and as if he were at last in his own country. He began to see tatters that matched his tatters. In Chatham Square there were aimless men strewn in front of saloons and lodging houses, standing sadly, patiently, reminding one vaguely of the attitudes of chickens in a storm. He aligned himself with these men, and turned slowly to occupy himself with the flowing life of the great street.

Through the mists of the cold and storming night, the cable cars went in silent procession, great affairs shining with red and brass, moving with formidable power, calm and irresistible, dangerful and gloomy, breaking silence only by the loud fierce cry of the gong. Two rivers of people swarmed along the sidewalks, spattered with black mud, which made each shoe leave a scar-like impression. Overhead elevated trains with a shrill grinding of the wheels stopped at the station, which upon its leglike pillars seemed to resemble some monstrous kind of crab squatting over the street. The quick fat puffings of the engines could be heard. Down an alley there were somber curtains of purple and black, on which street lamps dully glittered like embroidered flowers.

A saloon stood with a voracious air on a corner. A sign leaning against the front of the doorpost announced "Free hot soup tonight!" The swing doors, snapping to and fro like ravenous lips, made gratified smacks as the saloon gorged itself with plump men, eating with astounding and endless appetite, smiling in some indescribable manner as the men came from all directions like sacrifices to a heathenish superstition.

Caught by the delectable sign the young man allowed himself to be swallowed. A bartender placed a schooner of dark and portentous beer on the bar. Its monumental form upreared until the froth a-top was above the crown of the young man's brown derby.

"Soup over there, gents," said the bartender affably. A little yellow man in rags and the youth grasped their schooners and went with speed toward a lunch counter, where a man with oily but imposing whiskers ladled genially from a kettle until he had furnished his two mendicants with a soup that was steaming hot, and in which there were little floating suggestions of chicken. The young man, sipping his broth, felt the cordiality expressed by the warmth of the mixture, and he beamed at the man with oily but imposing whiskers, who was presiding like a priest behind an altar. "Have some more, gents?" he inquired

7

of the two sorry figures before him. The little yellow man accepted with a swift gesture, but the youth shook his head and went out, following a man whose wondrous seediness promised that he would have a knowledge of cheap lodging-houses.

On the sidewalk he accosted the seedy man. "Say, do you know a cheap place to sleep?"

The other hesitated for a time, gazing sideways. Finally he nodded in the direction of the street, "I sleep up there," he said, "when I've got the price."

"How much?"

"Ten cents."

The young man shook his head dolefully. "That's too rich for me."

At that moment there approached the two a reeling man in strange garments. His head was a fuddle of bushy hair and whiskers, from which his eyes peered with a guilty slant. In a close scrutiny it was possible to distinguish the cruel lines of a mouth which looked as if its lips had just closed with satisfaction over some tender and piteous morsel. He appeared like an assassin steeped in crimes performed awkwardly.

But at this time his voice was tuned to the coaxing key of an affectionate puppy. He looked at the men with wheedling eyes, and began to sing a little melody for charity.

"Say, gents, can't yeh give a poor feller a couple of cents t' git a bed? I got five, and I gits anudder two I gits me a bed. Now, on th' square, gents, can't yeh jest gimme two cents t' git a bed?

Now, yeh know how a respecter'ble gentlem'ns feels when he's down on his luck, an' I——"

The seedy man, staring with imperturbable countenance at a train which clattered overhead, interrupted in an expressionless voice—"Ah, go t' h——!"

But the youth spoke to the prayerful assassin in tones of astonishment and inquiry. "Say, you must be crazy! Why don't yeh strike somebody that looks as if they had money?"

The assassin, tottering about on his uncertain legs, and at intervals brushing imaginary obstacles from before his nose, entered into a long explanation of the psychology of the situation. It was so profound that it was unintelligible.

When he had exhausted the subject, the young man said to him: "Let's see th' five cents."

The assassin wore an expression of drunken woe at this sentence, filled with suspicion of him. With a deeply pained air he began to fumble in his clothing, his red hands trembling. Presently he announced in a voice of bitter grief, as if he had been betrayed—"There's only four."

"Four," said the young man thoughtfully. "Look here, I'm a stranger here, an' if ye'll steer me to your cheap joint I'll find the other three."

The assassin's countenance became instantly radiant with joy. His whiskers quivered with the wealth of his alleged emotions. He seized the young man's hand in a transport of delight and friendliness.

9

"B' Gawd," he cried, "if ye'll do that, b' Gawd, I'd say yeh was a damned good fellow, I would, an' I'd remember yeh all m' life, I would, b' Gawd, an' if I ever got a chance I'd return the compliment"—he spoke with drunken dignity—"b' Gawd, I'd treat yeh white, I would."

The young man drew back, looking at the assassin coldly. "Oh, that's all right," he said. "You show me th' joint—that's all y' got t' do."

The assassin, gesticulating gratitude, led the young man along a dark street. Finally he stopped before a little dusty door. He raised his hand impressively. "Look-a-here," he said, and there was a thrill of deep and ancient wisdom upon his face, "I've brought yeh here, an' that's my part, ain't it? If th' place don't suit yeh, yeh needn't git mad at me, need yeh? There won't be no bad feelin', will there?"

"No," said the young man.

The assassin waved his arm tragically, and led the march up the steep stairway. On the way the young man furnished the assassin with three pennies. At the top a man with benevolent spectacles looked at them through a hole in a board. He collected their money, wrote some names on a register, and speedily was leading the two men along a gloom-shrouded corridor.

Shortly after the beginning of this journey the young man felt his liver turn white, for from the dark and secret places of the building there suddenly came to his nostrils strange and unspeakable odors, that assailed him like malignant diseases with wings. They seemed to be from human bodies closely packed in dens; the exhalations from a hundred pairs of reeking lips; the fumes from a thousand bygone debauches; the expression of a thousand present miseries.

A man, naked save for a little snuff-colored undershirt, was parading sleepily along the corridor. He rubbed his eyes, and giving vent to a prodigious yawn, demanded to be told the time.

"Half-past one."

The man yawned again. He opened a door, and for a moment his form was outlined against a black, opaque interior. To this door came the three men, and as it was again opened the unholy odors rushed out like fiends, so the young man had to struggle as against an overpowering wind.

It was some time before the youth's eyes were good in the intense gloom within, but the man with benevolent spectacles led him skillfully, pausing but a moment to deposit the limp assassin upon a cot. He took the youth to a cot that lay tranquilly by the window, and showing him a tall locker for clothes that stood near the head with the ominous air of a tombstone, left him.

The youth sat on his cot and peered about him. There was a gas-jet in a distant part of the room, that burned a small flickering orange-hued flame. It caused vast masses of tumbled shadows in all parts of the place, save where, immediately about it, there was a little grey haze. As the

young man's eyes became used to the darkness,
he could see upon the cots that thickly littered
the floor the forms of men sprawled out, lying in
deathlike silence, or heaving and snoring with
tremendous effort, like stabbed fish.

The youth locked his derby and his shoes in the
mummy case near him, and then lay down with an
old and familiar coat around his shoulders. A
blanket he handled gingerly, drawing it over part
of the coat. The cot was covered with leather,
and as cold as melting snow. The youth was
obliged to shiver for some time on this affair,
which was like a slab. Presently, however, his
chill gave him peace, and during this period of
leisure from it he turned his head to stare at his
friend the assassin, whom he could dimly discern
where he lay sprawled on a cot in the abandon of a
man filled with drink. He was snoring with incredible vigor. His wet hair and beard dimly glistened, and his inflamed nose shone with subdued
lustre like a red light in a fog.

Within reach of the youth's hand was one who
lay with yellow breast and shoulders bare to the
cold drafts. One arm hung over the side of the
cot, and the fingers lay full length upon the wet
cement floor of the room. Beneath the inky
brows could be seen the eyes of the man exposed
by the partly opened lids. To the youth it seemed
that he and this corpse-like being were exchang-
ing a prolonged stare, and that the other threatened with his eyes. He drew back, watching his

neighbor from the shadows of his blanket edge. The man did not move once through the night, but lay in this stillness as of death like a body stretched out expectant of the surgeon's knife.

And all through the room could be seen the tawny hues of naked flesh, limbs thrust into the darkness, projecting beyond the cots; upreared knees, arms hanging long and thin over the cot edges. For the most part they were statuesque, carven, dead. With the curious lockers standing about like tombstones, there was a strange effect of a graveyard where bodies were merely flung.

Yet occasionally could be seen limbs wildly tossing in fantastic nightmare gestures, accompanied by guttural cries, grunts, oaths. And there was one fellow off in a gloomy corner, who in his dreams was oppressed by some frightful calamity, for of a sudden he began to utter long wails that went almost like yells from a hound, echoing wailfully and weird through this chill place of tombstones where men lay like the dead.

The sound in its high piercing beginnings, that dwindled to final melancholy moans, expressed a red and grim tragedy of the unfathomable possibilities of the man's dreams. But to the youth these were not merely the shrieks of a vision-pierced man: they were an utterance of the meaning of the room and its occupants. It was to him the protest of the wretch who feels the touch of the imperturbable granite wheels, and who then cries with an impersonal eloquence, with a strength not from him, giving voice to the wail of a whole section, a class, a people. This, weaving into the young man's brain, and mingling with his views of the vast and sombre shadows that, like mighty black fingers, curled around the naked bodies, made the young man so that he did not sleep, but lay carving the biographies for these men from his meagre experience. At times the fellow in the corner howled in a writhing agony of his imaginations.

Finally a long lance-point of grey light shot through the dusty panes of the window. Without, the young man could see roofs drearily white in the dawning. The point of light yellowed and grew brighter, until the golden rays of the morning sun came in bravely and strong. They touched with radiant color the form of a small fat man, who snored in stuttering fashion. His round and shiny bald head glowed suddenly with the valor of a decoration. He sat up, blinked at the sun, swore fretfully, and pulled his blanket over the ornamental splendors of his head.

The youth contentedly watched this rout of the shadows before the bright spears of the sun, and presently he slumbered. When he awoke he heard the voice of the assassin raised in valiant curses. Putting up his head, he perceived his comrade seated on the side of the cot engaged in scratching his neck with long finger-like nails that rasped like files.

"Hully Jee, dis is a new breed. They've got

14

can-openers on their feet." He continued in a violent tirade.

The young man hastily unlocked his closet and took out his shoes and hat. As he sat on the side of the cot lacing his shoes, he glanced about and saw that daylight had made the room comparatively commonplace and uninteresting. The men, whose faces seemed stolid, serene or absent, were engaging in dressing, while a great crackle of bantering conversation arose.

A few were parading in unconcerned nakedness. Here and there were men of brawn, whose skins shone clear and ruddy. They took splendid poses, standing massively like chiefs. When they had dressed in their ungainly garments there was an extraordinary change. They then showed bumps and deficiencies of all kinds.

There were others who exhibited many deformities. Shoulders were slanting, humped, pulled this way and pulled that way. And notable among these latter men was the little fat man who had refused to allow his head to be glorified. His pudgy form builded like a pear, bustled to and fro, while he swore in fishwife fashion. It appeared that some article of his apparel had vanished.

The young man attired speedily, and went to his friend the assassin. At first the latter looked dazed at the sight of the youth. The face seemed to be appealing to him through the cloud wastes of his memory. He scratched his neck and

reflected. At last he grinned, a broad smile gradually spreading until his countenance was a round
illumination. "Hello, Willie," he cried cheerily.

"Hello," said the young man. "Yeh ready t' fly?"

"Sure." The assassin tied his shoe carefully
with some twine and came ambling.

When he reached the street the young man
experienced no sudden relief from unholy atmos-
pheres. He had forgotten all about them, and
had been breathing naturally, and with no sen-
sation of discomfort or distress.

He was thinking of these things as he walked
along the street, when he was suddenly startled
by feeling the assassin's hand, trembling with
excitement, clutching his arm, and when the assassin spoke, his voice went into quavers from a
supreme agitation.

"I'll be hully, bloomin' blowed if there wasn't
a feller with a nightshirt on up in that joint."

The youth was bewildered for a moment, but
presently he turned to smile at the assassin's
humor. "Oh, you're a d——d liar," he merely said.

Whereupon the assassin began to gesture
extravagantly, and take oath by strange gods.
He frantically placed himself at the mercy of
remarkable fates if his tale were not true.

"Yes, he did! I cross m' heart thousan' times!"
he protested, and at the moment his eyes were
large with amazement, his mouth wrinkled in
unnatural glee.

"Yessir! A nightshirt! A hully white nightshirt!"

"You lie!"

"No, sir! I hope ter die b'fore I kin git anudder ball if there wasn't a jay wid a hully,
bloomin' white nightshirt!" His face was filled
with the infinite wonder of it. "A hully white
nightshirt," he continually repeated.

The young man saw the dark entrance to a
basement restaurant. There was a sign which
read "No mystery about our hash!" and there
were other age-stained and world-battered leg-
ends which told him that the place was within
his means. He stopped before it and spoke to
the assassin. "I guess I'll git somethin' t' eat."

At this the assassin, for some reason, appeared
to be embarrassed. He gazed at the seduc-
tive front of the eating place for a moment.
Then he started slowly up the street. "Well,
good-bye, Willie," he said bravely.

For an instant the youth studied the departing
figure. Then he called out, "Hol' on a minnet."
As they came together he spoke in a certain fierce
way, as if he feared that the other would think
him to be charitable. "Look-a-here, if yeh wanta
git some breakfas' I'll lend yeh three cents t'
do it with. But say, look-a-here, you've gota git
out an' hustle. I ain't goin' t' support yeh, or I'll
go broke b'fore night. I ain't no millionaire."

"I take me oath, Willie," said the assassin
earnestly, "th' on'y thing I really needs is a ball.
Me t'roat feels like a fryin'-pan. But as I can't
get a ball, why, th' next bes' thing is breakfast,

17

an' if yeh do that for me, b' Gawd, I say yeh was th' whitest lad I ever see."

They spent a few moments in dexterous exchanges of phrases, in which they each protested that the other was, as the assassin had originally said, "a respecter'ble gentlem'n." And they concluded with mutual assurances that they were the souls of intelligence and virtue. Then they went into a restaurant with a long counter, dimly lighted from hidden sources. Two or three men in soiled white aprons rushed here and there.

The youth bought a bowl of coffee for two cents and a roll for one cent. The assassin purchased the same. The bowls were webbed with brown seams, and the tin spoons wore an air of having emerged from the first pyramid. Upon them were black mosslike encrustations of age, and they were bent and scarred from the attacks of long-forgotten teeth. But over their repast the wanderers waxed warm and mellow. The assassin grew affable as the hot mixture went soothingly down his parched throat, and the young man felt courage flow in his veins.

Memories began to throng in on the assassin, and he brought forth long tales, intricate, incoherent, delivered with a chattering swiftness as from an old woman. "——great job out'n Orange. Boss keep yeh hustlin' though all time. I was there three days, and then I went an' ask 'im t' lend me a dollar. 'G-g-go ter the devil,' he ses, an' I lose me job."

"South no good. Damn niggers work for twenty-five an' thirty cents a day. Run white man out. Good grub, though. Easy livin'."

"Yas; uster work little in Toledo, raftin' logs. Make two or three dollars er day in the spring. Lived high. Cold as ice, though, in the winter."

"I was raised in northern N'York. O-a-ah, yes jest oughto live there. No beer ner whisky, though, way off in the woods. But all th' good hot grub yeh can eat. B'Gawd, I hung around there long as I could till th' ol' man fired me. 'Git t' hell outa here, yeh wuthless skunk, git t' hell outa here, an' go die,' he ses. 'You're a hell of a father,' I ses, 'you are,' an' I quit 'im."

As they were passing from the dim eating place, they encountered an old man who was trying to steal forth with a tiny package of food, but a tall man with an indomitable moustache stood dragon fashion, barring the way of escape. They heard the old man raise a plaintive protest. "Ah, you always want to know what I take out, and you never see that I usually bring a package in here from my place of business."

As the wanderers trudged slowly along Park Row, the assassin began to expand and grow blithe. "B'Gawd, we've been livin' like kings," he said, smacking appreciative lips.

"Look out, or we'll have t' pay fer it t'night," said the youth with gloomy warning.

But the assassin refused to turn his gaze toward the future. He went with limping step, into which he injected a suggestion of lamblike gambols. His mouth was wreathed in a red grin.

In the City Hall Park the two wanderers sat down in the little circle of benches sanctified by traditions of their class. They huddled in their old garments, slumbrously conscious of the march of the hours which for them had no meaning.

The people of the street hurrying hither and thither made a blend of black figures changing yet frieze-like. They walked in their good clothes as upon important missions, giving no gaze to the two wanderers seated upon the benches. They expressed to the young man his infinite distance from all that he valued. Social position, comfort, the pleasures of living, were unconquerable kingdoms. He felt a sudden awe.

And in the background a multitude of buildings, of pitiless hues and sternly high, were to him emblematic of a nation forcing its regal head into the clouds, throwing no downward glances; in the sublimity of its aspirations ignoring the wretches who may flounder at its feet. The roar of the city in his ear was to him the confusion of strange tongues, babbling heedlessly; it was the clink of coin, the voice of the city's hopes which were to him no hopes.

He confessed himself an outcast, and his eyes from under the lowered rim of his hat began to glance guiltily, wearing the criminal expression that comes with certain convictions.

# THE BRIGADE COMMANDER

BY J. W. DE FOREST

# THE BRIGADE COMMANDER

BY J. W. DE FOREST

THE Colonel was the idol of his bragging old regiment and of the bragging brigade which for the last six months he had commanded.

He was the idol, not because he was good and gracious, not because he spared his soldiers or treated them as fellow-citizens, but because he had led them to victory and made them famous. If a man will win battles and give his brigade a right to brag loudly of its doings, he may have its admiration and even its enthusiastic devotion, though he be as pitiless and as wicked as Lucifer.

"It's nothin' to me what the Currnell is in prrivit, so long as he shows us how to whack the rrebs," said Major Gahogan, commandant of the "Old Tenth." "Moses saw God in the burrnin' bussh, an' bowed down to it, an' worrshipt it. It wasn't the bussh he worrshipt; it was his God that was in it. An' I worrship this villin of a Currnell (if he is a villin) because he's almighty and gives us the vict'ry. He's nothin' but a human burrnin' bussh, perhaps, but he's got the god of war in um. Adjetant

By permission of "The New York Times."

Wallis, it's a —— long time between dhrinks, as I think ye was sayin', an' with rayson. See if ye can't confiscate a canteen of whiskee somewhere in the camp. Bedad, if I can't buy it I'll stale it. We're goin' to fight tomorry, an' it may be it's the last chance we'll have for a dhrink, unless there's more lik'r now in the other worrld than Dives got."

The brigade was bivouacked in some invisible region, amid the damp, misty darkness of a September night. The men lay in their ranks, each with his feet to the front and his head rearward, each covered by his overcoat and pillowed upon his haversack, each with his loaded rifle nestled close beside him. Asleep as they were, or dropping placidly into slumber, they were ready to start in order to their feet and pour out the red light and harsh roar of combat. There were two lines of battle, each of three regiments of infantry, the first some two hundred yards in advance of the second. In the space between them lay two four-gun batteries, one of them brass twelve-pounder "Napoleons," and the other rifled Parrotts. To the rear of the infantry were the recumbent troopers and picketed horses of a regiment of cavalry. All around, in the far, black distance, invisible and inaudible, paced or watched stealthily the sentinels of the grand guards.

There was not a fire, not a torch, nor a starbeam in the whole bivouac to guide the feet of

# THE BRIGADE COMMANDER

Adjutant Wallis in his pilgrimage after whiskey. The orders from brigade headquarters had been strict against illuminations, for the Confederates were near at hand in force, and a surprise was proposed as well as feared. A tired and sleepy youngster, almost dropping with the heavy somnolence of wearied adolescence, he stumbled on through the trials of an undiscernible and unfamiliar footing, lifting his heavy riding-boots sluggishly over imaginary obstacles, and fearing the while lest his toil were labor misspent. It was a dry camp, he felt dolefully certain, or there would have been more noise in it. He fell over a sleeping sergeant, and said to him hastily, "Steady, man—a friend!" as the half-roused soldier clutched his rifle. Then he found a lieutenant, and shook him in vain; further on a captain, and exchanged saddening murmurs with him; further still a camp-follower of African extraction, and blasphemed him.

"It's a God-forsaken camp, and there isn't a horn in it," said Adjutant Wallis to himself as he pursued his groping journey. "Bet you I don't find the first drop," he continued, for he was a betting boy, and frequently argued by wagers, even with himself. "Bet you two to one I don't. Bet you three to one—ten to one."

Then he saw, an indefinite distance beyond him, burning like red-hot iron through the darkness, a little scarlet or crimson gleam, as of a lighted cigar.

"That's Old Grumps, of the Bloody Fourteenth," he thought. "I've raided into his happy sleeping-grounds. I'll draw on him."

But Old Grumps, otherwise Colonel Lafayette Gildersleeve, had no rations—that is, no whiskey.

"How do you suppose an officer is to have a drink, Lieutenant?" he grumbled. "Don't you know that our would-be Brigadier sent all the commissary to the rear day before yesterday? A canteenful can't last two days. Mine went empty about five minutes ago."

"Oh, thunder!" groaned Wallis, saddened by that saddest of all thoughts, "Too late!" "Well, least said soonest mended. I must wobble back to my Major."

"He'll send you off to some other camp as dry as this one. Wait ten minutes, and he'll be asleep. Lie down on my blanket and light your pipe. I want to talk to you about official business—about our would-be Brigadier."

"Oh, *your* turn will come some day," mumbled Wallis, remembering Gildersleeve's jealousy of the brigade commander—a jealousy which only gave tongue when aroused by "commissary." "If you do as well as usual to-morrow you can have your own brigade."

"I suppose you think we are all going to do well to-morrow," scoffed Old Grumps, whose utterance by this time stumbled. "I suppose you expect to whip and to have a good time. I suppose you brag on fighting and enjoy it."

26

"I like it well enough when it goes right; and it generally does go right with this brigade. I should like it better if the rebs would fire higher and break quicker."

"That depends on the way those are commanded whose business it is to break them," growled Old Grumps. I don't say but what we are rightly commanded," he added, remembering his duty to superiors. "I concede and acknowledge that our would-be Brigadier knows his military business. But the blessing of God, Wallis! I believe in Waldron as a soldier. But as a man and a Christian, faugh!"

Gildersleeve had clearly emptied his canteen unassisted; he never talked about Christianity when perfectly sober.

"What was your last remark?" inquired Wallis, taking his pipe from his mouth to grin. Even a superior officer might be chaffed a little in the darkness.

"I made no last remark," asserted the Colonel with dignity. "I'm not a-dying yet. If I said anything last it was a mere exclamation of disgust—the disgust of an officer and gentleman. I suppose you know something about our would-be Brigadier. I suppose you think you know something about him."

"Bet you I know *all* about him," affirmed Wallis. "He enlisted in the Old Tenth as a common soldier. Before he had been a week in camp they found that he knew his biz, and they

made him a sergeant. Before we started for the
field the Governor got his eye on him and shoved
him into a lieutenancy. The first battle h'isted
him to a captain. And the second—bang! whiz!
he shot up to colonel right over the heads of
everybody, line and field. Nobody in the Old
Tenth grumbled. They saw that he knew his
biz. I know *all* about him. What'll you bet?"

"I'm not a betting man, Lieutenant, except
in a friendly game of poker," sighed Old
Grumps. "You don't know anything about
your Brigadier," he added in a sepulchral murmur, the echo of an empty canteen. "I have only
been in this brigade a month, and I know more
than you do, far, very far more, sorry to say it.
He's a reformed clergyman. He's an apostatized minister." The Colonel's voice as he said
this was solemn and sad enough to do credit to
an undertaker. "It's a bad sort, Wallis," he
continued, after another deep sigh, a very highly
perfumed one, the sigh of a barkeeper. "When
a clergyman falls, he falls for life and eternity,
like a woman or an angel. I never knew a back-
slidden shepherd to come to good. Sooner or
later he always goes to the devil, and takes down
whomsoever hangs to him."

"He'll take down the Old Tenth, then," asserted Wallis. "It hangs to him. Bet you two
to one he takes it along."

"You're right, Adjutant; spoken like a soldier," swore Gildersleeve. "And the Bloody

28

Fourteenth, too. It will march into the burning pit as far as any regiment; and the whole brigade, yes, sir! But a backslidden shepherd, my God! Have we come to that? I often say to myself, in the solemn hours of the night, as I remember my Sabbath-school days, 'Great Scott! have we come to that?' A reformed clergyman! An apostatized minister! Think of it, Wallis, think of it! Why, sir, his very wife ran away from him. They had but just buried their first boy," pursued Old Grumps, his hoarse voice sinking to a whimper. "They drove home from the burial-place, where lay the new-made grave. Arrived at their door, *he* got out and extended his hand to help *her* out. Instead of accepting, instead of throwing herself into his arms and weeping there, she turned to the coachman and said, 'Driver, drive me to my father's house.' That was the end of their wedded life, Wallis."

The Colonel actually wept at this point, and the maudlin tears were not altogether insincere. His own wife and children he heartily loved, and remembered them now with honest tenderness. At home he was not a drinker and a rough; only amid the hardships and perils of the field.

"That was the end of it, Wallis," he repeated. "And what was it while it lasted? What does a woman leave her husband for? Why does she separate from him over the grave of her innocent first-born? There are twenty reasons, but they must all of them be good ones. I am sorry to give it as my decided opinion, Wallis, in perfect confidence, that they must all be whopping good ones. Well, that was the beginning; only the beginning. After that he held on for a while, breaking the bread of life to a skedaddling flock, and then he bolted. The next known of him, three years later, he enlisted in your regiment, a smart but seedy recruit, smelling strongly of whiskey."

"I wish I smelt half as strong of it myself," grumbled Wallis. "It might keep out the swamp fever."

"That's the true story of Col. John James Waldron," continued Old Grumps, with a groan which was very somnolent, as if it were a twin to a snore. "That's the true story."

"I don't believe the first word of it—that is to say, Colonel, I think you have been misinformed —and I'll bet you two to one on it. If he was nothing more than a minister, how did he know drill and tactics?"

"Oh, I forgot to say he went through West Point—that is, nearly through. They graduated him in his third year by the back door, Wallis."

"Oh, that was it, was it? He was a West Pointer, was he? Well, then, the backsliding was natural, and oughtn't to count against him. A member of Benny Haven's church has a right to backslide anywhere, especially as the Colonel doesn't seem to be any worse than some of the rest of us, who haven't fallen from grace the least particle, but took our stand at the start just where we are now. A fellow that begins with a handful of trumps has a right to play a risky game."

"I know what euchered him, Wallis. It was the old Little Joker; and there's another of the same on hand now."

"On hand where? What are you driving at, Colonel?"

"He looks like a boy. I mean she looks like a boy. You know what I mean, Wallis; I mean the boy that makes believe to wait on him. And her brother is in camp, got here to-night. There'll be an explanation to-morrow, and there'll be bloodshed."

"Good-night, Colonel, and sleep it off," said Wallis, rising from the side of a man whom he believed to be sillily drunk and altogether untrustworthy. "You know we get after the rebs at dawn."

"I know it—goo-night, Adjutant—gawbless-you," mumbled Old Grumps. "We'll lick those rebs, won't we?" he chuckled. Goo-night, ole fellow, an' gawblessyou."

Whereupon Old Grumps fell asleep, very absurdly overcome by liquor, we extremely regret to concede, but nobly sure to do his soldierly duty as soon as he should awake.

Stumbling wearily blanketward, Wallis found his Major and regimental commander, the genial and gallant Gahogan, slumbering in a peace like that of the just. He stretched himself anear, put out his hand to touch his sabre and revolver, drew his caped great-coat over him, moved once to free his back of a root or pebble, glanced languidly at a single struggling star, thought for an instant of his far-away mother, turned his head with a sigh and slept. In the morning he was to fight, and perhaps to die; but the boyish veteran was too seasoned, and also too tired, to mind that; he could mind but one thing—nature's pleading for rest.

In the iron-gray dawn, while the troops were falling dimly and spectrally into line, and he was mounting his horse to be ready for orders, he remembered Gildersleeve's drunken tale concerning the commandant, and laughed aloud. But turning his face toward brigade headquarters (a sylvan region marked out by the branches of a great oak), he was surprised to see a strange officer, a fair young man in captain's uniform, riding slowly toward it.

"Is that the boy's brother?" he said to himself; and in the next instant he had forgotten the whole subject; it was time to form and present the regiment.

Quietly and without tap of drum the small, battle-worn battalions filed out of their bivouacs into the highway, ordered arms and waited for the word to march. With a dull rumble the field-pieces trundled slowly after, and halted in rear of the infantry. The cavalry trotted off circuitously through the fields, emerged upon a road in advance and likewise halted, all but a single company, which pushed on for half a mile, spreading out as it went into a thin line of skirmishers.

Meanwhile a strange interview took place near the great oak which had sheltered brigade headquarters. As the unknown officer, whom Wallis had noted, approached it, Col. Waldron was standing by his horse ready to mount. The commandant was a man of medium size, fairly handsome in person and features, and apparently about twenty-eight years of age. Perhaps it was the singular breadth of his forehead which made the lower part of his face look so unusually slight and feminine. His eyes were dark hazel, as clear, brilliant, and tender as a girl's, and brimming full of a pensiveness which seemed both loving and melancholy. Few persons, at all events few women, who looked upon him ever looked beyond his eyes. They were very fascinating, and in a man's countenance very strange. They were the kind of eyes which reveal passionate romances, and which make them.

By his side stood a boy, a singularly interesting and beautiful boy, fair-haired and blue-eyed, and delicate in color. When this boy saw the stranger approach he turned as pale as marble, slid away from the brigade commander's side, and disappeared behind a group of staff officers and orderlies. The new-comer also became deathly white as he glanced after the retreating youth. Then he dismounted, touched his cap slightly and, as if mechanically, advanced a few steps, and said hoarsely, "I believe this is Colonel Waldron. I am Captain Fitz Hugh, of the —th Delaware."

Waldron put his hand to his revolver, withdrew it instantaneously, and stood motionless.

"I am on leave of absence from my regiment, Colonel," continued Fitz Hugh, speaking now with an elaborate ceremoniousness of utterance significant of a struggle to suppress violent emotion. "I suppose you can understand why I made use of it in seeking you."

Waldron hesitated; he stood gazing at the earth with the air of one who represses deep pain; at last, after a profound sigh, he raised his eyes and answered:

"Captain, we are on the eve of a battle. I must attend to my public duties first. After the battle we will settle our private affair."

"There is but one way to settle it, Colonel."

"You shall have your way if you will. You shall do what you will. I only ask what good will it do to *her?*"

"It will do good to *me,* Colonel," whispered Fitz Hugh, suddenly turning crimson. "You forget *me.*"

Waldron's face also flushed, and an angry sparkle shot from under his lashes in reply to

34

this utterance of hate, but it died out in an instant.

"I have done a wrong, and I will accept the consequences," he said. "I pledge you my word that I will be at your disposal if I survive the battle. Where do you propose to remain meanwhile?"

"I will take the same chance, sir. I propose to do my share in the fighting if you will use me."

"I am short of staff officers. Will you act as my aid?"

"I will, Colonel," bowed Fitz Hugh, with a glance which expressed surprise, and perhaps admiration, at this confidence.

Waldron turned, beckoned his staff officers to approach, and said, "Gentlemen, this is Captain Fitz Hugh of the —th Delaware. He has volunteered to join us for the day, and will act as my aid. And now, Captain, will you ride to the head of the column and order it forward? There will be no drum-beat and no noise. When you have given your order and seen it executed, you will wait for me."

Fitz Hugh saluted, sprang into his saddle and galloped away. A few minutes later the whole column was plodding on silently toward its bloody goal. To a civilian, unaccustomed to scenes of war, the tranquillity of these men would have seemed very wonderful. Many of the soldiers were still munching the hard bread and

raw pork of their meagre breakfasts, or drinking
the cold coffee with which they had filled their
canteens the day previous.  Many more were
chatting in an undertone, grumbling over their
sore feet and other discomfits, chaffing each
other, and laughing.  The general bearing, however, was grave, patient, quietly enduring, and
one might almost say stolid.  You would have
said, to judge by their expressions, that these sunburned fellows were merely doing hard work,
and thoroughly commonplace work, without a
prospect of adventure, and much less of danger.
The explanation of this calmness, so brutal perhaps to the eye of a sensitive soul, lies mainly in
the fact that they were all veterans, the survivors of marches, privations, maladies, sieges,
and battles.  Not a regiment present numbered
four hundred men, and the average was not
above three hundred.  The whole force, including artillery and cavalry, might have been about
twenty-five hundred sabres and bayonets.

At the beginning of the march Waldron fell
into the rear of his staff and mounted orderlies.
Then the boy who had fled from Fitz Hugh
dropped out of the tramping escort, and rode up
to his side.

"Well, Charlie," said Waldron, casting a pity-
ing glance at the yet pallid face and anxious
eyes of the youth, "you have had a sad fright.  I
make you very miserable."

"He has found us at last," murmured Charlie

in a tremulous soprano voice. "What did he say?"

"We are to talk to-morrow. He acts as my aide-de-camp to-day. I ought to tell you frankly that he is not friendly."

"Of course, I knew it," sighed Charlie, while the tears fell.

"It is only one more trouble—one more danger, and perhaps it may pass. So many *have* passed."

"Did you tell him anything to quiet him? Did you tell him that we were married?"

"But we are not married yet, Charlie. We shall be, I hope."

"But you ought to have told him that we were. It might stop him from doing something—mad. Why didn't you tell him so? Why didn't you think of it?"

"My dear little child, we are about to have a battle. I should like to carry some honor and truth into it."

"Where is he?" continued Charlie, unconvinced and unappeased. "I want to see him. Is he at the head of the column? I want to speak to him, just one word. He won't hurt me."

She suddenly spurred her horse, wheeled into the fields, and dashed onward. Fitz Hugh was lounging in his saddle, and sombrely surveying the passing column, when she galloped up to him.

"Carrol!" she said, in a choked voice, reining

in by his side, and leaning forward to touch his sleeve.

He threw one glance at her—a glance of aversion, if not of downright hatred, and turned his back in silence.

"He is my husband, Carrol," she went on rapidly. "I knew you didn't understand it. I ought to have written you about it. I thought I would come and tell you before you did anything absurd. We were married as soon as he heard that his wife was dead."

"What is the use of this?" he muttered hoarsely. "She is not dead. I heard from her a week ago. She was living a week ago."

"Oh, Carrol!" stammered Charlie. "It was some mistake then. Is it possible! And he was so sure! But he can get a divorce, you know. She abandoned him. Or *she* can get one. No, *he* can get it—of course, when she abandoned him. But, Carrol, she *must* be dead—he was *so* sure."

"She is *not* dead, I tell you. And there can be no divorce. Insanity bars all claim to a divorce. She is in an asylum. She had to leave him, and then she went mad."

"Oh, no, Carrol, it is all a mistake; it is not so. Carrol," she murmured in a voice so faint that he could not help glancing at her, half in fury and half in pity. She was slowly falling from her horse. He sprang from his saddle, caught her in his arms, and laid her on the turf, wishing the while that it covered her grave. Just then one of Waldron's orderlies rode up and exclaimed: "What is the matter with the—the boy? Hullo, Charlie."

Fitz Hugh stared at the man in silence, tempted to tear him from his horse. "The boy is ill," he answered when he recovered his self-command. "Take charge of him yourself." He remounted, rode onward out of sight beyond a thicket, and there waited for the brigade commander, now and then fingering his revolver. As Charlie was being placed in an ambulance by the orderly and a sergeant's wife, Waldron came up, reined in his horse violently, and asked in a furious voice, "Is that boy hurt?

"Ah — fainted," he added immediately. "Thank you, Mrs. Gunner. Take good care of him—the best of care, my dear woman, and don't let him leave you all day."

Further on, when Fitz Hugh silently fell into his escort, he merely glanced at him in a furtive way, and then cantered on rapidly to the head of the cavalry. There he beckoned to the tall, grave, iron-gray Chaplain of the Tenth, and rode with him for nearly an hour, apart, engaged in low and seemingly impassioned discourse. From this interview Mr. Colquhoun returned to the escort with a strangely solemnized, tender countenance, while the commandant, with a more cheerful air than he had yet worn that day, gave himself to his martial duties, inspecting the landscape incessantly with his glass, and sending frequently for news to the advance scouts. It may properly be stated here that the Chaplain never divulged to any one the nature of the conversation which he had held with his Colonel.

Nothing further of note occurred until the little army, after two hours of plodding march, wound through a sinuous, wooded ravine, entered a broad, bare, slightly undulating valley, and for the second time halted. Waldron galloped to the summit of a knoll, pointed to a long eminence which faced him some two miles distant, and said tranquilly, "There is our battle-ground."

"Is that the enemy's position?" returned Captain Ives, his adjutant-general. "We shall have a tough job if we go at it from here."

Waldron remained in deep thought for some minutes, meanwhile scanning the ridge and all its surroundings.

"What I want to know," he observed, at last, "is whether they have occupied the wooded knolls in front of their right and around their right flank."

Shortly afterward the commander of the scouting squadron came riding back at a furious pace.

"They are on the hill, Colonel," he shouted.

"Yes, of course," nodded Waldron; "but have they occupied the woods which veil their right front and flank?"

"Not a bit of it; my fellows have cantered all through, and up to the base of the hill."

"Ah!" exclaimed the brigade commander, with a rush of elation. "Then it will be easy work. Go back, Captain, and scatter your men through the wood, and hold it, if possible. Adjutant, call up the regimental commanders at once. I want them to understand my plan fully."

In a few minutes, Gahogan, of the Tenth; Gildersleeve, of the Fourteenth; Peck, of the First; Thomas, of the Seventh; Taylor, of the Eighth, and Colburn, of the Fifth, were gathered around their commander. There, too, was Bradley, the boyish, red-cheeked chief of the artillery; and Stilton, the rough, old, bearded regular, who headed the cavalry. The staff was at hand, also, including Fitz Hugh, who sat his horse a little apart, downcast and sombre and silent, but nevertheless keenly interested. It is worthy of remark, by the way, that Waldron took no special note of him, and did not seem conscious of any disturbing presence. Evil as the man may have been, he was a thoroughly good soldier, and just now he thought but of his duties.

"Gentlemen," he said, "I want you to see your field of battle. The enemy occupy that long ridge. How shall we reach it?"

"I think, if we got at it straight from here, we shan't miss it," promptly judged Old Grumps, his red-oak countenance admirably cheerful and hopeful, and his jealousy all dissolved in the interest of approaching combat.

"Nor they won't miss us nuther," laughed

Major Gahogan. "Betther slide our infantree into thim wuds, push up our skirmishers, play wid our guns for an hour, an' thin rowl in a couple o' col'ms."

There was a general murmur of approval. The limits of volunteer invention in tactics had been reached by Gahogan. The other regimental commanders looked upon him as their superior in the art of war.

"That would be well, Major, if we could do nothing better," said Waldron. "But I do not feel obliged to attack the front seriously at all. The rebels have been thoughtless enough to leave that long semicircle of wooded knolls unoccupied, even by scouts. It stretches from the front of their centre clear around their right flank. I shall use it as a veil to cover us while we get into position. I shall throw out a regiment, a battery, and five companies of cavalry, to make a feint against their centre and left. With the remainder of the brigade I shall skirt the woods, double around the right of the position, and close in upon it front and rear."

"Loike scissors blades upon a snip o' paper," shouted Gahogan, in delight. Then he turned to Fitz Hugh, who happened to be nearest him, and added, "I tell ye he's got the God o' War in um. He's the burnin' bussh of humanity, wid a God o' Battles inside on't."

"But how if they come down on our thin right wing?" asked a cautious officer, Taylor, of the

Eighth. They might smash it and seize our line of retreat."

"Men who have taken up a strong position, a position obviously chosen for defence, rarely quit it promptly for an attack," replied Waldron. "There is not one chance in ten that these gentlemen will make a considerable forward movement early in the fight. Only the greatest geniuses jump from the defensive to the offensive. Besides, we must hold the wood. So long as we hold the wood in front of their centre we save the road."

Then came personal and detailed instructions. Each regimental commander was told whither he should march, the point where he should halt to form line, and the direction by which he should attack. The mass of the command was to advance in marching column toward a knoll where the highway entered and traversed the wood. Some time before reaching it Taylor was to deploy the Eighth to the right, throw out a strong skirmish line and open fire on the enemy's centre and left, supported by the battery of Parrotts, and, if pushed, by five companies of cavalry. The remaining troops would reach the knoll, file to the left under cover of the forest, skirt it for a mile as rapidly as possible, infold the right of the Confederate position, and then move upon it concentrically. Counting from the left, the Tenth, the Seventh, and the Fourteenth were to constitute the first line of battle, while five companies of cavalry, then the First, and then the Fifth formed the second line. Not until Gahogan might have time to wind into the enemy's right rear should Gildersleeve move out of the wood and commence the real attack.

"You will go straight at the front of their right," said Waldron, with a gay smile, to this latter Colonel. "Send up two companies as skirmishers. The moment they are clearly checked, lead up the other eight in line. It will be rough work. But keep pushing. You won't have fifteen minutes of it before Thomas, on your left, will be climbing the end of the ridge to take the rebels in flank. In fifteen minutes more Gahogan will be running in on their backs. Of course, they will try to change front and meet us. But they have extended their line a long way in order to cover the whole ridge. They will not be quick enough. We shall get hold of their right, and we shall roll them up. Then, Colonel Stilton, I shall expect to see the troopers jumping into the gaps and making prisoners."

"All right, Colonel," answered Stilton in that hoarse growl which is apt to mark the old cavalry officer. "Where shall we find you if we want a fresh order?"

"I shall be with Colburn, in rear of Gildersleeve. That is our centre. But never mind me; you know what the battle is to be, and you know how to fight it. The whole point with the infantry is to fold around the enemy's right, go in

44

upon it concentrically, smash it, and roll up their line. The cavalry will watch against the infantry being flanked, and when the latter have seized the hill, will charge for prisoners. The artillery will reply to the enemy's guns with shell, and fire grape at any offensive demonstration. You all know your duties, now, gentlemen. Go to your commands, and march!"

The colonels saluted and started off at a gallop. In a few minutes twenty-five hundred men were in simultaneous movement. Five companies of cavalry wheeled into column of companies, and advanced at a trot through the fields, seeking to gain the shelter of the forest. The six infantry regiments slid up alongside of each other, and pushed on in six parallel columns of march, two on the right of the road and four on the left. The artillery, which alone left the highway, followed at a distance of two or three hundred yards. The remaining cavalry made a wide detour to the right as if to flank the enemy's left.

It was a mile and a quarter—it was a march of fully twenty minutes—to the edge of the woodland, the proposed cover of the column. Ten minutes before this point was reached a tiny puff of smoke showed on the brow of the hostile ridge; then, at an interval of several seconds, followed the sound of a distant explosion; then, almost immediately, came the screech of a rifled shell. Every man who heard it swiftly asked himself, "Will it strike *me?*" But even as the words were thought out it had passed, high in air, clean to the rear, and burst harmlessly. A few faces turned upward and a few eyes glanced backward, as if to see the invisible enemy. But there was no pause in the column; it flowed onward quietly, eagerly, and with business-like precision; it gave forth no sound but the trampling of feet and the muttering of the officers. "Steady, men! Forward, men!"

The Confederates, however, had got their range. A half minute later four puffs of smoke dotted the ridge, and a flight of hoarse humming shrieks tore the air. A little aureole cracked and splintered over the First, followed by loud cries of anguish and a brief, slight confusion. The voice of an officer rose sharply out of the flurry, "Close up, Company A! Forward, men!" The battalion column resumed its even formation in an instant, and tramped unitedly onward, leaving behind it two quivering corpses and a wounded man who tottered rearward.

Then came more screeches, and a shell exploded over the highroad, knocking a gunner lifeless from his carriage. The brigade commander glanced anxiously along his batteries, and addressed a few words to his chief of artillery. Presently the four Napoleons set forward at a gallop for the wood, while the four Parrotts wheeled to the right, deployed, and advanced across the fields, inclining toward the left of the enemy. Next Taylor's regiment (the Eighth)

halted, fronted, faced to the right, and filed off
in column of march at a double-quick until it had
gained the rear of the Parrotts, when it fronted
again, and pushed on in support. A quarter of a
mile further on these guns went into battery behind the brow of a little knoll, and opened fire.
Four companies of the Eighth spread out to the
right as skirmishers, and commenced stealing
toward the ridge, from time to time measuring
the distance with rifle-balls. The remainder of
the regiment lay down in line between the Parrotts and the forest. Far away to the right, five
companies of cavalry showed themselves, ma-
nœuvring as if they proposed to turn the left
flank of the Southerners. The attack on this side
was in form and in operation.

Meantime the Confederate fire had divided.
Two guns pounded away at Taylor's feint, while
two shelled the main column. The latter was
struck repeatedly; more than twenty men
dropped silent or groaning out of the hurrying
files; but the survivors pushed on without falter-
ing and without even caring for the wounded.
At last a broad belt of green branches rose between the regiments and the ridge; and the rebel
gunners, unable to see their foe, dropped suddenly into silence.

Here it appeared that the road divided. The
highway traversed the forest, mounted the slope
beyond and dissected the enemy's position, while
a branch road turned to the left and skirted the

exterior of the long curve of wooded hillocks. At the fork the battery of Napoleons had halted, and there it was ordered to remain for the present in quiet. There, too, the Fourteenth filed in among the dense greenery, threw out two companies of skirmishers toward the ridge, and pushed slowly after them into the shadows.

"Get sight of the enemy at once!" was Waldron's last word to Gildersleeve. "If they move down the slope, drive them back. But don't commence your attack under half an hour."

Next he filed the Fifth into the thickets, saying to Colburn, "I want you to halt a hundred yards to the left and rear of Gildersleeve. Cover his flank if he is attacked; but otherwise lie quiet. As soon as he charges, move forward to the edge of the wood, and be ready to support him. But make no assault yourself until further orders."

The next two regiments—the Seventh and First—he placed in *échelon,* in like manner, a quarter of a mile further along. Then he galloped forward to the cavalry, and a last word with Stilton. "You and Gahogan must take care of yourselves. Push on four or five hundred yards, and then face to the right. Whatever Gahogan finds let him go at it. If he can't shake it, help him. You two *must* reach the top of the ridge. Only, look out for your left flank. Keep a squadron or two in reserve on that side."

"Currnel, if we don't raich the top of the hill, it'll be because it hasn't got wan," answered

Gahogan. Stilton only laughed and rode forward.

Waldron now returned toward the fork of the road. On the way he sent a staff officer to the Seventh with renewed orders to attack as soon as possible after Gildersleeve. Then another staff officer was hurried forward to Taylor with directions to push his feint strongly, and drive his skirmishers as far up the slope as they could get. A third staff officer set the Parrotts in rear of Taylor to firing with all their might. By the time that the commandant had returned to Colburn's ambushed ranks, no one was with him but his enemy, Fitz Hugh.

"You don't seem to trust me with duty, Colonel," said the young man.

"I shall use you only in case of extremity, Captain," replied Waldron. "We have business to settle to-morrow."

"I ask no favors on that account. I hope you will offer me none."

"In case of need I shall spare no one," declared Waldron.

Then he took out his watch, looked at it impatiently, put it to his ear, restored it to his pocket, and fell into an attitude of deep attention. Evidently his whole mind was on his battle, and he was waiting, watching, yearning for its outburst.

"If he wins this fight," thought Fitz Hugh, "how can I do him a harm? And yet," he added, "how can I help it?"

Minutes passed. Fitz Hugh tried to think of his injury, and to steel himself against his chief. But the roar of battle on the right, and the suspense and imminence of battle on the left, absorbed the attention of even this wounded and angry spirit, as, indeed, they might have absorbed that of any being not more or less than human. A private wrong, insupportable though it might be, seemed so small amid that deadly clamor and awful expectation! Moreover, the intellect which worked so calmly and vigorously by his side, and which alone of all things near appeared able to rule the coming crisis, began to dominate him, in spite of his sense of injury. A thought crossed him to the effect that the great among men are too valuable to be punished for their evil deeds. He turned to the absorbed brigade commander, now not only his ruler, but even his protector, with a feeling that he must accord him a word of peace, a proffer in some form of possible forgiveness and friendship. But the man's face was clouded and stern with responsibility and authority. He seemed at that moment too lofty to be approached with a message of pardon. Fitz Hugh gazed at him with a mixture of profound respect and smothered hate. He gazed, turned away, and remained silent.

Minutes more passed. Then a mounted orderly dashed up at full speed, with the words, "Colonel, Major Gahogan has fronted."

"Has he?" answered Waldron, with a smile

which thanked the trooper and made him happy. "Ride on through the thicket here, my man, and tell Colonel Gildersleeve to push up his skirmishers."

With a thud of hoofs and a rustling of parting foliage the cavalryman disappeared amid the underwood. A minute or two later a thin, dropping rattle of musketry, five hundred yards or so to the front, announced that the sharpshooters of the Fourteenth were at work. Almost immediately there was an angry response, full of the threatenings and execution of death. Through the lofty leafage tore the screech of a shell, bursting with a sharp crash as it passed overhead, and scattering in humming slivers. Then came another, and another, and many more, chasing each other with hoarse hissings through the trembling air, a succession of flying serpents. The enemy doubtless believed that nearly the whole attacking force was massed in the wood around the road, and they had brought at least four guns to bear upon that point, and were working them with the utmost possible rapidity. Presently a large chestnut, not fifty yards from Fitz Hugh, was struck by a shot. The solid trunk, nearly three feet in diameter, parted asunder as if it were the brittlest of vegetable matter. The upper portion started aside with a monstrous groan, dropped in a standing posture to the earth, and then toppled slowly, sublimely prostrate, its branches crashing and all its leaves wailing. Ere long, a little further to the front, another Anak of the forest went down; and, mingled with the noise of its sylvan agony, there arose sharp cries of human suffering. Then Colonel Colburn, a broad-chested and ruddy man of thirty-five, with a look of indignant anxiety in his iron-gray eyes, rode up to the brigade commander.

"This is very annoying, Colonel," he said. "I am losing my men without using them. That last tree fell into my command."

"Are they firing toward our left?" asked Waldron.

"Not a shot."

"Very good," said the chief, with a sigh of contentment. "If we can only keep them occupied in this direction! By the way, let your men lie down under the fallen tree, as far as it will go. It will protect them from others."

Colburn rode back to his regiment. Waldron looked impatiently at his watch. At that moment a fierce burst of line firing arose in front, followed and almost overborne by a long-drawn yell, the scream of charging men. Waldron put up his watch, glanced excitedly at Fitz Hugh, and smiled.

"I must forgive or forget," the latter could not help saying to himself. "All the rest of life is nothing compared with this."

"Captain," said Waldron, "ride off to the left at full speed. As soon as you hear firing at the shoulder of the ridge, return instantly and let me know."

Fitz Hugh dashed away. Three minutes carried him into perfect peace, beyond the whistling of ball or the screeching of shell. On the right was a tranquil, wide waving of foliage, and on the left a serene landscape of cultivated fields, with here and there an embowered farm-house. Only for the clamor of artillery and musketry far behind him, he could not have believed in the near presence of battle, of blood and suffering and triumphant death. But suddenly he heard to his right, assaulting and slaughtering the tranquillity of nature, a tumultuous outbreak of file firing, mingled with savage yells. He wheeled, drove spurs into his horse, and flew back to Waldron. As he re-entered the wood he met wounded men streaming through it, a few marching alertly upright, many more crouching and groaning, some clinging to their less injured comrades, but all haggard in face and ghastly.

"Are we winning?" he hastily asked of one man who held up a hand with three fingers gone and the bones projecting in sharp spikes through mangled flesh.

"All right, sir; sailing in," was the answer.

"Is the brigade commander all right?" he inquired of another who was winding a bloody handkerchief around his arm.

"Straight ahead, sir; hurrah for Waldron!"

responded the soldier, and almost in the same instant fell lifeless with a fresh ball through his head.

"Hurrah for him!" Fitz Hugh answered frantically, plunging on through the underwood. He found Waldron with Colburn, the two conversing tranquilly in their saddles amid hissing bullets and dropping branches.

"Move your regiment forward now," the brigade commander was saying; "but halt it in the edge of the wood."

"Shan't I relieve Gildersleeve if he gets beaten?" asked the subordinate officer eagerly.

"No. The regiments on the left will help him out. I want your men and Peck's for the fight on top of the hill. Of course the rebels will try to retake it; then I shall call for you."

Fitz Hugh now approached and said, "Colonel, the Seventh has attacked in force."

"Good!" answered Waldron, with that sweet smile of his which thanked people who brought him pleasant news. "I thought I heard his fire. Gahogan will be on their right rear in ten minutes. Then we shall get the ridge. Ride back now to Major Bradley, and tell him to bring his Napoleons through the wood, and set two of them to shelling the enemy's centre. Tell him my idea is to amuse them, and keep them from changing front."

Again Fitz Hugh galloped off as before on a comfortably safe errand, safer at all events than many errands of that day. "This man is sparing my life," he said to himself. "Would to God I knew how to spare his!"

He found Bradley lunching on a gun caisson, and delivered his orders. "Something to do at last, eh?" laughed the rosy-cheeked youngster. "The smallest favors thankfully received. Won't you take a bite of rebel chicken, Captain? This rebellion must be put down. No? Well, tell the Colonel I am moving on, and John Brown's soul not far ahead."

When Fitz Hugh returned to Waldron he found him outside of the wood, at the base of the long incline which rose into the rebel position. About the slope were scattered prostrate forms, most numerous near the bottom, some crawling slowly rearward, some quiescent. Under the brow of the ridge, decimated and broken into a mere skirmish line sheltered in knots and singly, behind rocks and knolls, and bushes, lay the Fourteenth Regiment, keeping up a steady, slow fire. From the edge above, smokily dim against a pure, blue heaven, answered another rattle of musketry, incessant, obstinate, and spiteful. The combatants on both sides were lying down; otherwise neither party could have lasted ten minutes. From Fitz Hugh's point of view not a Confederate uniform could be seen. But the smoke of their rifles made a long gray line, which was disagreeably visible and permanent; and the sharp *whit! whit!* of their bullets continually

passed him, and cheeped away in the leafage behind.

"Our men can't get on another inch," he ven-
tured to say to his commander. "Wouldn't it be
well for me to ride up and say a cheering word?"

"Every battle consists largely in waiting," replied Waldron thoughtfully. "They have un-
doubtedly brought up a reserve to face Thomas.
But when Gahogan strikes the flank of the reserve, we shall win."

"I wish you would take shelter," begged Fitz
Hugh. "Everything depends on your life."

"My life has been both a help and a hurt to my
fellow-creatures," sighed the brigade commander. "Let come what will to it."

He glanced upward with an expression of profound emotion; he was evidently fighting two
battles, an outward and an inward one.

Presently he added, "I think the musketry is
increasing on the left. Does it strike you so?"

He was all eagerness again, leaning forward
with an air of earnest listening, his face deeply
flushed and his eye brilliant. Of a sudden the
combat above rose and swelled into higher vio-
lence. There was a clamor far away—it seemed
nearly a mile away—over the hill. Then the
nearer musketry—first Thomas's on the shoulder
of the ridge, next Gildersleeve's in front—
caught fire and raged with new fury.

Waldron laughed outright. "Gahogan has
reached them," he said to one of his staff who had

just rejoined him. "We shall all be up there in five minutes. Tell Colburn to bring on his regiment slowly."

Then, turning to Fitz Hugh, he added, "Captain, we will ride forward."

They set off at a walk, now watching the smoking brow of the eminence, now picking their way among dead and wounded. Suddenly there was a shout above them and a sudden diminution of the firing; and looking upward they saw the men of the Fourteenth running confusedly toward the summit. Without a word the brigade commander struck spurs into his horse and dashed up the long slope at a run, closely followed by his enemy and aid. What they saw when they overtook the straggling, running, panting, screaming pellmell of the Fourteenth was victory!

The entire right wing of the Confederates, attacked on three sides at once, placed at enormous disadvantage, completely outgeneraled, had given way in confusion, was retreating, breaking, and flying. There were lines yet of dirty gray or butternut; but they were few, meagre, fluctuating, and recoiling, and there were scattered and scurrying men in hundreds. Three veteran and gallant regiments had gone all to wreck under the shock of three similar regiments far more intelligently directed. A strong position had been lost because the heroes who held it could not perform the impossible feat of forming successively two fresh fronts under a concentric fire of musketry. The inferior brain power had confessed the superiority of the stronger one.

On the victorious side there was wild, clamorous, fierce exultation. The hurrying, shouting, firing soldiers, who noted their commander riding among them, swung their rifles or their tattered hats at him, and screamed "Hurrah!" No one thought of the Confederate dead underfoot, nor of the Union dead who dotted the slope behind. "What are you here for, Colonel?" shouted rough old Gildersleeve, one leg of his trousers dripping blood. "We can do it alone."

"It is a battle won," laughed Fitz Hugh, almost worshiping the man whom he had come to slay.

"It is a battle won, but not used," answered Waldron. "We haven't a gun yet, nor a flag. Where is the cavalry? Why isn't Stilton here? He must have got afoul of the enemy's horse, and been obliged to beat it off. Can anybody hear anything of Stilton?"

"Let him go," roared Old Grumps. "The infantry don't want any help."

"Your regiment has suffered, Colonel," answered Waldron, glancing at the scattered files of the Fourteenth. "Halt it and reorganize it, and let it fall in with the right of the First when Peck comes up. I shall replace you with the Fifth. Send your Adjutant back to Colburn and tell him to hurry along. Those fellows are making a new front over there," he added, pointing to the centre of the hill. "I want the Fifth, Seventh and Tenth in *échelon* as quickly as possible. And I want that cavalry. Lieutenant," turning to one of his staff, "ride off to the left and find Colonel Stilton. Tell him that I need a charge in ten minutes."

Presently cannon opened from that part of the ridge still held by the Confederates, the shell tearing through or over the dissolving groups of their right wing, and cracking viciously above the heads of the victorious Unionists. The explosions followed each other with stunning rapidity, and the shrill whirring of the splinters was ominous. Men began to fall again in the ranks or to drop out of them wounded. Of all this Waldron took no further note than to ride hastily to the brow of the ridge and look for his own artillery.

"See how he attinds to iverything himself," said Major Gahogan, who had cantered up to the side of Fitz Hugh. "It's just a matther of plain business, an' he looks after it loike a business man. Did ye see us, though, Captin, whin we come in on their right flank? By George, we murthered um. There's more'n a hundred lyin' in hapes back there. As for old Stilton, I just caught sight of um behind that wood to our left, an' he's makin' for the enemy's right rair. He'll have lots o' prisoners in half an hour."

When Waldron returned to the group he was told of his cavalry's whereabouts, and responded to the information with a smile of satisfaction.

"Bradley is hurrying up," he said, "and Taylor is pushing their left smartly. They will make one more tussle to recover their line of retreat; but we shall smash them from end to end and take every gun."

He galloped now to his infantry, and gave the word "Forward!" The three regiments which composed the *échelon* were the Fifth on the right, the Seventh fifty yards to the rear and left of the Fifth, the Tenth to the rear and left of the Seventh. It was behind the Fifth, that is, the foremost battalion, that the brigade commander posted himself.

"Do *you* mean to stay here, Colonel?" asked Fitz Hugh, in surprise and anxiety.

"It is a certain victory now," answered Waldron, with a singular glance upward. "My life is no longer important. I prefer to do my duty to the utmost in the sight of all men."

"I shall follow you and do mine, sir," said the Captain, much moved, he could scarcely say by what emotions, they were so many and conflicting.

"I want you otherwheres. Ride to Colonel Taylor at once, and hurry him up the hill. Tell him the enemy have greatly weakened their left. Tell him to push up everything, infantry, and cavalry, and artillery, and to do it in haste."

"Colonel, this is saving my life against my will," remonstrated Fitz Hugh.

60

# THE BRIGADE COMMANDER

"Go!" ordered Waldron, imperiously. "Time is precious."

Fitz Hugh dashed down the slope to the right at a gallop. The brigade commander turned tranquilly, and followed the march of his *échelon*. The second and decisive crisis of the little battle was approaching, and to understand it we must glance at the ground on which it was to be fought. Two hostile lines were marching toward each other along the broad, gently rounded crest of the hill and at right angles to its general course. Between these lines, but much the nearest to the Union troops, a spacious road came up out of the forest in front, crossed the ridge, swept down the smooth decline in rear, and led to a single wooden bridge over a narrow but deep rivulet. On either hand the road was hedged in by a close board fence, four feet or so in height. It was for the possession of this highway that the approaching lines were about to shed their blood. If the Confederates failed to win it all their artillery would be lost, and their army captured or dispersed.

The two parties came on without firing. The soldiers on both sides were veterans, cool, obedient to orders, intelligent through long service, and able to reserve all their resources for a short-range and final struggle. Moreover, the fences as yet partially hid them from each other, and would have rendered all aim for the present vague and uncertain.

61

"Forward, Fifth!" shouted Waldron. "Steady. Reserve your fire." Then, as the regiment came up to the fence, he added, "Halt; right dress. Steady, men."

Meantime he watched the advancing array with an eager gaze. It was a noble sight, full of moral sublimity, and worthy of all admiration. The long, lean, sunburned, weather-beaten soldiers, in ragged gray stepped forward, superbly, their ranks loose, but swift and firm, the men leaning forward in their haste, their tattered slouch hats pushed backward, their whole aspect business-like and virile. Their line was three battalions strong, far outflanking the Fifth, and at least equal to the entire *échelon*. When within thirty or forty yards of the further fence they increased their pace to nearly a double-quick, many of them stooping low in hunter fashion, and a few firing. Then Waldron rose in his stirrups and yelled, "Battalion! ready—aim—aim low. Fire!"

There was a stunning roar of three hundred and fifty rifles, and a deadly screech of bullets. But the smoke rolled out, the haste to reload was intense, and none could mark what execution was done. Whatever the Confederates may have suffered, they bore up under the volley, and they came on. In another minute each of those fences, not more than twenty-five yards apart, was lined by the shattered fragment of a regiment, each firing as fast as possible into the face of the other.

The Fifth bled fearfully: it had five of its ten company commanders shot dead in three minutes; and its loss in other officers and in men fell scarcely short of this terrible ratio. On its left the Seventh and the Tenth were up, pouring in musketry, and receiving it in a fashion hardly less sanguinary. No one present had ever seen, or ever afterward saw, such another close and deadly contest.

But the strangest thing in this whole wonderful fight was the conduct of the brigade commander. Up and down the rear of the lacerated Fifth Waldron rode thrice, spurring his plunging and wounded horse close to the yelling and fighting file-closers, and shouting in a piercing voice encouragement to his men. Stranger still, considering the character which he had borne in the army, and considering the evil deed for which he was to account on the morrow, were the words which he was distinctly and repeatedly heard to utter. "Stand steady, men—God is with us!" was the extraordinary battle-cry of this back-slidden clergyman, this sinner above many.

And it was a prophecy of victory. Bradley ran up his Napoleons on the right in the nick of time, and, although only one of them could be brought to bear, it was enough; the grape raked the Confederate left, broke it, and the battle was over. In five minutes more their whole array was scattered, and the entire position open to galloping cavalry, seizing guns, standards, and prisoners.

It was in the very moment of triumph, just as the stubborn Southern line reeled back from the fence in isolated clusters, that the miraculous immunity of Waldron terminated, and he received his death wound. A quarter of an hour later Fitz Hugh found a sorrowful group of officers gazing from a little distance upon their dying commander.

"Is the Colonel hit?" he asked, shocked and grieved, incredible as the emotion may seem.

"Don't go near him," called Gildersleeve, who, it will be remembered, knew or guessed his errand in camp. "The chaplain and surgeon are there. Let him alone."

"He's going to render his account," added Gahogan. "An' whativer he's done wrong, he's made it square to-day. Let um lave it to his brigade."

Adjutant Wallis, who had been blubbering aloud, who had cursed the rebels and the luck energetically, and who had also been trying to pray inwardly, groaned out, "This is our last victory. You see if it ain't. Bet you two to one."

"Hush, man!" replied Gahogan. "We'll win our share of um, though we'll have to work harder for it. We'll have to do more ourselves, an' get less done for us in the way of tactics."

"That's so, Major," whimpered a drummer, looking up from his duty of attending to a wounded comrade. "He knowed how to put his men in the right place, and his men knowed when they was in the right place. But it's goin' to be uphill through the steepest part of hell the rest of the way."

Soldiers, some of them weeping, some of them bleeding, arrived constantly to inquire after their commander, only to be sent quietly back to their ranks or to the rear. Around lay other men— dead men, and senseless, groaning men—all for the present unnoticed. Everything, except the distant pursuit of the cavalry, waited for Waldron to die. Fitz Hugh looked on silently with the tears of mingled emotions in his eyes, and with hopes and hatreds expiring in his heart. The surgeon supported the expiring victor's head, while Chaplain Colquhoun knelt beside him, holding his hand and praying audibly. Of a sudden the petition ceased, both bent hastily toward the wounded man, and after what seemed a long time exchanged whispers. Then the Chaplain rose, came slowly toward the now advancing group of officers, his hands outspread toward heaven in an attitude of benediction, and tears running down his haggard white face.

"I trust, dear friends," he said, in a tremulous voice, "that all is well with our brother and commander. His last words were, 'God is with us.'"

"Oh! but, man, *that* isn't well," broke out Gahogan, in a groan. "What did ye pray for his soul for? Why didn't ye pray for his loife?"

Fitz Hugh turned his horse and rode silently away. The next day he was seen journeying rearward by the side of an ambulance, within which lay what seemed a strangely delicate boy, insensible, and, one would say, mortally ill.

# THE DENVER EXPRESS

BY A. A. HAYES

# THE DENVER EXPRESS

## BY A. A. HAYES

NY one who has seen an outward-bound
clipper ship getting under way, and heard
the "shanty-songs" sung by the sailors
as they toiled at capstan and halliards, will probably remember that rhymeless but melodious refrain—

> "I'm bound to see its muddy waters,
> Yeo ho! that rolling river;
> Bound to see its muddy waters,
> Yeo ho! the wild Missouri."

Only a happy inspiration could have impelled
Jack to apply the adjective "wild" to that ill-be-
haved and disreputable river which, tipsily bearing its enormous burden of mud from the far
Northwest, totters, reels, runs its tortuous course
for hundreds on hundreds of miles and which,
encountering the lordly and thus far well-behaved
Mississippi at Alton, and forcing its company
upon this splendid river (as if some drunken fellow should lock arms with a dignified pedestrian), contaminates it all the way to the Gulf of
Mexico.

At a certain point on the banks of this river, or
rather—as it has the habit of abandoning and
destroying said banks—at a safe distance there-

From "Belgravia" for January, 1884.

69

from, there is a town from which a railroad takes its departure, for its long climb up the natural incline of the Great Plains, to the base of the mountains; hence the importance to this town of the large but somewhat shabby building serving as terminal station. In its smoky interior, late in the evening and not very long ago, a train was nearly ready to start. It was a train possessing a certain consideration. For the benefit of a public easily gulled and enamored of grandiloquent terms, it was advertised as the "Denver Fast Express"; sometimes, with strange unfitness, as the "Lightning Express"; "elegant" and "palatial" cars were declared to be included therein; and its departure was one of the great events of the twenty-four hours in the country round about. A local poet described it in the "live" paper of the town, cribbing from an old Eastern magazine and passing off as original the lines—

"Again we stepped into the street,
  A train came thundering by,
Drawn by the snorting iron steed
  Swifter than eagles fly.
Rumbled the wheels, the whistle shrieked,
  Far rolled the smoky cloud,
Echoed the hills, the valleys shook,
  The flying forests bowed."

The trainmen, on the other hand, used no fine phrases. They called it simply "Number Seventeen"; and, when it started, said it had "pulled out."

On the evening in question, there it stood,

nearly ready.  Just behind the great hissing loco-motive, with its parabolic headlight and its coal-laden tender, came the baggage, mail, and ex-press cars; then the passenger coaches, in which the social condition of the occupants seemed to be in inverse ratio to their distance from the engine.  First came emigrants, "honest miners," "cowboys," and laborers; Irishmen, Germans, Welshmen, Mennonites from Russia, quaint of garb and speech, and Chinamen.  Then came along cars full of people of better station, and last the great Pullman "sleepers," in which the busy black porters were making up the berths for well-to-do travelers of diverse nationalities and occupations.

It was a curious study for a thoughful ob-server, this motley crowd of human beings sink-ing all differences of race, creed, and habits in the common purpose to move westward—to the mountain fastnesses, the sage-brush deserts and the Golden Gate.

The warning bell had sounded, and the fireman leaned far out for the signal.  The gong struck sharply, the conductor shouted, "All aboard," and raised his hand; the tired ticket-seller shut his window, and the train moved out of the sta-tion, gathered way as it cleared the outskirts of the town, rounded a curve, entered on an abso-lutely straight line, and, with one long whistle from the engine, settled down to its work.  Through the night hours it sped on, past lonely ranches and infrequent stations, by and across shallow streams fringed with cottonwood trees, over the greenish-yellow buffalo grass near the old trail where many a poor emigrant, many a bold frontiersman, many a brave soldier, had laid his bones but a short time before.

Familiar as they may be, there is something strangely impressive about all-night journeys by rail, and those forming part of an American transcontinental trip are almost weird. From the windows of a night express in Europe or the older portions of the United States, one looks on houses and lights, cultivated fields, fences, and hedges; and, hurled as he may be through the darkness, he has a sense of companionship and semi-security. Far different is it when the long train is running over those two rails which, seen before night sets in, seem to meet on the horizon. Within all is as if between two great seaboard cities; the neatly dressed people, the uniformed officials, the handsome fittings, the various appliances for comfort. Without are now long dreary levels, now deep and wild canyons, now an environment of strange and grotesque rock-formations, castles, battlements, churches, statues. The antelope fleetly runs, and the coyote skulks away from the track, and the gray wolf howls afar off. It is for all the world, to one's fancy, as if a bit of civilization, a family or community, its belongings and surroundings complete, were flying through regions barbarous and inhospitable.

# THE DENVER EXPRESS

From the cab of Engine No. 32, the driver of the Denver Express saw, showing faintly in the early morning, the buildings grouped about the little station ten miles ahead, where breakfast awaited his passengers. He looked at his watch; he had just twenty minutes in which to run the distance, as he had run it often before. Something, however, traveled faster than he. From the smoky station out of which the train passed the night before, along the slender wire stretched on rough poles at the side of the track, a spark of that mysterious something which we call electricity flashed at the moment he returned the watch to his pocket; and in five minutes' time the station-master came out on the platform, a little more thoughtful than his wont, and looked eastward for the smoke of the train. With but three of the passengers in that train has this tale especially to do, and they were all in the new and comfortable Pullman "City of Cheyenne." One was a tall, well-made man of about thirty—blond, blue-eyed, bearded, straight, sinewy, alert. Of all in the train he seemed the most thoroughly at home, and the respectful greeting of the conductor, as he passed through the car, marked him as an officer of the road. Such was he—Henry Sinclair, assistant engineer, quite famed on the line, high in favor with the directors, and a rising man in all ways. It was known on the road that he was expected in Denver, and there were rumors that he was to organize the parties for the survey

of an important "extension." Beside him sat his
pretty young wife. She was a New Yorker—
one could tell at first glance—from the feather of
her little bonnet, matching the gray traveling
dress, to the tips of her dainty boots; and one,
too, at whom old Fifth Avenue promenaders
would have turned to look. She had a charming
figure, brown hair, hazel eyes, and an expression
at once kind, intelligent, and spirited. She had
cheerfully left a luxurious home to follow the
young engineer's fortunes; and it was well known
that those fortunes had been materially advanced
by her tact and cleverness.

The third passenger in question had just been
in conversation with Sinclair and the latter was
telling his wife of their curious meeting. Entering the toilet-room at the rear of the car, he said,
he had begun his ablutions by the side of another
man, and it was as they were sluicing their faces
with water that he heard the cry:

"Why, Major, is that you? Just to think of
meeting you here!"

A man of about twenty-eight years of age,
slight, muscular, wiry, had seized his wet hand
and was wringing it. He had black eyes, keen
and bright, swarthy complexion, black hair and
mustache. A keen observer might have seen
about him some signs of a *jeunesse orageuse,* but
his manner was frank and pleasing. Sinclair
looked him in the face, puzzled for a moment.

"Don't you remember Foster?" asked the man.

"Of course I do," replied Sinclair. "For a moment I could not place you. Where have you been and what have you been doing?"

"Oh," replied Foster, laughing, "I've braced up and turned over a new leaf. I'm a respectable member of society, have a place in the express company, and am going to Denver to take charge."

"I am very glad to hear it, and you must tell me your story when we have had our breakfast."

The pretty young woman was just about to ask who Foster was, when the speed of the train slackened, and the brakeman opened the door of the car and cried out in stentorian tones:

"Pawnee Junction; twenty minutes for refreshments!"

## II

When the celebrated Rocky Mountain gold excitement broke out, more than twenty years ago, and people painted "PIKE'S PEAK OR BUST" on the canvas covers of their wagons and started for the diggings, they established a "trail" or "trace" leading in a southwesterly direction from the old one to California.

At a certain point on this trail a frontiersman named Barker built a forlorn ranch-house and *corral,* and offered what is conventionally called "entertainment for man and beast."

For years he lived there, dividing his time between fighting the Indians and feeding the pass-

ing emigrants and their stock. Then the first
railroad to Denver was built, taking another
route from the Missouri, and Barker's occupation
was gone. He retired with his gains to St. Louis
and lived in comfort.

Years passed on, and the "extension" over
which our train is to pass was planned. The old
pioneers were excellent natural engineers and
their successors could find no better route than
they had chosen. Thus it was that "Barker's"
became, during the construction period, an important point, and the frontiersman's name came
to figure on time-tables. Meanwhile the place
passed through a process of evolution which
would have delighted Darwin. In the party of
engineers which first camped there was Sinclair,
and it was by his advice that the contractors
selected it for division headquarters. Then came
drinking "saloons" and gambling houses—alike
the inevitable concomitant and the bane of Western settlements; then scattered houses and shops
and a shabby so-called hotel, in which the letting
of miserable rooms (divided from each other by
canvas partitions) was wholly subordinated to
the business of the bar. Before long, Barker's
had acquired a worse reputation than even other
towns of its type, the abnormal and uncanny ag-
gregations of squalor and vice which dotted the
plains in those days; and it was at its worst when
Sinclair returned thither and took up his quarters in the engineers' building. The passion for

gambling was raging, and to pander thereto were collected as choice a lot of desperadoes as ever "stacked" cards or loaded dice. It came to be noticed that they were on excellent terms with a man called "Jeff" Johnson, who was lessee of the hotel; and to be suspected that said Johnson, in local parlance, "stood in with" them. With this man had come to Barker's his daughter Sarah, commonly known as "Sally," a handsome girl, with a straight, lithe figure, fine features, reddish auburn hair, and dark-blue eyes. It is but fair to say that even the "toughs" of a place like Barker's show some respect for the other sex, and Miss Sally's case was no exception to the rule. The male population admired her; they said she "put on heaps of style"; but none of them had seemed to make any progress in her good graces.

On a pleasant afternoon just after the track had been laid some miles west of Barker's, and construction trains were running with some regularity to and from the end thereof, Sinclair sat on the rude veranda of the engineers' quarters, smoking his well-colored meerschaum and looking at the sunset. The atmosphere had been so clear during the day that glimpses were had of Long's and Pike's peaks, and as the young engineer gazed at the gorgeous cloud display he was thinking of the miners' quaint and pathetic idea that the dead "go over the Range."

"Nice-looking, ain't it, Major?" asked a voice

at his elbow, and he turned to see one of the contractors' officials taking a seat near him.

"More than nice-looking to my mind, Sam," he replied. "What is the news to-day?"

"Nothin' much. There's a sight of talk about the doin's of them faro an' keno sharps. The boys is gettin' kind o' riled, fur they allow the game ain't on the square wuth a cent. Some of 'em down to the tie-camp wuz a-talkin' about a vigilance committee, an' I wouldn't be surprised ef they meant business. Hev yer heard about the young feller that come in a week ago from Laramie an' set up a new faro-bank?"

"No. What about him?"

"Wa'al, yer see he's a feller thet's got a lot of sand an' ain't afeard of nobody, an' he's allowed to hev the deal to his place on the square every time. Accordin' to my idee, gamblin's about the wust racket a feller kin work, but it takes all sorts of men to make a world, an' ef the boys is bound to hev a game, I calkilate they'd like to patronize his bank. Thet's made the old crowd mighty mad an' they're a-talkin' about puttin' up a job of cheatin' on him an' then stringin' him up. Besides, I kind o' think there's some cussed jealousy on another lay as comes in. Yer see the young feller—Cyrus Foster's his name—is sweet on thet gal of Jeff Johnson's. Jeff was to Laramie before he come here, an' Foster knowed Sally up thar. I allow he moved here to see her. Hello! Ef thar they ain't a-coming now."

Down a path leading from the town past the railroad buildings, and well on the prairie, Sinclair saw the girl walking with the "young feller." He was talking earnestly to her and her eyes were cast down. She looked pretty and, in a way, graceful; and there was in her attire a noticeable attempt at neatness, and a faint reminiscence of bygone fashions. A smile came to Sinclair's lips as he thought of a couple walking up Fifth Avenue during his leave of absence not many months before, and of a letter many times read, lying at that moment in his breast-pocket.

"Papa's bark is worse than his bite," ran one of its sentences. "Of course he does not like the idea of my leaving him and going away to such dreadful and remote places as Denver and Omaha and I don't know what else; but he will not oppose me in the end, and when you come on again—"

"By thunder!" exclaimed Sam; "ef thar ain't one of them cussed sharps a-watchin' 'em."

Sure enough a rough-looking fellow, his hat pulled over his eyes, half concealed behind a pile of lumber, was casting a sinister glance toward the pair.

"The gal's well enough," continued Sam; "but I don't take a cent's wuth of stock in thet thar father of her'n. He's in with them sharps, sure pop, an' it don't suit his book to hev Foster hangin' round. It's ten to one he sent that cuss to watch 'em. Wa'al, they're a queer lot, an' I'm

afeared thar's plenty of trouble ahead among 'em.
Good luck to you, Major," and he pushed back
his chair and walked away.

After breakfast next morning, when Sinclair
was sitting at the table in his office, busy with
maps and plans, the door was thrown open, and
Foster, panting for breath, ran in.

"Major Sinclair," he said, speaking with difficulty, "I've no claim on you, but I ask you to
protect me. The other gamblers are going to
hang me. They are more than ten to one. They
will track me here; unless you harbor me, I'm a
dead man."

Sinclair rose from his chair in a second and
walked to the window. A party of men were
approaching the building. He turned to Foster:

"I do not like your trade," said he; "but I will
not see you murdered if I can help it. You are
welcome here." Foster said "Thank you," stood
still a moment, and then began to pace the room,
rapidly clinching his hands, his whole frame
quivering, his eyes flashing fire—"for all the
world," Sinclair said, in telling the story afterward, "like a fierce caged tiger."

"My God!" he muttered, with concentrated
intensity, "to be *trapped,* TRAPPED like this!"

Sinclair stepped quickly to the door of his bedroom and motioned Foster to enter. Then there
came a knock at the outer door, and he opened it
and stood on the threshold erect and firm. Half
a dozen "toughs" faced him.

"Major," said their spokesman, "we want that man."

"You can not have him, boys."

"Major, we're a-goin' to take him."

"You had better not try," said Sinclair, with perfect ease and self-possession, and in a pleasant voice. "I have given him shelter, and you can only get him over my dead body. Of course you can kill me, but you won't do even that without one or two of you going down; and then you know perfectly well, boys, what will happen. You *know* that if you lay your finger on a railroad man it's all up with you. There are five hundred men in the tie-camp, not five miles away, and you don't need to be told that in less than one hour after they get word there won't be a piece of one of you big enough to bury."

The men made no reply. They looked him straight in the eyes for a moment. Had they seen a sign of flinching they might have risked the issue, but there was none. With muttered curses, they slunk away. Sinclair shut and bolted the door, then opened the one leading to the bedroom.

"Foster," he said, "the train will pass here in half an hour. Have you money enough?"

"Plenty, Major."

"Very well; keep perfectly quiet and I will try to get you safely off." He went to an adjoining room and called Sam, the contractor's man. He took in the situation at a glance.

"Wa'al Foster," said he, "kind o' 'close call' for yer, warn't it? Guess yer'd better be gittin' up an' gittin' pretty lively. The train boys will take yer through an' yer kin come back when this racket's worked out."

Sinclair glanced at his watch, then he walked to the window and looked out. On a small *mesa,* or elevated plateau, commanding the path to the railroad, he saw a number of men with rifles.

"Just as I expected," said he. "Sam, ask one of the boys to go down to the track and, when the train arrives, tell the conductor to come here."

In a few minutes the whistle was heard and the conductor entered the building. Receiving his instructions, he returned, and immediately on engine, tender, and platform appeared the train-men, with *their* rifles covering the group on the bluff. Sinclair put on his hat.

"Now, Foster," said he, "we have no time to lose. Take Sam's arm and mine, and walk between us."

The trio left the building and walked deliberately to the railroad. Not a word was spoken. Besides the men in sight on the train, two behind the window-blinds of the one passenger coach, and unseen, kept their fingers on the triggers of their repeating carbines. It seemed a long time, counted by anxious seconds, until Foster was safe in the coach.

"All ready, conductor," said Sinclair. "Now, Foster, good-by. I am not good at lecturing, but if I were you, I would make this the turning-point in my life."

Foster was much moved.

"I will do it, Major," said he; "and I shall never forget what you have done for me to-day. I am sure we shall meet again."

With another shriek from the whistle the train started. Sinclair and Sam saw the men quietly returning the firearms to their places as it gathered way. Then they walked back to their quarters. The men on the *mesa,* balked of their purpose, had withdrawn.

Sam accompanied Sinclair to his door, and then sententiously remarked: "Major, I think I'll light out and find some of the boys. You ain't got no call to know anything about it, but I allow it's about time them cusses was bounced."

Three nights after this, a powerful party of *Vigilantes,* stern and inexorable, made a raid on all the gambling dens, broke the tables and apparatus, and conducted the men to a distance from the town, where they left them with an emphatic and concise warning as to the consequences of any attempt to return. An exception was made in Jeff Johnson's case—but only for the sake of his daughter—for it was found that many a "little game" had been carried on in his house.

Ere long he found it convenient to sell his business and retire to a town some miles to the eastward, where the railroad influence was not as strong as at Barker's. At about this time, Sinclair made his arrangements to go to New York, with the pleasant prospect of marrying the young lady in Fifth Avenue. In due time he arrived at Barker's with his young and charming wife and remained for some days. The changes were astounding. Commonplace respectability had replaced abnormal lawlessness. A neat station stood where had been the rough contractor's buildings. At a new "Windsor" (or was it "Brunswick"?) the performance of the kitchen contrasted sadly (alas! how common is such contrast in these regions) with the promise of the *menu*. There was a tawdry theatre yclept "Academy of Music," and there was not much to choose in the way of ugliness between two "meeting-houses."

"Upon my word, my dear," said Sinclair to his wife, "I ought to be ashamed to say it, but I prefer Barker's *au naturel.*"

One evening, just before the young people left the town, and as Mrs. Sinclair sat alone in her room, the frowsy waitress announced "a lady," and was requested to bid her enter. A woman came with timid mien into the room, sat down, as invited, and removed her veil. Of course the young bride had never known Sally Johnson, the whilom belle of Barker's, but her husband would have noticed at a glance how greatly she was changed from the girl who walked with Foster past the engineers' quarters. It would be hard to find a more striking contrast than was presented by the two women as they sat facing each other: the one in the flush of health and beauty, calm, sweet, self-possessed; the other still retaining some of the shabby finery of old days, but pale and haggard, with black rings under her eyes, and a pathetic air of humiliation.

"Mrs. Sinclair," she hurriedly began, "you do not know me, nor the like of me. I've got no right to speak to you, but I couldn't help it. Oh! please believe me, I am not real downright bad. I'm Sally Johnson, daughter of a man whom they drove out of the town. My mother died when I was little, and I *never* had a show; and folks think because I live with my father, and he makes me know the crowd he travels with, that I must be in with them, and be of their sort. I never had a woman speak a kind word to me, and I've had so much trouble that I'm just drove wild, and like to kill myself; and then I was at the station when you came in, and I saw your sweet face and the kind look in your eyes, and it came in my heart that I'd speak to you if I died for it." She leaned eagerly forward, her hands nervously closing on the back of a chair. "I suppose your husband never told you of me; like enough he never knew me; but I'll never forget him as long as I live. When he was here before, there was a young man"—here a faint color came in the wan cheeks—"who was fond of me, and I thought the world of him, and my father was down on him, and the men that father was in with wanted to kill him; and Mr. Sinclair saved his life. He's gone away, and I've waited and waited for him to come back—and perhaps I'll never see him again. But oh! dear lady, I'll never forget what your husband did. He's a good man, and he deserves the love of a dear good woman like you, and if I dared I'd pray for you both, night and day."

She stopped suddenly and sank back in her seat, pale as before, and as if frightened by her own emotion. Mrs. Sinclair had listened with sympathy and increasing interest.

"My poor girl," she said, speaking tenderly (she had a lovely, soft voice) and with slightly heightened color, "I am delighted that you came to see me, and that my husband was able to help you. Tell me, can we not do more for you? I do not for one moment believe you can be happy with your present surroundings. Can we not assist you to leave them?"

The girl rose, sadly shaking her head. "I thank you for your words," she said. "I don't suppose I'll ever see you again, but I'll say, God bless you!"

She caught Mrs. Sinclair's hand, pressed it to her lips, and was gone.

Sinclair found his wife very thoughtful when he came home, and he listened with much interest to her story.

"Poor girl!" said he; "Foster is the man to

help her. I wonder where he is? I must inquire about him."

The next day they proceeded on their way to San Francisco, and matters drifted on at Barker's much as before. Johnson had, after an absence of some months, come back and lived without molestation amid the shifting population. Now and then, too, some of the older residents fancied they recognized, under slouched sombreros, the faces of some of his former "crowd" about the "Ranchman's Home," as his gaudy saloon was called.

Late on the very evening on which this story opens, and they had been "making up" the Denver Express in the train-house on the Missouri, "Jim" Watkins, agent and telegrapher at Barker's, was sitting in his little office, communicating with the station rooms by the ticket window. Jim was a cool, silent, efficient man, and not much given to talk about such episodes in his past life as the "wiping out" by Indians of the construction party to which he belonged, and his own rescue by the scouts. He was smoking an old and favorite pipe, and talking with one of "the boys" whose head appeared at the wicket. On a seat in the station sat a woman in a black dress and veil, apparently waiting for a train.

"Got a heap of letters and telegrams there, ain't yer, Jim?" remarked the man at the window.

"Yes," replied Jim; "they're for Engineer Sinclair, to be delivered to him when he passes through here. He left on No. 17, to-night." The inquirer did not notice the sharp start of the woman near him.

"Is that good-lookin' wife of his'n a-comin' with him?" asked he.

"Yes, there's letters for her, too."

"Well, good-night, Jim. See yer later," and he went out. The woman suddenly rose and ran to the window.

"Mr. Watkins," cried she, "can I see you for a few moments where no one can interrupt us? It's a matter of life and death." She clutched the sill with her thin hands, and her voice trembled. Watkins recognized Sally Johnson in a moment. He unbolted a door, motioned her to enter, closed and again bolted it, and also closed the ticket window. Then he pointed to a chair, and the girl sat down and leaned eagerly forward.

"If they knew I was here," she said in a hoarse whisper, "my life wouldn't be safe five minutes. I was waiting to tell you a terrible story, and then I heard who was on the train due here to-morrow night. Mr. Watkins, don't, for God's sake, ask me how I found out, but I hope to die if I ain't telling you the living truth! They're going to wreck that train—No. 17—at Dead Man's Crossing, fifteen miles east, and rob the passengers and the express car. It's the worst gang in the country, *Perry's*. They're going to

88

throw the train off the track, the passengers will be maimed and killed—and Mr. Sinclair and his wife on the cars! Oh! my God! Mr. Watkins, send them warning!"

She stood upright, her face deadly pale, her hands clasped. Watkins walked deliberately to the railroad map which hung on the wall and scanned it. Then he resumed his seat, laid his pipe down, fixed his eyes on the girl's face, and began to question her. At the same time his right hand, with which he had held the pipe, found its way to the telegraph key. None but an expert could have distinguished any change in the *clicking* of the instrument, which had been almost incessant; but Watkins had "called" the head office on the Missouri. In two minutes the "sounder" rattled out *All right! What is it?"*

Watkins went on with his questions, his eyes still fixed on the poor girl's face, and all the time his fingers, as it were, playing with the key. If he were imperturbable, so was *not* a man sitting at a receiving instrument nearly five hundred miles away. He had "taken" but a few words when he jumped from his chair and cried:

"Shut that door, and call the superintendent and be quick! Charley, brace up—lively—and come and write this out!" With his wonderful electric pen, the handle several hundreds of miles long, Watkins, unknown to his interlocutor, was printing in the Morse alphabet this startling message:

"Inform'n rec'd. Perry gang going to throw No. 17 off track near —xth mile-post, this division, about nine to-morrow (Thursday) night, kill passengers, and rob express and mail. Am alone here. No chance to verify story, but believe it to be on square. Better make arrangements from your end to block game. No Sheriff here now. Answer."

The superintendent, responding to the hasty summons, heard the message before the clerk had time to write it out. His lips were closely compressed as he put his own hand on the key and sent these laconic sentences: *"O. K. Keep perfectly dark. Will manage from this end."*

Watkins, at Barker's, rose from his seat, opened the door a little way, saw that the station was empty, and then said to the girl, brusquely, but kindly:

"Sally, you've done the square thing, and saved that train. I'll take care that you don't suffer and that you get well paid. Now come home with me, and my wife will look out for you."

"Oh! no," cried the girl, shrinking back, "I must run away. You're mighty kind, but I daren't go with you." Detecting a shade of doubt in his eye, she added: "Don't be afeared; I'll die before they'll know I've given them away to you!" and she disappeared in the darkness.

At the other end of the wire, the superintendent had quietly impressed secrecy on his operator and clerk, ordered his fast mare harnessed, and gone to his private office.

"Read that!" said he to his secretary. "It was about time for some trouble of this kind, and now

I'm going to let Uncle Sam take care of his mails. If I don't get to the reservation before the General's turned in, I shall have to wake him up. Wait for me, please."

The gray mare made the six miles to the military reservation in just half an hour. The General was smoking his last cigar, and was alert in an instant; and before the superintendent had finished the jorum of "hot Scotch" hospitably tendered, the orders had gone by wire to the commanding officer at Fort ——, some distance east of Barker's, and been duly acknowledged.

Returning to the station, the superintendent remarked to the waiting secretary:

"The General's all right. Of course we can't tell that this is not a sell; but if those Perry hounds mean business they'll get all the fight they want—and if they've got any souls—which I doubt—may the Lord have mercy on them!"

He prepared several despatches, two of which were as follows:

"MR. HENRY SINCLAIR:
    "On No. 17, Pawnee Junction:
    This telegram your authority to take charge of train on which you are, and demand obedience of all officials and trainmen on road. Please do so, and act in accordance with information wired station agent at Pawnee Junction."

To the Station Agent:

"Reported Perry gang will try wreck and rob No. 17 near ——xth mile-post, Denver Division, about nine Thursday night. Troops will await train at Fort ——. Car ordered ready for them. Keep everything secret, and act in accordance with orders of Mr. Sinclair."

"It's worth about ten thousand dollars," sententiously remarked he, "that Sinclair's on that train. He's got both sand and brains. Goodnight," and he went to bed and slept the sleep of the just.

## III

The sun never shone more brightly and the air was never more clear and bracing than when Sinclair helped his wife off the train at Pawnee Junction. The station-master's face fell as he saw the lady, but he saluted the engineer with as easy an air as he could assume, and watched for an opportunity to speak to him alone. Sinclair read the despatches with an unmoved countenance, and after a few minutes' reflection simply said: "All right. Be sure to keep the matter perfectly quiet." At breakfast he was *distrait*—so much so that his wife asked him what was the matter. Taking her aside, he at once showed her the telegrams.

"You see my duty," he said. "My only thought is about you, my dear child. Will you stay here?"

She simply replied, looking into his face without a tremor:

"My place is with you." Then the conductor called "All aboard," and the train once more started.

Sinclair asked Foster to join him in the smoking compartment and tell him the promised story, which the latter did. His rescue at Barker's, he frankly and gratefully said, *had* been the turning point in his life. In brief, he had "sworn off" from gambling and drinking, had found honest employment, and was doing well.

"I've two things to do now, Major," he added; "first, I must show my gratitude to you; and next"—he hesitated a little—"I want to find that poor girl that I left behind at Barker's. She was engaged to marry me, and when I came to think of it, and what a life I'd have made her lead, I hadn't the heart till now to look for her; but, seeing I'm on the right track, I'm going to find her, and get her to come with me. Her father's an —old scoundrel, but that ain't her fault, and I ain't going to marry *him*."

"Foster," quietly asked Sinclair, "do you know the Perry gang?"

The man's brow darkened.

"Know them?" said he. "I know them much too well. Perry is as ungodly a cutthroat as ever killed an emigrant in cold blood, and he's got in his gang nearly all those hounds that tried to hang me. Why do you ask, Major?"

Sinclair handed him the despatches. "You are the only man on the train to whom I have shown them," said he.

Foster read them slowly, his eyes lighting up as he did so. "Looks as if it was true," said he. "Let me see! Fort ——. Yes, that's the —th infantry. Two of their boys were killed at Sidney last summer by some of the same gang, and the regiment's sworn vengeance. Major, if this story's on the square, that crowd's goose is cooked, and *don't you forget it!* I say, you must give me a hand in."

"Foster," said Sinclair, "I am going to put responsibility on your shoulders. I have no doubt that, if we be attacked, the soldiers will dispose of the gang; but I must take all possible precautions for the safety of the passengers. We must not alarm them. They can be made to think that the troops are going on a scout, and only a certain number of resolute men need be told of what we expect. Can you, late this afternoon, go through the cars, and pick them out? I will then put you in charge of the passenger cars, and you can post your men on the platforms to act in case of need. My place will be ahead."

"Major, you can depend on me," was Foster's reply. "I'll go through the train and have my eye on some boys of the right sort, and that's got their shooting-irons with them."

Through the hours of that day on rolled the train, still over the crisp buffalo grass, across the well-worn buffalo trails, past the prairie-dog villages. The passengers chatted, dozed, played cards, read, all unconscious, with the exception of three, of the coming conflict between the good and the evil forces bearing on their fate; of the fell preparations making for their disaster; of the grim preparations making to avert such disaster;

of all of which the little wires alongside of them had been talking back and forth. Watkins had telegraphed that he still saw no reason to doubt the good faith of his warning, and Sinclair had reported his receipt of authority and his acceptance thereof. Meanwhile, also, there had been set in motion a measure of that power to which appeal is so reluctantly made in time of peace. At Fort ——, a lonely post on the plains, the orders had that morning been issued for twenty men under Lieutenant Halsey to parade at 4 P. M., with overcoats, two days' rations, and ball cartridges; also for Assistant Surgeon Kesler to report for duty with the party. Orders as to destination were communicated direct to the lieutenant from the post commander, and on the minute the little column moved, taking the road to the station. The regiment from which it came had been in active service among the Indians on the frontier for a long time, and the officers and men were tried and seasoned fighters. Lieutenant Halsey had been well known at the West Point balls as the "leader of the german." From the last of these balls he had gone straight to the field, and three years had given him an enviable reputation for *sang-froid* and determined bravery. He looked every inch the soldier as he walked along the trail, his cloak thrown back and his sword tucked under his arm. The doctor, who carried a Modoc bullet in some inaccessible part of his scarred body, growled good-naturedly at the need of walking, and the men, enveloped in their army-blue overcoats, marched easily by fours. Reaching the station, the lieutenant called the agent aside, and with him inspected, on a siding, a long platform car on which benches had been placed and secured. Then he took his seat in the station and quietly waited, occasionally twisting his long blond mustache. The doctor took a cigar with the agent, and the men walked about or sat on the edge of the platform. One of them, who obtained a surreptitious glance at his silent commander, told his companions that there was trouble ahead for somebody.

"That's just the way the leftenant looked, boys," said he, "when we was laying for them Apaches that raided Jones's Ranch and killed the women and little children."

In a short time the officer looked at his watch, formed his men, and directed them to take their places on the seats of the car. They had hardly done so when the whistle of the approaching train was heard. When it came up, the conductor, who had his instructions from Sinclair, had the engine detached and backed on the siding for the soldiers' car, which thus came between it and the foremost baggage car when the train was again made up. As arranged, it was announced that the troops were to be taken a certain distance to join a scouting party, and the curiosity of the passengers was but slightly excited. The soldiers sat quietly in their seats, their repeating rifles held between their knees, and the officer in front. Sinclair joined the latter, and had a few words with him as the train moved on. A little later, when the stars were shining brightly overhead, they passed into the express car, and sent for the conductor and other trainmen, and for Foster. In a few words Sinclair explained the position of affairs. His statement was received with perfect coolness, and the men only asked what they were to do.

"I hope, boys," said Sinclair, "that we are going to put this gang to-night where they will make no more trouble. Lieutenant Halsey will bear the brunt of the fight, and it only remains for you to stand by the interests committed to your care. Mr. Express Agent, what help do you want?" The person addressed, a good-natured giant, girded with a cartridge belt, smiled as he replied:

"Well, sir, I'm wearing a watch which the company gave me for standing off the James gang in Missouri for half an hour, when we hadn't the ghost of a soldier about. I'll take the contract, and welcome, to hold *this* fort alone."

"Very well," said Sinclair. "Foster, what progress have you made?"

"Major, I've got ten or fifteen as good men as ever drew a bead, and just red-hot for a fight."

"That will do very well. Conductor, give the trainmen the rifles from the baggage car and let them act under Mr. Foster. Now, boys, I am sure you will do your duty. That is all."

From the next station Sinclair telegraphed "All ready" to the superintendent, who was pacing his office in much suspense. Then he said a few words to his brave but anxious wife, and walked to the rear platform. On it were several armed men, who bade him good-evening, and asked "when the fun was going to begin." Walking through the train, he found each platform similarly occupied, and Foster going from one to the other. The latter whispered as he passed him:

"Major, I found Arizona Joe, the scout, in the smokin' car, and he's on the front platform. That lets me out, and although I know as well as you that there ain't any danger about that rear sleeper where the madam is, I ain't a-going to be far off from her." Sinclair shook him by the hand; then he looked at his watch. It was half-past eight. He passed through the baggage and express cars, finding in the latter the agent sitting behind his safe, on which lay two large revolvers. On the platform car he found the soldiers and their commander sitting silent and unconcerned as before. When Sinclair reached the latter and nodded, he rose and faced the men, and his fine voice was clearly heard above the rattle of the train.

"Company, 'ten*tion!*" The soldiers straightened themselves in a second.

"With ball cartridge, *load!*" It was done with the precision of a machine. Then the lieutenant spoke, in the same clear, crisp, tones that the troops had heard in more than one fierce battle.

"Men," said he, "in a few minutes the Perry gang, which you will remember, are going to try to run this train off the track, wound and kill the passengers, and rob the cars and the United States mail. It is our business to prevent them. Sergeant Wilson" (a gray-bearded non-commissioned officer stood up and saluted), "I am going on the engine. See that my orders are repeated. Now, men, aim low, and don't waste any shots." He and Sinclair climbed over the tender and spoke to the engine-driver.

"How are the air-brakes working?" asked Sinclair.

"First-rate."

"Then, if you slowed down now, you could stop the train in a third of her length, couldn't you?"

"Easy, if you don't mind being shaken up a bit."

"That is good. How is the country about the —xth mile-post?"

"Dead level, and smooth."

"Good again. Now, Lieutenant Halsey, this is a splendid head-light, and we can see a long way with my night glass. I will have a—"

"—2d mile-pole just past," interrupted the engine-driver.

"Only one more to pass, then, before we ought to strike them. Now, lieutenant, I undertake to stop the train within a very short distance of the gang. They will be on both sides of the track, no doubt; and the ground, as you hear, is quite level. You will best know what to do."

The officer stepped back. "Sergeant," called he, "do you hear me plainly?"

"Yes, sir."

"Have the men fix bayonets. When the train stops, and I wave my sword, let half jump off each side, run up quickly, and form line *abreast of the engine*—not ahead."

"Jack," said Sinclair to the engine-driver, "is your hand steady?" The man held it up with a smile. "Good. Now stand by your throttle and your air-brake. Lieutenant, better warn the men to hold on tight, and tell the sergeant to pass the word to the boys on the platforms, or they will be knocked off by the sudden stop. Now for a look ahead!" and he brought the binocular to his eyes.

The great parabolic head-light illuminated the track a long way in advance, all behind it being of course in darkness. Suddenly Sinclair cried out:

"The fools have a light there, as I am a living man; and there is a little red one near us. What can that be? All ready, Jack! By heaven! they have taken up two rails. Now *hold on, all!* STOP HER!!"

The engine-driver shut his throttle-valve with a jerk. Then, holding hard by it, he sharply turned a brass handle. There was a fearful jolt —a grating—and the train's way was checked. The lieutenant, standing sidewise, had drawn his sword. He waved it, and almost before he could get off the engine the soldiers were up and forming, still in shadow, while the bright light was thrown on a body of men ahead.

"Surrender, or you are dead men!" roared the officer. Curses and several shots were the reply. Then came the orders, quick and sharp:

*"Forward! Close up! Double-quick! Halt!* FIRE!" . . . It was speedily over. Left on the car with the men, the old sergeant had said:

"Boys, you hear. It's that —— Perry gang. Now, don't forget Larry and Charley that they murdered last year," and there had come from the soldiers a sort of fierce, subdued *growl*. The volley was followed by a bayonet charge, and it required all the officer's authority to save the lives even of those who "threw up their hands." Large as the gang was (outnumbering the troops), well armed and desperate as they were, every one was dead, wounded, or a prisoner when the men who guarded the train platforms ran up. The surgeon, with professional coolness, walked up to the robbers, his instrument case under his arm.

"Not much for me to do here, Lieutenant," said he. "That practice for Creedmoor is telling on the shooting. Good thing for the gang, too.

Bullets are better than rope, and a Colorado jury will give them plenty of that."

Sinclair had sent a man to tell his wife that all was over. Then he ordered a fire lighted, and the rails relaid. The flames lit a strange scene as the passengers flocked up. The lieutenant posted men to keep them back.

"Is there a telegraph station not far ahead, Sinclair?" asked he. "Yes? All right." He drew a small pad from his pocket, and wrote a despatch to the post commander.

"Be good enough to send that for me," said he, "and leave orders at Barker's for the night express eastward to stop for us, and bring a posse to take care of the wounded and prisoners. And now, my dear Sinclair, I suggest that you get the passengers into the cars, and go on as soon as those rails are spiked. When they realize the situation, some of them will feel precious ugly, and you know we can't have any lynching."

Sinclair glanced at the rails and gave the word at once to the conductor and brakemen, who began vociferating, "All aboard!" Just then Foster appeared, an expression of intense satisfaction showing clearly on his face, in the firelight.

"Major," said he, "I didn't use to take much stock in special Providence, or things being ordered; but I'm darned if I don't believe in them from this day. I was bound to stay where you put me, but I was uneasy, and wild to be in the scrimmage; and, if I had been there, I wouldn't have taken notice of a little red light that wasn't much behind the rear platform when we stopped. When I saw there was no danger there I ran back, and what do you think I found? There was a woman in a dead faint, and just clutching a lantern that she had tied up in a red scarf, poor little thing! And, Major, it was Sally! It was the little girl that loved me out at Barker's, and has loved me and waited for me ever since! And when she came to, and knew me, she was so glad she 'most fainted away again; and she let on as it was her that gave away the job. And I took her into the sleeper, and the madam, God bless her!—she knew Sally before and was good to her —she took care of her and is cheering her up. And now, Major, I'm going to take her straight to Denver, and send for a parson and get her married to me, and she'll brace up, sure pop."

The whistle sounded, and the train started. From the window of the "sleeper" Sinclair and his wife took their last look at the weird scene. The lieutenant, standing at the side of the track, wrapped in his cloak, caught a glimpse of Mrs. Sinclair's pretty face, and returned her bow. Then, as the car passed out of sight, he tugged at his mustache and hummed:

> "Why, boys, why,
> Should we be melancholy, boys,
> Whose business 'tis to die?"

In less than an hour, telegrams having in the meantime been sent in both directions, the train ran alongside the platform at Barker's; and Watkins, imperturbable as usual, met Sinclair, and gave him his letters.

"Perry gang wiped out, I hear, Major," said he. "Good thing for the country. That's a lesson the 'toughs' in these parts won't forget for a long time. Plucky girl that give 'em away, wasn't she? Hope she's all right."

"She is all right," said Sinclair with a smile.

"Glad of that. By the way, that father of her'n passed in his checks to-night. He'd got one warning from the Vigilantes, and yesterday they found out he was in with this gang, and they was a-going for him; but when the telegram come, he put a pistol to his head and saved them all trouble. Good riddance to everybody, I say. The sheriff's here now, and is going east on the next train to get them fellows. He's got a big posse together, and I wouldn't wonder if they was hard to hold in, after the 'boys in blue' is gone."

In a few minutes the train was off, and its living freight—the just and the unjust, the reformed and the rescued, the happy and the anxious. With many of the passengers the episode of the night was already a thing of the past. Sinclair sat by the side of his wife, to whose cheeks the color had all come back; and Sally Johnson lay in her berth, faint still, but able to give an occasional smile to Foster. In the station on the Missouri the reporters were gathered about the happy superintendent, smoking his cigars, and

104

filling their note-books with items.  In Denver, their brethren would gladly have done the same, but Watkins failed to gratify them.  He was a man of few words.  When the train had gone, and a friend remarked: "Hope they'll get through all right, now," he simply said: "Yes, likely.  Two shots don't most always go in the same hole."  Then he went to the telegraph instrument.  In a few minutes he could have told a story as wild as a Norse *saga,* but what he said, when Denver had responded, was only—

*"No.* 17, *fifty-five minutes late."*

# THE AMBITIOUS GUEST

BY NATHANIEL HAWTHORNE

# THE AMBITIOUS GUEST[1]

BY NATHANIEL HAWTHORNE

ONE September night a family had gathered round their hearth and piled it high with the driftwood of mountain streams, the dry cones of the pine, and the splintered ruins of great trees, that had come crashing down the precipice. Up the chimney roared the fire, and brightened the room with its broad blaze. The faces of the father and mother had a sober gladness; the children laughed. The eldest daughter was the image of Happiness at seventeen, and the aged grandmother, who sat knitting in the warmest place, was the image of Happiness grown old. They had found the "herb heart's-ease" in the bleakest spot of all New England. This family were situated in the Notch of the White Hills,[2] where the wind was sharp throughout the year and pitilessly cold in the winter, giving their cottage all its fresh inclemency before it descended on the valley of the Saco. They dwelt in a cold spot and a dangerous one, for a mountain towered above their heads so steep that the stones would often rumble down its sides and startle them at midnight.

[1] From *Twice-Told Tales*, published in 1837.
[2] White Hills: better known as the White Mountains.

The daughter had just uttered some simple jest that filled them all with mirth, when the wind came through the Notch and seemed to pause before their cottage, rattling the door with a sound of wailing and lamentation before it passed into the valley. For a moment it saddened them, though there was nothing unusual in the tones. But the family were glad again when they perceived that the latch was lifted by some traveler whose footsteps had been unheard amid the dreary blast which heralded his approach and wailed as he was entering, and went moaning away from the door.

Though they dwelt in such a solitude, these people held daily converse with the world. The romantic pass of the Notch is a great artery through which the life-blood of internal commerce is continually throbbing between Maine on one side and the Green Mountains and the shores of the St. Lawrence on the other. The stage coach always drew up before the door of the cottage. The wayfarer with no companion but his staff paused here to exchange a word, that the sense of loneliness might not utterly overcome him ere he could pass through the cleft of the mountain or reach the first house in the valley. And here the teamster on his way to Portland market would put up for the night, and, if a bachelor, might sit an hour beyond the usual bedtime and steal a kiss from the mountain maid at parting. It was one of those primitive

THE AMBITIOUS GUEST

taverns where the traveler pays only for food
and lodging, but meets with a homely kindness
beyond all price. When the footsteps were heard,
therefore, between the outer door and the inner
one, the whole family rose up, grandmother, children and all, as if about to welcome some one
who belonged to them, and whose fate was linked
with theirs.

The door was opened by a young man. His
face at first wore the melancholy expression,
almost despondency, of one who travels a wild
and bleak road at nightfall and alone, but soon
brightened up when he saw the kindly warmth
of his reception. He felt his heart spring forward
to meet them all, from the old woman who wiped
the chair with her apron to the little child that
held out its arms to him. One glance and smile
placed the stranger on a footing of innocent
familiarity with the eldest daughter.

"Ah! this fire is the right thing," cried he,
"especially when there is such a pleasant circle
round it. I am quite benumbed, for the Notch is
just like the pipe of a great pair of bellows;
it has blown a terrible blast in my face all the
way from Bartlett."

"Then you are going toward Vermont?" said
the master of the house as he helped to take a
light knapsack off the young man's shoulders.

"Yes, to Burlington, and far enough beyond,"
replied he. "I meant to have been at Ethan
Crawford's tonight, but a pedestrian lingers
111

along such a road as this. It is no matter; for
when I saw this good fire and all your cheerful
faces, I felt as if you had kindled it on purpose
for me and were waiting my arrival. So I shall
sit down among you and make myself at home."

The frank-hearted stranger had just drawn
his chair to the fire when something like a heavy
footstep was heard without, rushing down the
steep side of the mountain as with long and
rapid strides, and taking such a leap in passing
the cottage as to strike the opposite precipice.
The family held their breath, because they knew
the sound, and their guest held his by instinct.

"The old mountain has thrown a stone at us
for fear we should forget him," said the land-
lord, recovering himself. "He sometimes nods
his head and threatens to come down, but we are
old neighbors, and agree together pretty well
upon the whole. Besides, we have a sure place
of refuge hard by if he should be coming in
good earnest."

Let us now suppose the stranger to have finished his supper of bear's meat, and by his natural
felicity of manner to have placed himself on a
footing of kindness with the whole family; so
that they talked as freely together as if he belonged to their mountain brood. He was of a
proud yet gentle spirit, haughty and reserved
among the rich and great, but ever ready to
stoop his head to the lowly cottage door and
be like a brother or a son at the poor man's fire-

side. In the household of the Notch he found warmth and simplicity of feeling, the pervading intelligence of New England, and a poetry of native growth which they had gathered when they little thought of it from the mountain-peaks and chasms, and at the very threshold of their romantic and dangerous abode. He had traveled far and alone; his whole life, indeed, had been a solitary path, for, with the lofty caution of his nature, he had kept himself apart from those who might otherwise have been his companions. The family, too, though so kind and hospitable, had that consciousness of unity among themselves and separation from the world at large which in every domestic circle should still keep a holy place where no stranger may intrude. But this evening a prophetic sympathy impelled the refined and educated youth to pour out his heart before the simple mountaineers, and constrained them to answer him with the same free confidence. And thus it should have been. Is not the kindred of a common fate a closer tie than that of birth?

The secret of the young man's character was a high and abstracted ambition. He could have borne to live an undistinguished life, but not to be forgotten in the grave. Yearning desire had been transformed to hope, and hope, long cherished, had become like certainty that, obscurely as he journeyed now, a glory was to beam on all his pathway, though not, perhaps, while he was treading it. But when posterity should gaze back into the gloom of what was now the present, they would trace the brightness of his footsteps, brightening as meaner glories faded, and confess that a gifted one had passed from his cradle to his tomb with none to recognize him.

"As yet," cried the stranger, his cheek glowing and his eye flashing with enthusiasm—" as yet I have done nothing. Were I to vanish from the earth tomorrow, none would know so much of me as you—that a nameless youth came up at nightfall from the valley of the Saco, and opened his heart to you in the evening, and passed through the Notch by sunrise, and was seen no more. Not a soul would ask, 'Who was he? Whither did the wanderer go?' But I cannot die till I have achieved my destiny. Then let Death come; I shall have built my monument."

There was a continual flow of natural emotion gushing forth amid abstracted reverie which enabled the family to understand this young man's sentiments, though so foreign from their own. With quick sensibility of the ludicrous, he blushed at the ardor into which he had been betrayed.

"You laugh at me," said he, taking the eldest daughter's hand and laughing himself. "You think my ambition as nonsensical as if I were to freeze myself to death on the top of Mount Washington only that people might spy at me from the country round-about. And truly that would be a noble pedestal for a man's statue."

"It is better to sit here by this fire," answered the girl, blushing, "and be comfortable and contented, though nobody thinks about us."

"I suppose," said her father, after a fit of musing, "there is something natural in what the young man says; and if my mind had been turned that way, I might have felt just the same. It is strange, wife, how his talk has set my head running on things that are pretty certain never to come to pass."

Perhaps they may," observed the wife. "Is the man thinking what he will do when he is a widower?"

"No, no!" cried he, repelling the idea with reproachful kindness. "When I think of your death, Esther, I think of mine, too. But I was wishing we had a good farm in Bartlett or Bethlehem or Littleton, or some other township round the White Mountains, but not where they could tumble on our heads. I should want to stand well with my neighbors and be called squire and sent to General Court for a term or two; for a plain, honest man may do as much good there as a lawyer. And when I should be grown quite an old man, and you an old woman, so as not to be long apart, I might die happy enough in my bed, and leave you all crying around me. A slate gravestone would suit me as well as a marble one, with just my name and age, and a verse of a hymn, and something to let people know that I lived an honest man and died a Christian."

"There, now!" exclaimed the stranger; "it is our nature to desire a monument, be it slate or marble, or a pillar of granite, or a glorious memory in the universal heart of man."

"We're in a strange way tonight," said the wife, with tears in her eyes. "They say it's a sign of something when folks' minds go a-wandering so. Hark to the children!"

They listened accordingly. The younger children had been put to bed in another room, but with an open door between; so that they could be heard talking busily among themselves. One and all seemed to have caught the infection from the fireside circle, and were outvying each other in wild wishes and childish projects of what they would do when they came to be men and women. At length a little boy, instead of addressing his brothers and sisters, called out to his mother:

"I'll tell you what I wish, mother," cried he: "I want you and father and grandma'm, and all of us, and the stranger, too, to start right away and go and take a drink out of the basin of the Flume."

Nobody could help laughing at the child's notion of leaving a warm bed and dragging them from a cheerful fire to visit the basin of the Flume—a brook which tumbles over the precipice deep within the Notch.

The boy had hardly spoken, when a wagon rattled along the road and stopped a moment before the door. It appeared to contain two or three men who were cheering their hearts with the rough chorus of a song which resounded in broken notes between the cliffs, while the singers hesitated whether to continue their journey or put up here for the night.

"Father," said the girl, "they are calling you."

But the good man doubted whether they had really called him, and was unwilling to show himself too solicitous of gain by inviting people to patronize his house. He therefore did not hurry to the door, and, the lash being soon applied, the travelers plunged into the Notch, still singing and laughing, though their music and mirth came back drearily from the heart of the mountain.

"There, mother!" cried the boy again; "they'd have given us a ride to the Flume."

Again they laughed at the child's pertinacious fancy for a night ramble. But it happened that a light cloud passed over the daughter's spirit; she looked gravely into the fire and drew a breath that was almost a sigh. It forced its way, in spite of a little struggle to repress it. Then, starting and blushing, she looked quickly around the circle, as if they had caught a glimpse into her bosom. The stranger asked what she had been thinking of.

"Nothing," answered she, with a downcast smile; "only I felt lonesome just then."

"Oh, I have always had a gift of feeling what is in other people's hearts," said he, half seriously.

"Shall I tell the secrets of yours? For I know what to think when a girl shivers by a warm hearth and complains of lonesomeness at her mother's side. Shall I put these feelings into words?"

"They would not be a girl's feelings any longer if they could be put into words," replied the mountain nymph, laughing, but avoiding his eye.

All this was said apart. Perhaps a germ of love was springing in their hearts so pure that it might blossom in Paradise, since it could not be matured on earth; for women worship such gentle dignity as his, and the proud, contemplative, yet kindly, soul is oftenest captivated by simplicity like hers. But while they spoke softly, and he was watching the happy sadness, the lightsome shadows, the shy yearnings of a maiden's nature, the wind through the Notch took a deeper and drearier sound. It seemed, as the fanciful stranger said, like the choral strain of the spirits of the blast who in old Indian times had their dwelling among these mountains, and made their heights and recesses a sacred region. There was a wail along the road as if a funeral were passing. To chase away the gloom, the family threw pine-branches on their fire till the dry leaves crackled and the flame arose, discovering once again a scene of peace and humble happiness. The light hovered about them fondly and caressed them all. There were the little faces of the children peeping from their bed apart, and here the father's frame of strength, the mother's subdued and careful mien, the high-browed youth, the budding girl, and the good old grandam still knitting in the warmest place.

The aged woman looked up from her task, and with fingers ever busy was the next to speak.

"Old folks have their notions," said she, "as well as young ones. You've been wishing and planning and letting your heads run on one thing and another till you've set my mind a-wandering too. Now, what should an old woman wish for when she can go but a step or two before she comes to her grave? Children, it will haunt me night and day till I tell you."

"What is it, mother?" cried the husband and wife, at once.

Then the old woman, with an air of mystery which drew the circle closer round the fire, informed them that she had provided her grave-clothes some years before—a nice linen shroud, a cap with a muslin ruff, and everything of a finer sort than she had worn since her wedding day. But this evening an old superstition had strangely recurred to her. It used to be said in her younger days that if anything were amiss with a corpse, if only the ruff were not smooth or the cap did not set right, the corpse, in the coffin and beneath the clods, would strive to put up its cold hands and arrange it. The bare thought made her nervous.

"Don't talk so, grandmother," said the girl, shuddering.

"Now," continued the old woman with singular earnestness, yet smiling strangely at her own folly, "I want one of you, my children, when your mother is dressed and in the coffin,—I want one of you to hold a looking-glass over my face. Who knows but I may take a glimpse at myself, and see whether all's right."

"Old and young, we dream of graves and monuments," murmured the stranger youth. "I wonder how mariners feel when the ship is sinking and they, unknown and undistinguished, are to be buried together in the ocean, that wide and nameless sepulchre?"

For a moment the old woman's ghastly conception so engrossed the minds of her hearers that a sound abroad in the night, rising like the roar of a blast, had grown broad, deep and terrible before the fated group were conscious of it. The house and all within it trembled; the foundations of the earth seemed to be shaken, as if this awful sound were the peal of the last trump. Young and old exchanged one wild glance and remained an instant pale, affrighted, without utterance or power to move. Then the same shriek burst from all their lips:

"The slide! The slide!"

The simplest words must intimate, but not portray, the unutterable horror of the catastrophe. The victims rushed from their cottage, and sought refuge in what they deemed a safer spot, where, in contemplation of such an emergency, a sort of barrier had been reared. Alas! they had quitted their security and fled right into the pathway of destruction. Down came the whole side of the mountain in a cataract of ruin. Just before it reached the house the stream broke into two branches, shivered not a window there, but overwhelmed the whole vicinity, blocked up the road and annihilated everything in its dreadful course. Long ere the thunder of that great slide had ceased to roar among the mountains the mortal agony had been endured and the victims were at peace. Their bodies were never found.

The next morning the light smoke was seen stealing from the cottage chimney, up the mountain-side. Within, the fire was yet smouldering on the hearth, and the chairs in a circle round it, as if the inhabitants had but gone forth to view the devastation of the slide, and would shortly return to thank Heaven for their miraculous escape. All had left separate tokens by which those who had known the family were made to shed a tear for each. Who has not heard their name? The story has been told far and wide, and will forever be a legend of these mountains. Poets have sung their fate.

There were circumstances which led some to suppose that a stranger had been received into the cottage on this awful night, and had shared the catastrophe of all its inmates; others denied that there were sufficient grounds for such a conjecture. Woe for the high-souled youth with his dream of earthly immortality! His name and person utterly unknown, his history, his way of life, his plans, a mystery never to be solved, his death and his existence equally a doubt,—whose was the agony of that death moment?

The Ambitious Guest story founded upon an actual occurrence, the death of the Willey family, is narrated in J. H. Spaulding's *Historical Relics of the White Mountains:*

"Some time in June, before the great slide in August, 1826, there came a great storm, and the old veteran, Abel Crawford, coming down the Notch, noticed the trees slipping down, standing upright, and as he was passing Mr. Willey's he called and informed him of the wonderful fact. Immediately, in a less exposed place, Mr. Willey prepared a shelter to which to flee in case of immediate danger, and in the night of August 28 in that year he was, with his whole family, awakened by the thundering crash of the coming avalanche. Attempting to escape, that family, nine in number, rushed from the house and were overtaken and buried alive under a vast pile of rocks, earth, and water. By a remarkable coincidence the house remained uninjured, as the slide divided about four rods back of the house, against a high flat rock, and came down on either side with overwhelming power."

# MY TERMINAL MORAINE

BY FRANK R. STOCKTON

# MY TERMINAL MORAINE

BY FRANK R. STOCKTON

A MAN'S birth is generally considered the most important event of his existence, but I truly think that what I am about to relate was more important to me than my entrance into this world; because, had not these things happened, I am of the opinion that my life would have been of no value to me and my birth a misfortune.

My father, Joshua Cuthbert, died soon after I came to my majority, leaving me what he had considered a comfortable property. This consisted of a large house and some forty acres of land, nearly the whole of which lay upon a bluff, which upon three sides descended to a little valley, through which ran a gentle stream. I had no brothers or sisters. My mother died when I was a boy, and I, Walter Cuthbert, was left the sole representative of my immediate family.

My estate had been a comfortable one to my father, because his income from the practice of his profession as a physician enabled him to keep it up and provide satisfactorily for himself and me. I had no profession and but a very small income, the result of a few investments my father

Copyright, 1892, by P. F. Collier.

had made. Left to myself, I felt no inducement to take up any profession or business. My wants were simple, and for a few years I lived without experiencing any inconvenience from the economies which I was obliged to practice. My books, my dog, my gun and my rod made life pass very pleasantly to me, and the subject of an increase of income never disturbed my mind.

But as time passed on the paternal home began to present an air of neglect and even dilapidation, which occasionally attracted my attention and caused, as I incidentally discovered, a great deal of unfavorable comment among my neighbors, who thought that I should go to work and at least earn money enough to put the house and grounds in a condition which should not be unworthy the memory of the good Dr. Cuthbert. In fact, I began to be looked upon as a shiftless young man; and, now and then, I found a person old enough and bold enough to tell me so.

But, instead of endeavoring to find some suitable occupation by which I might better my condition and improve my estate, I fell in love, which, in the opinion of my neighbors, was the very worst thing that could have happened to me at this time. I lived in a thrifty region, and for a man who could not support himself to think of taking upon him the support of a wife, especially such a wife as Agnes Havelot would be, was considered more than folly and looked upon as a crime. Everybody knew that I was in love with Miss Havelot, for I went to court her as boldly as I went to fish or shoot. There was a good deal of talk about it, and this finally came to the ears of Mr. Havelot, my lady's father, who, thereupon, promptly ordered her to have no more to do with me.

The Havelot estate, which adjoined mine, was a very large one, containing hundreds and hundreds of acres; and the Havelots were rich, rich enough to frighten any poor young man of marrying intent. But I did not appreciate the fact that I was a poor young man. I had never troubled my head about money as it regarded myself, and I now did not trouble my head about it as it regarded Agnes. I loved her, I hoped she loved me, and all other considerations were thrown aside. Mr. Havelot, however, was a man of a different way of thinking.

It was a little time before I became convinced that the decision of Agnes's father, that there should be no communication between that dear girl and myself, really meant anything. I had never been subjected to restrictions, and I did not understand how people of spirit could submit to them; but I was made to understand it when Mr. Havelot, finding me wandering about his grounds, very forcibly assured me that if I should make my appearance there again, or if he discovered any attempt on my part to communicate with his daughter in any way, he would send her from home. He concluded the very brief interview by stating that if I had any real regard for his daughter's happiness I would cease attentions which would meet with the most decided disapprobation from her only surviving parent and which would result in exiling her from home. I begged for one more interview with Miss Havelot, and if it had been granted I should have assured her of the state of my affections, no matter if there were reasons to suppose that I would never see her again; but her father very sternly forbade anything of the kind, and I went away crushed.

It was a very hard case, for if I played the part of a bold lover and tried to see Agnes without regard to the wicked orders of her father, I should certainly be discovered; and then it would be not only myself, but the poor girl, who would suffer. So I determined that I would submit to the Havelot decree. No matter if I never saw her again, never heard the sound of her voice, it would be better to have her near me, to have her breathe the same air, cast up her eyes at the same sky, listen to the same birds, that I breathed, looked at and listened to, than to have her far away, probably in Kentucky, where I knew she had relatives, and where the grass was blue and the sky probably green, or at any rate would appear so to her if in the least degree she felt as I did in regard to the ties of home and the affinities between the sexes.

I now found myself in a most doleful and even

desperate condition of mind. There was nothing in the world which I could have for which I cared. Hunting, fishing, and the rambles through woods and fields that had once been so delightful to me now became tasks which I seldom undertook. The only occupation in which I felt the slightest interest was that of sitting in a tower of my house with a telescope, endeavoring to see my Agnes on some portion of her father's grounds; but, although I diligently directed my glass at the slightest stretch of lawn or bit of path which I could discern through openings in the foliage, I never caught sight of her. I knew, however, by means of daily questions addressed to my cook, whose daughter was a servant in the Havelot house, that Agnes was yet at home. For that reason I remained at home. Otherwise, I should have become a wanderer.

About a month after I had fallen into this most unhappy state an old friend came to see me. We had been school-fellows, but he differed from me in almost every respect. He was full of ambition and energy, and, although he was but a few years older than myself, he had already made a name in the world. He was a geologist, earnest and enthusiastic in his studies and his investigations. He told me frankly that the object of his visit was twofold. In the first place, he wanted to see me, and, secondly, he wanted to make some geological examinations on my grounds, which were situated, as he informed me, upon a terminal moraine, a formation which he had not yet had an opportunity of practically investigating.

I had not known that I lived on a moraine, and now that I knew it, I did not care. But Tom Burton glowed with high spirits and lively zeal as he told me how the great bluff on which my house stood, together with the other hills and wooded terraces which stretched away from it along the side of the valley, had been formed by the minute fragments of rock and soil, which, during ages and ages, had been gradually pushed down from the mountains by a great glacier which once occupied the country to the northeast of my house. "Why, Walter, my boy," he cried, "if I had not read it all in the books I should have known for myself, as soon as I came here, that there had once been a glacier up there, and as it gradually moved to the southwest it had made this country what it is. Have you a stream down there in that dell which I see lies at right angles with the valley and opens into it?"

"No," said I; "I wish there were one. The only stream we have flows along the valley and not on my property."

Without waiting for me Tom ran down into my dell, pushed his way through the underbrush to its upper end, and before long came back flushed with heat and enthusiasm.

"Well, sir," he said, "that dell was once the

bed of a glacial stream, and you may as well clear it out and plant corn there if you want to, for there never will be another stream flowing through it until there is another glacier out in the country beyond. And now I want you to let me dig about here. I want to find out what sort of stuff the glacier brought down from the mountains. I will hire a man and will promise you to fill up all the holes I make."

I had no objection to my friend's digging as much as he pleased, and for three days he busied himself in getting samples of the soil of my estate. Sometimes I went out and looked at him, and gradually a little of his earnest ardor infused itself into me, and with some show of interest I looked into the holes he had made and glanced over the mineral specimens he showed me.

"Well, Walter," said he, when he took leave of me, "I am very sorry that I did not discover that the glacier had raked out the bed of a gold mine from the mountains up there and brought it down to you, or at any rate, some valuable iron ore. But I am obliged to say it did not do anything of the sort. But I can tell you one thing it brought you, and, although it is not of any great commercial value, I should think you could make good use of it here on your place. You have one of the finest deposits of gravel on this bluff that I have met with, and if you were to take out a lot of it and spread it over your

driveways and paths, it would make it a great
deal pleasanter for you to go about here in bad
weather and would wonderfully improve your
property. Good roads always give an idea of
thrift and prosperity." And then he went away
with a valise nearly full of mineral specimens
which he assured me were very interesting.

My interest in geological formations died
away as soon as Tom Burton had departed, but
what he said about making gravel roads giving
the place an air of thrift and prosperity had its
effect upon my mind. It struck me that it would
be a very good thing if people in the neighborhood, especially the Havelots, were to perceive
on my place some evidences of thrift and prosperity. Most palpable evidences of unthrift and
inpecuniosity had cut me off from Agnes, and
why might it not be that some signs of improved
circumstances would remove, to a degree at least,
the restrictions which had been placed between
us? This was but a very little thing upon which
to build hopes; but ever since men and women
have loved they have built grand hopes upon
very slight foundations. I determined to put
my roadways in order.

My efforts in this direction were really evidence of anything but thriftiness, for I could
not in the least afford to make my drives and
walks resemble the smooth and beautiful roads
which wound over the Havelot estate, although
to do this was my intention, and I set about the

work without loss of time. I took up this occupation with so much earnestness that it seriously interfered with my observations from the tower.

I hired two men and set them to work to dig a gravel-pit. They made excavations at several places, and very soon found what they declared to be a very fine quality of road-gravel. I ordered them to dig on until they had taken out what they believed to be enough to cover all my roads. When this had been done, I would have it properly spread and rolled. As this promised to be a very good job, the men went to work in fine spirits and evidently made up their minds that the improvements I desired would require a vast deal of gravel.

When they had dug a hole so deep that it became difficult to throw up the gravel from the bottom, I suggested that they should dig at some other place. But to this they objected, declaring that the gravel was getting better and better, and it would be well to go on down as long as the quality continued to be so good. So, at last, they put a ladder into the pit, one man carrying the gravel up in a hod, while the other dug it; and when they had gone down so deep that this was no longer practicable, they rigged up a derrick and windlass and drew up the gravel in a bucket.

Had I been of a more practical turn of mind I might have perceived that this method of working made the job a very long and, consequently, to the laborers, a profitable one; but no such idea entered into my head, and not noticing whether they were bringing up sand or gravel I allowed them to proceed.

One morning I went out to the spot where the excavation was being made and found that the men had built a fire on the ground near the opening of the pit, and that one of them was bending over it warming himself. As the month was July this naturally surprised me, and I inquired the reason for so strange a performance.

"Upon my soul," said the man, who was rubbing his hands over the blaze, "I do not wonder you are surprised, but it's so cold down at the bottom of that pit that me fingers is almost frosted; and we haven't struck any wather neither, which couldn't be expected, of course, a-diggin' down into the hill like this."

I looked into the hole and found it was very deep. "I think it would be better to stop digging here," said I, "and try some other place."

"I wouldn't do that just now," said the other man, who was preparing to go down in the bucket; "to be sure, it's a good deal more like a well than a gravel-pit, but it's bigger at the top than at the bottom, and there's no danger of its cavin' in, and now that we've got everything rigged up all right, it would be a pity to make a change yet awhile."

So I let them go on; but the next day when I

went out again I found that they had come to the conclusion that it was time to give up digging in that hole. They both declared that it almost froze their feet to stand on the ground where they worked at the bottom of the excavation. The slow business of drawing up the gravel by means of a bucket and windlass was, therefore, reluctantly given up. The men now went to work to dig outward from this pit toward the edge of the bluff which overlooked my little dell, and gradually made a wide trench, which they deepened until—and I am afraid to say how long they worked before this was done—they could walk to the original pit from the level of the dell. They then deepened the inner end of the trench, wheeling out the gravel in barrows, until they had made an inclined pathway from the dell to the bottom of the pit. The wheeling now became difficult, and the men soon declared that they were sure that they had quite gravel enough.

When they made this announcement, and I had gone into some financial calculations, I found that I would be obliged to put an end to my operations, at least for the present, for my available funds were gone, or would be when I had paid what I owed for the work. The men were very much disappointed by the sudden ending of this good job, but they departed, and I was left to gaze upon a vast amount of gravel, of which, for the present at least, I could not afford to make the slightest use.

The mental despondency which had been somewhat lightened during my excavating operations now returned, and I became rather more gloomy and downcast than before. My cook declared that it was of no use to prepare meals which I never ate, and suggested that it would save money if I discharged her. As I had not paid her anything for a long time, I did not see how this would benefit me.

Wandering about one day with my hat pulled down over my eyes and my hands thrust deep into my pockets, I strolled into the dell and stood before the wide trench which led to the pit in which I had foolishly sunk the money which should have supported me for months. I entered this dismal passage and walked slowly and carefully down the incline until I reached the bottom of the original pit, where I had never been before. I stood here looking up and around me and wondering how men could bring themselves to dig down into such dreary depths simply for the sake of a few dollars a week, when I involuntarily began to stamp my feet. They were very cold, although I had not been there more than a minute. I wondered at this and took up some of the loose gravel in my hand. It was quite dry, but it chilled my fingers. I did not understand it, and I did not try to, but walked up the trench and around into the dell, thinking of Agnes.

I was very fond of milk, which, indeed, was

almost the only food I now cared for, and I was consequently much disappointed at my noonday meal when I found that the milk had soured and was not fit to drink.

"You see, sir," said Susan, "ice is very scarce and dear, and we can not afford to buy much of it. There was no freezin' weather last winter, and the price has gone up as high as the thermometer, sir, and so, between the two of 'em, I can't keep things from spoilin'."

The idea now came to me that if Susan would take the milk, and anything else she wished to keep cool in this hot weather, to the bottom of the gravel-pit, she would find the temperature there cold enough to preserve them without ice, and I told her so.

The next morning Susan came to me with a pleased countenance and said, "I put the butter and the milk in that pit last night, and the butter's just as hard and the milk's as sweet as if it had been kept in an ice-house. But the place is as cold as an ice-house, sir, and unless I am mistaken, there's ice in it. Anyway, what do you call that?" And she took from a little basket a piece of grayish ice as large as my fist. "When I found it was so cold down there, sir," she said, "I thought I would dig a little myself and see what made it so; and I took a fire-shovel and hatchet, and, when I had scraped away some of the gravel, I came to something hard and chopped off this piece of it, which is real ice, sir, or I know nothing about it. Perhaps there used to be an ice-house there, and you might get some of it if you dug, though why anybody should put it down so deep and then cover it up, I'm sure I don't know. But as long as there's any there, I think we should get it out, even if there's only a little of it; for I can not take everything down to that pit, and we might as well have it in the refrigerator."

This seemed to me like very good sense, and if I had had a man I should have ordered him to go down to the pit and dig up any lumps of ice he might find and bring them to the house. But I had no man, and I therefore became impressed with the opinion that if I did not want to drink sour milk for the rest of the summer, it might be a good thing for me to go down there and dig out some of the ice myself. So with pickaxe and shovel I went to the bottom of the pit and set myself to work.

A few inches below the surface I found that my shovel struck something hard, and, clearing away the gravel from this for two or three square feet, I looked down upon a solid mass of ice. It was dirty and begrimed, but it was truly ice. With my pick I detached some large pieces of it. These, with some discomfort, I carried out into the dell where Susan might come with her basket and get them.

For several days Susan and I took out ice from the pit, and then I thought that perhaps

Tom Burton might feel some interest in this frozen deposit in my terminal moraine, and so I wrote to him about it. He did not answer my letter, but instead arrived himself the next afternoon.

"Ice at the bottom of a gravel-pit," said he, "is a thing I never heard of. Will you lend me a spade and a pickaxe?"

When Tom came out of that pit—it was too cold a place for me to go with him and watch his proceedings—I saw him come running toward the house.

"Walter," he shouted, "we must hire all the men we can find and dig, dig, dig. If I am not mistaken something has happened on your place that is wonderful almost beyond belief. But we must not stop to talk. We must dig, dig, dig; dig all day and dig all night. Don't think of the cost. I'll attend to that. I'll get the money. What we must do is to find men and set them to work."

"What's the matter?" said I. "What has happened?"

"I haven't time to talk about it now; besides I don't want to, for fear that I should find that I am mistaken. But get on your hat, my dear fellow, and let's go over to the town for men."

The next day there were eight men working under the direction of my friend Burton, and although they did not work at night as he wished them to do, they labored steadfastly for ten days or more before Tom was ready to announce what it was he had hoped to discover, and whether or not he had found it. For a day or two I watched the workmen from time to time, but after that I kept away, preferring to await the result of my friend's operations. He evidently expected to find something worth having, and whether he was successful or not, it suited me better to know the truth all at once and not by degrees.

On the morning of the eleventh day Tom came into the room where I was reading and sat down near me. His face was pale, his eyes glittering. "Old friend," said he, and as he spoke I noticed that his voice was a little husky, although it was plain enough that his emotion was not occasioned by bad fortune—"my good old friend, I have found out what made the bottom of your gravel-pit so uncomfortably cold. You need not doubt what I am going to tell you, for my excavations have been complete and thorough enough to make me sure of what I say. Don't you remember that I told you that ages ago there was a vast glacier in the country which stretches from here to the mountains? Well, sir, the foot of that glacier must have reached further this way than is generally supposed. At any rate a portion of it did extend in this direction as far as this bit of the world which is now yours. This end or spur of the glacier, nearly a quarter of a mile in width, I should say, and pushing before it a portion of the terminal

140

moraine on which you live, came slowly toward
the valley until suddenly it detached itself from
the main glacier and disappeared from sight.
That is to say, my boy"—and as he spoke Tom
sprang to his feet, too excited to sit any longer
—"it descended to the bowels of the earth, at
least for a considerable distance in that direction.
Now you want to know how this happened.
Well, I'll tell you. In this part of the country
there are scattered about here and there great
caves. Geologists know one or two of them,
and it is certain that there are others undis-
covered. Well, sir, your glacier spur discovered
one of them, and when it had lain over the top
of it for an age or two, and had grown bigger
and bigger, and heavier and heavier, it at last
burst through the rock roof of the cave, snapping
itself from the rest of the glacier and falling in
one vast mass to the bottom of the subterranean
abyss. Walter, it is there now. The rest of the
glacier came steadily down; the moraines were
forced before it; they covered up this glacier
spur, this broken fragment, and by the time the
climate changed and the average of temperature
rose above that of the glacial period, this vast
sunken mass of ice was packed away below the
surface of the earth, out of the reach of the action
of friction, or heat, or moisture, or anything else
which might destroy it. And through all the
long procession of centuries that broken end of
the glacier has been lying in your terminal

moraine. It is there now. It is yours, Walter Cuthbert. It is an ice-mine. It is wealth, and so far as I can make out, it is nearly all upon your land. To you is the possession, but to me is the glory of the discovery. A bit of the glacial period kept in a cave for us! It is too wonderful to believe! Walter, have you any brandy?"

It may well be supposed that by this time I was thoroughly awakened to the importance and the amazing character of my friend's discovery, and I hurried with him to the scene of operations. There he explained everything and showed me how, by digging away a portion of the face of the bluff, he had found that this vast fragment of the glacier, which had been so miraculously preserved, ended in an irregularly perpendicular wall, which extended downward he knew not how far, and the edge of it on its upper side had been touched by my workmen in digging their pit. "It was the gradual melting of the upper end of this glacier," said Tom, "probably more elevated than the lower end, that made your dell. I wondered why the depression did not extend further up toward the spot where the foot of the glacier was supposed to have been. This end of the fragment, being sunk in deeper and afterward covered up more completely, probably never melted at all."

"It is amazing—astounding," said I; "but what of it, now that we have found it?"

"What of it?" cried Tom, and his whole form

trembled as he spoke. "You have here a source of wealth, of opulence which shall endure for the rest of your days. Here at your very door, where it can be taken out and transported with the least possible trouble, is ice enough to supply the town, the county, yes, I might say, the State, for hundreds of years. No, sir, I can not go in to supper. I can not eat. I leave to you the business and practical part of this affair. I go to report upon its scientific features."

"Agnes," I exclaimed, as I walked to the house with my hands clasped and my eyes raised to the sky, "the glacial period has given thee to me!"

This did not immediately follow, although I went that very night to Mr. Havelot and declared to him that I was now rich enough to marry his daughter. He laughed at me in a manner which was very annoying, and made certain remarks which indicated that he thought it probable that it was not the roof of the cave, but my mind, which had given way under the influence of undue pressure.

The contemptuous manner in which I had been received aroused within me a very unusual state of mind. While talking to Mr. Havelot I heard not far away in some part of the house a voice singing. It was the voice of Agnes, and I believed she sang so that I could hear her. But as her sweet tones reached my ear there came to me at the same time the harsh, contemptuous words of her father. I left the house determined to

crush that man to the earth beneath a superin-
cumbent mass of ice—or the evidence of the results of the ownership of such a mass—which
would make him groan and weep as he apologized
to me for his scornful and disrespectful utterances and at the same time offered me the hand
of his daughter.

When the discovery of the ice-mine, as it grew
to be called, became generally known, my
grounds were crowded by sightseers, and reporters of newspapers were more plentiful than
squirrels. But the latter were referred to Burton, who would gladly talk to them as long as
they could afford to listen, and I felt myself at
last compelled to shut my gates to the first.

I had offers of capital to develop this novel
source of wealth, and I accepted enough of this
assistance to enable me to begin operations on a
moderate scale. It was considered wise not to
uncover any portion of the glacier spur, but to
construct an inclined shaft down to its wall-like
end and from this tunnel into the great mass.
Immediately the leading ice company of the
neighboring town contracted with me for all the
ice I could furnish, and the flood-gates of afflu-
ence began slowly to rise.

The earliest, and certainly one of the greatest,
benefits which came to me from this bequest from
the unhistoric past was the new energy and vigor
with which my mind and body were now infused.
My old, careless method of life and my recent

melancholy, despairing mood were gone, and I now began to employ myself upon the main object of my life with an energy and enthusiasm almost equal to that of my friend, Tom Burton. This present object of my life was to prepare my home for Agnes.

The great piles of gravel which my men had dug from the well-like pit were spread upon the roadways and rolled smooth and hard; my lawn was mowed; my flower-beds and borders put in order; useless bushes and undergrowth cut out and cleared away; my outbuildings were repaired and the grounds around my house rapidly assumed their old appearance of neatness and beauty.

Ice was very scarce that summer, and, as the wagons wound away from the opening of the shaft which led down to the glacier, carrying their loads to the nearest railway station, so money came to me; not in large sums at first, for preparations had not yet been perfected for taking out the ice in great quantities, but enough to enable me to go on with my work as rapidly as I could plan it. I set about renovating and brightening and newly furnishing my house. Whatever I thought that Agnes would like I bought and put into it. I tried to put myself in her place as I selected the paper-hangings and the materials with which to cover the furniture.

Sometimes, while thus employed selecting ornaments or useful articles for my house, and using as far as was possible the taste and judgment of another instead of my own, the idea came to me that perhaps Agnes had never heard of my miraculous good fortune. Certainly her father would not be likely to inform her, and perhaps she still thought of me, if she thought at all, as the poor young man from whom she had been obliged to part because he was poor.

But whether she knew that I was growing rich, or whether she thought I was becoming poorer and poorer, I thought only of the day when I could go to her father and tell him that I was able to take his daughter and place her in a home as beautiful as that in which she now lived, and maintain her with all the comforts and luxuries which he could give her.

One day I asked my faithful cook, who also acted as my housekeeper and general supervisor, to assist me in making out a list of china which I intended to purchase.

"Are you thinking of buying china, sir?" she asked. "We have now quite as much as we really need."

"Oh, yes," said I, "I shall get complete sets of everything that can be required for a properly furnished household."

Susan gave a little sigh. "You are spendin' a lot of money, sir, and some of it for things that a single gentleman would be likely not to care very much about; and if you was to take it into your head to travel and stay away for a year or two,

there's a good many things you've bought that
would look shabby when you come back, no matter how careful I might be in dustin' 'em and
keepin' 'em covered."

"But I have no idea of traveling," said I.
"There's no place so pleasant as this to me."

Susan was silent for a few moments, and then
she said: "I know very well why you are doing
all this, and I feel it my bounden duty to say to
you that there's a chance of its bein' no use. I
do not speak without good reason, and I would
not do it if I didn't think that it might make
trouble lighter to you when it comes."

"What are you talking about, Susan; what do
you mean?"

"Well, sir, this is what I mean: It was only
last night that my daughter Jane was in Mr.
Havelot's dining-room after dinner was over,
and Mr. Havelot and a friend of his were sitting
there, smoking their cigars and drinking their
coffee. She went in and come out again as she
was busy takin' away the dishes, and they paid
no attention to her, but went on talkin' without
knowing, most likely, she was there. Mr. Havelot and the gentleman were talkin' about you,
and Jane she heard Mr. Havelot say as plain as
anything, and she said she couldn't be mistaken,
that even if your nonsensical ice-mine proved to
be worth anything, he would never let his daughter marry an ice-man. He spoke most disrespectful of ice-men, sir, and said that it would

make him sick to have a son-in-law whose business it was to sell ice to butchers, and hotels, and
grog-shops, and pork-packers, and all that sort
of people, and that he would as soon have his
daughter marry the man who supplied a hotel
with sausages as the one who supplied it with ice
to keep those sausages from spoiling. You see,
sir, Mr. Havelot lives on his property as his
father did before him, and he is a very proud
man, with a heart as hard and cold as that ice
down under your land; and it's borne in on me
very strong, sir, that it would be a bad thing for
you to keep on thinkin' that you are gettin' this
house all ready to bring Miss Havelot to when
you have married her. For if Mr. Havelot
keeps on livin', which there's every chance of his
doin', it may be many a weary year before you
get Miss Agnes, if you ever get her. And havin'
said that, sir, I say no more, and I would not
have said this much if I hadn't felt it my bounden
duty to your father's son to warn him that most
likely he was workin' for what he might never
get, and so keep him from breakin' his heart
when he found out the truth all of a sudden."

With that Susan left me, without offering
any assistance in making out a list of china. This
was a terrible story; but, after all, it was founded
only upon servants' gossip. In this country,
even proud, rich men like Mr. Havelot did not
have such absurd ideas regarding the source of
wealth. Money is money, and whether it is de-

rived from the ordinary products of the earth, from which came much of Mr. Havelot's revenue, or from an extraordinary project such as my glacier spur, it truly could not matter so far as concerned the standing in society of its possessor. What utter absurdity was this which Susan had told me! If I were to go to Mr. Havelot and tell him that I would not marry his daughter because he supplied brewers and bakers with the products of his fields, would he not consider me an idiot? I determined to pay no attention to the idle tale. But alas! determinations of that sort are often of little avail. I did pay attention to it, and my spirits drooped.

The tunnel into the glacier spur had now attained considerable length, and the ice in the interior was found to be of a much finer quality than that first met with, which was of a grayish hue and somewhat inclined to crumble. When the workmen reached a grade of ice as good as they could expect, they began to enlarge the tunnel into a chamber, and from this they proposed to extend tunnels in various directions after the fashion of a coal-mine. The ice was hauled out on sledges through the tunnel and then carried up a wooden railway to the mouth of the shaft.

It was comparatively easy to walk down the shaft and enter the tunnel, and when it happened that the men were not at work I allowed visitors to go down and view this wonderful ice-cavern. The walls of the chamber appeared semi-transparent, and the light of the candles or lanterns gave the whole scene a weird and beautiful aspect. It was almost possible to imagine one's self surrounded by limpid waters, which might at any moment rush upon him and ingulf him.

Every day or two Tom Burton came with a party of scientific visitors, and had I chosen to stop the work of taking out ice, admitted the public and charged a price for admission, I might have made almost as much money as I at that time derived from the sale of the ice. But such a method of profit was repugnant to me.

For several days after Susan's communication to me I worked on in my various operations, endeavoring to banish from my mind the idle nonsense she had spoken of; but one of its effects upon me was to make me feel that I ought not to allow hopes so important to rest upon uncertainties. So I determined that as soon as my house and grounds should be in a condition with which I should for the time be satisfied, I would go boldly to Mr. Havelot, and, casting out of my recollection everything that Susan had said, invite him to visit me and see for himself the results of the discovery of which he had spoken with such derisive contempt. This would be a straightforward and business-like answer to his foolish objections to me, and I believed that in his heart the old gentleman would properly appreciate my action.

About this time there came to my place Aaron

Boyce, an elderly farmer of the neighborhood, and, finding me outside, he seized the opportunity to have a chat with me.

"I tell you what it is, Mr. Cuthbert," said he, "the people in this neighborhood hasn't give you credit for what's in you. The way you have fixed up this place, and the short time you have took to do it, is enough to show us now what sort of a man you are; and I tell you, sir, we're proud of you for a neighbor. I don't believe there's another gentleman in this county of your age that could have done what you have done in so short a time. I expect now you will be thinking of getting married and startin' housekeepin' in a regular fashion. That comes just as natural as to set hens in the spring. By the way, have you heard that old Mr. Havelot's thinkin' of goin' abroad? I didn't believe he would ever do that again, because he's gettin' pretty well on in years, but old men will do queer things as well as young ones."

"Going abroad!" I cried. "Does he intend to take his daughter with him?"

Mr. Aaron Boyce smiled grimly. He was a great old gossip, and he had already obtained the information he wanted. "Yes," he said, "I've heard it was on her account he's going. She's been kind of weakly lately, they tell me, and hasn't took to her food, and the doctors has said that what she wants is a sea voyage and a change to foreign parts."

Going abroad! Foreign parts! This was more terrible than anything I had imagined. I would go to Mr. Havelot that very evening, the only time which I would be certain to find him at home, and talk to him in a way which would be sure to bring him to his senses, if he had any. And if I should find that he had no sense of propriety or justice, no sense of his duty to his fellow-man and to his offspring, then I would begin a bold fight for Agnes, a fight which I would not give up until, with her own lips, she told me that it would be useless. I would follow her to Kentucky, to Europe, to the uttermost ends of the earth. I could do it now. The frozen deposits in my terminal moraine would furnish me with the means. I walked away and left the old farmer standing grinning. No doubt my improvements and renovations had been the subject of gossip in the neighborhood, and he had come over to see if he could find out anything definite in regard to the object of them. He had succeeded, but he had done more: he had nerved me to instantly begin the conquest of Agnes, whether by diplomacy or war.

I was so anxious to begin this conquest that I could scarcely wait for the evening to come. At the noon hour, when the ice-works were deserted, I walked down the shaft and into the ice-chamber to see what had been done since my last visit. I decided to insist that operations upon a larger scale should be immediately begun, in order that

I might have plenty of money with which to carry on my contemplated campaign. Whether it was one of peace or war, I should want all the money I could get.

I took with me a lantern and went around the chamber, which was now twenty-five or thirty feet in diameter, examining the new inroads which had been made upon its walls. There was a tunnel commenced opposite the one by which the chamber was entered, but it had not been opened more than a dozen feet, and it seemed to me that the men had not been working with any very great energy. I wanted to see a continuous stream of ice-blocks from that chamber to the mouth of the shaft.

While grumbling thus I heard behind me a sudden noise like thunder and the crashing of walls, and, turning quickly, I saw that a portion of the roof of the chamber had fallen in. Nor had it ceased to fall. As I gazed, several great masses of ice came down from above and piled themselves upon that which had already fallen.

Startled and frightened, I sprang toward the opening of the entrance tunnel; but, alas! I found that that was the point where the roof had given way, and between me and the outer world was a wall of solid ice through which it would be as impossible for me to break as if it were a barrier of rock. With the quick instinct which comes to men in danger I glanced about to see if the workmen had left their tools; but there were none.

They had been taken outside. Then I stood and gazed stupidly at the mass of fallen ice, which, even as I looked upon it, was cracking and snapping, pressed down by the weight above it, and forming itself into an impervious barrier without crevice or open seam.

Then I madly shouted. But of what avail were shouts down there in the depths of the earth? I soon ceased this useless expenditure of strength, and, with my lantern in my hand, began to walk around the chamber, throwing the light upon the walls and the roof. I became impressed with the fear that the whole cavity might cave in at once and bury me here in a tomb of ice. But I saw no cracks, nor any sign of further disaster. But why think of anything more? Was not this enough? For, before that ice-barrier could be cleared away, would I not freeze to death?

I now continued to walk, not because I expected to find anything or do anything, but simply to keep myself warm by action. As long as I could move about I believed that there was no immediate danger of succumbing to the intense cold; for, when a young man, traveling in Switzerland, I had been in the cave of a glacier, and it was not cold enough to prevent some old women from sitting there to play the zither for the sake of a few coppers from visitors. I could not expect to be able to continue walking until I should be rescued, and if I sat down, or by chance slept from exhaustion, I must perish.

The more I thought of it, the more sure I became that in any case I must perish. A man in a block of ice could have no chance of life. And Agnes! Oh, Heavens! what demon of the ice had leagued with old Havelot to shut me up in this frozen prison? For a long time I continued to walk, beat my body with my arms and stamp my feet. The instinct of life was strong within me. I would live as long as I could, and think of Agnes. When I should be frozen I could not think of her.

Sometimes I stopped and listened. I was sure I could hear noises, but I could not tell whether they were above me or not. In the centre of the ice-barrier, about four feet from the ground, was a vast block of the frozen substance which was unusually clear and seemed to have nothing on the other side of it; for through it I could see flickers of light, as though people were going about with lanterns. It was quite certain that the accident had been discovered; for, had not the thundering noise been heard by persons outside, the workmen would have seen what had happened as soon as they came into the tunnel to begin their afternoon operations.

At first I wondered why they did not set to work with a will and cut away this barrier and let me out. But there suddenly came to my mind a reason for this lack of energy which was more chilling than the glistening walls around me: Why should they suppose that I was in the ice-chamber? I was not in the habit of coming here very often, but I was in the habit of wandering off by myself at all hours of the day. This thought made me feel that I might as well lie down on the floor of this awful cave and die at once. The workmen might think it unsafe to mine any further in this part of the glacier, and begin operations at some other point. I did sit down for a moment, and then I rose involuntarily and began my weary round. Suddenly I thought of looking at my watch. It was nearly five o'clock. I had been more than four hours in that dreadful place, and I did not believe that I could continue to exercise my limbs very much longer. The lights I had seen had ceased. It was quite plain that the workmen had no idea that any one was imprisoned in the cave.

But soon after I had come to this conclusion I saw through the clear block of ice a speck of light, and it became stronger and stronger, until I believed it to be close to the other side of the block. There it remained stationary; but there seemed to be other points of light which moved about in a strange way, and near it. Now I stood by the block watching. When my feet became very cold, I stamped them; but there I stood fascinated, for what I saw was truly surprising. A large coal of fire appeared on the other side of the block; then it suddenly vanished and was succeeded by another coal. This disappeared, and another took its place, each one seeming to come nearer and nearer to me. Again and again did these coals appear. They reached the centre of the block; they approached my side of it. At last one was so near to me that I thought it was about to break through, but it vanished. Then there came a few quick thuds and the end of a piece of iron protruded from the block. This was withdrawn, and through the aperture there came a voice which said: "Mr. Cuthbert, are you in there?" It was the voice of Agnes!

Weak and cold as I was, fire and energy rushed through me at these words. "Yes," I exclaimed, my mouth to the hole; "Agnes, is that you?"

"Wait a minute," came from the other side of the aperture. "I must make it bigger. I must keep it from closing up."

Again came the coals of fire, running backward and forward through the long hole in the block of ice. I could see now what they were. They were irons used by plumbers for melting solder and that sort of thing, and Agnes was probably heating them in a little furnace outside, and withdrawing them as fast as they cooled. It was not long before the aperture was very much enlarged; and then there came grating through it a long tin tube nearly two inches in diameter, which almost, but not quite, reached my side of the block.

Now came again the voice of Agnes: "Oh, Mr. Cuthbert, are you truly there? Are you crushed? Are you wounded? Are you nearly frozen? Are you starved? Tell me quickly if you are yet safe."

Had I stood in a palace padded with the softest silk and filled with spicy odors from a thousand rose gardens, I could not have been better satisfied with my surroundings than I was at that moment. Agnes was not two feet away! She was telling me that she cared for me! In a very few words I assured her that I was uninjured. Then I was on the point of telling her I loved her, for I believed that not a moment should be lost in making this avowal. I could not die without her knowing that. But the appearance of a mass of paper at the other end of the tube prevented the expression of my sentiments. This was slowly pushed on until I could reach it. Then there came the words: "Mr. Cuthbert, these are sandwiches. Eat them immediately and walk about while you are doing it. You must keep yourself warm until the men get to you."

Obedient to the slightest wish of this dear creature, I went twice around the cave, devouring the sandwiches as I walked. They were the most delicious food that I had ever tasted. They were given to me by Agnes. I came back to the opening. I could not immediately begin my avowal. I must ask a question first. "Can they get to me?" I inquired. "Is anybody trying to do that? Are they working there by you? I do not hear them at all."

"Oh, no," she answered; they are not working

here. They are on top of the bluff, trying to dig down to you. They were afraid to meddle with the ice here for fear that more of it might come down and crush you and the men, too. Oh, there has been a dreadful excitement since it was found that you were in there!"

"How could they know I was here?" I asked.

"It was your old Susan who first thought of it. She saw you walking toward the shaft about noon, and then she remembered that she had not seen you again; and when they came into the tunnel here they found one of the lanterns gone and the big stick you generally carry lying where the lantern had been. Then it was known that you must be inside. Oh, then there was an awful time! The foreman of the ice-men examined everything, and said they must dig down to you from above. He put his men to work; but they could do very little, for they had hardly any spades. Then they sent into town for help and over to the new park for the Italians working there. From the way these men set to work you might have thought that they would dig away the whole bluff in about five minutes; but they didn't. Nobody seemed to know what to do, or how to get to work; and the hole they made when they did begin was filled up with men almost as fast as they even threw out the stones and gravel. I don't believe anything would have been done properly if your friend, Mr. Burton, hadn't happened to

come with two scientific gentlemen, and since that
he has been directing everything. You can't
think what a splendid fellow he is! I fairly
adored him when I saw him giving his orders and
making everybody skip around in the right way."

"Tom is a very good man," said I; "but it is
his business to direct that sort of work, and it is
not surprising that he knows how to do it. But,
Agnes, they may never get down to me, and we
do not know that this roof may not cave in upon
me at any moment; and before this or anything
else happens I want to tell you—"

"Mr. Cuthbert," said Agnes, "is there plenty
of oil in your lantern? It would be dreadful if it
were to go out and leave you there in the dark.
I thought of that and brought you a little bottle
of kerosene so that you can fill it. I am going to
push the bottle through now, if you please."
And with this a large phial, cork end foremost,
came slowly through the tube, propelled by one
of the soldering irons. Then came Agnes's voice:
"Please fill your lantern immediately, because if
it goes out you can not find it in the dark; and
then walk several times around the cave, for you
have been standing still too long already."

I obeyed these injunctions, but in two or three
minutes was again at the end of the tube.
"Agnes," said I, "how did you happen to come
here? Did you contrive in your own mind this
method of communicating with me?"

"Oh, yes; I did," she said. "Everybody said

that this mass of ice must not be meddled with, but I knew very well it would not hurt it to make a hole through it."

"But how did you happen to be here?" I asked.

"Oh, I ran over as soon as I heard of the accident. Everybody ran here. The whole neighborhood is on top of the bluff; but nobody wanted to come into the tunnel, because they were afraid that more of it might fall in. So I was able to work here all by myself, and I am very glad of it. I saw the soldering iron and the little furnace outside of your house where the plumbers had been using them, and I brought them here myself. Then I thought that a simple hole through the ice might soon freeze up again, and if you were alive inside I could not do anything to help you; and so I ran home and got my diploma case, that had had one end melted out of it, and I brought that to stick in the hole. I'm so glad that it is long enough, or almost."

"Oh, Agnes," I cried, "you thought of all this for me?"

"Why, of course, Mr. Cuthbert," she answered, before I had a chance to say anything more. "You were in great danger of perishing before the men got to you, and nobody seemed to think of any way to give you immediate relief. And don't you think that a collegiate education is a good thing for girls—at least, that it was for me?"

"Agnes," I exclaimed, "please let me speak. I want to tell you, I must tell you—"

But the voice of Agnes was clearer than mine and it overpowered my words. "Mr. Cuthbert," she said, "we can not both speak through this tube at the same time in opposite directions. I have here a bottle of water for you, but I am very much afraid it will not go through the diploma case."

"Oh, I don't want any water," I said. "I can eat ice if I am thirsty. What I want is to tell you—"

"Mr. Cuthbert," said she, "you must not eat that ice. Water that was frozen countless ages ago may be very different from the water of modern times, and might not agree with you. Don't touch it, please. I am going to push the bottle through if I can. I tried to think of everything that you might need and brought them all at once; because, if I could not keep the hole open, I wanted to get them to you without losing a minute."

Now the bottle came slowly through. It was a small beer-bottle, I think, and several times I was afraid it was going to stick fast and cut off communication between me and the outer world —that is to say, between me and Agnes. But at last the cork and the neck appeared, and I pulled it through. I did not drink any of it, but immediately applied my mouth to the tube.

"Agnes," I said, "my dear Agnes, really you must not prevent me from speaking. I can not delay another minute. This is an awful position for me to be in, and as you don't seem to realize—"

"But I do realize, Mr. Cuthbert, that if you don't walk about you will certainly freeze before you can be rescued. Between every two or three words you want to take at least one turn around that place. How dreadful it would be if you were suddenly to become benumbed and stiff! Everybody is thinking of that. The best diggers that Mr. Burton had were three colored men; but after they had gone down nothing like as deep as a well, they came up frightened and said they would not dig another shovelful for the whole world. Perhaps you don't know it, but there's a story about the neighborhood that the negro hell is under your property. You know many of the colored peoeple expect to be everlastingly punished with ice and not with fire—"

"Agnes," I interrupted, "I am punished with ice and fire both. Please let me tell you—"

"I was going on to say, Mr. Cuthbert," she interrupted, "that when the Italians heard why the colored men had come out of the hole they would not go in either, for they are just as afraid of everlasting ice as the negroes are, and were sure that if the bottom came out of that hole they would fall into a frozen lower world. So there was nothing to do but to send for paupers, and they are working now. You know paupers have to do what they are told without regard to their beliefs. They got a dozen of them from the poorhouse. Somebody said they just threw them into the hole. Now I must stop talking, for it is time for you to walk around again. Would you like another sandwich?"

"Agnes," said I, endeavoring to speak calmly, "all I want is to be able to tell you—"

"And when you walk, Mr. Cuthbert, you had better keep around the edge of the chamber, for there is no knowing when they may come through. Mr. Burton and the foreman of the ice-men measured the bluff so that they say the hole they are making is exactly over the middle of the chamber you are in, and if you walk around the edge the pieces may not fall on you."

"If you don't listen to me, Agnes," I said, "I'll go and sit anywhere, everywhere, where death may come to me quickest. Your coldness is worse than the coldness of the cave. I can not bear it."

"But, Mr. Cuthbert," said Agnes, speaking, I thought, with some agitation, "I have been listening to you, and what more can you possibly have to say? If there is anything you want, let me know. I will run and get it for you."

"There is no need that you should go away to get what I want," I said. "It is there with you. It is you."

"Mr. Cuthbert," said Agnes, in a very low voice, but so distinctly that I could hear every word, "don't you think it would be better for you to give your whole mind to keeping yourself warm and strong? For if you let yourself get benumbed you may sink down and freeze."

"Agnes," I said, "I will not move from this little hole until I have told you that I love you, that I have no reason to care for life or rescue unless you return my love, unless you are willing to be mine. Speak quickly to me, Agnes, because I may not be rescued and may never know whether my love for you is returned or not."

At this moment there was a tremendous crash behind me, and, turning, I saw a mass of broken ice upon the floor of the cave, with a cloud of dust and smaller fragments still falling. And then with a great scratching and scraping, and a howl loud enough to waken the echoes of all the lower regions, down came a red-headed, drunken shoemaker. I can not say that he was drunk at that moment, but I knew the man the moment I saw his carroty poll, and it was drink which had sent him to the poorhouse.

But the sprawling and howling cobbler did not reach the floor. A rope had been fastened around his waist to prevent a fall in case the bottom of the pit should suddenly give way, and he hung dangling in mid air with white face and distended eyes, cursing and swearing and vociferously entreating to be pulled up. But before he received any answer from above, or I could speak to him, there came through the hole in the roof of the cave a shower of stones and gravel, and with them a frantic Italian, his legs and arms outspread, his face wild with terror.

Just as he appeared in view he grasped the rope of the cobbler, and, though in a moment he came down heavily upon the floor of the chamber, this broke his fall, and he did not appear to be hurt. Instantly he crouched low and almost upon all fours, and began to run around the chamber, keeping close to the walls and screaming, I suppose to his saints, to preserve him from the torments of the frozen damned.

In the midst of this hubbub came the voice of Agnes through the hole: "Oh, Mr. Cuthbert, what has happened? Are you alive?"

I was so disappointed by the appearance of these wretched interlopers at the moment it was about to be decided whether my life—should it last for years, or but for a few minutes—was to be black or bright, and I was so shaken and startled by the manner of their entry upon the scene, that I could not immediately shape the words necessary to inform Agnes what had happened. But, collecting my faculties, I was about to speak, when suddenly, with the force of the hind leg of a mule, I was pushed away from the aperture, and the demoniac Italian clapped his great mouth to the end of the tube and roared through it a volume of oaths and supplications. I attempted to thrust aside the wretched being, but I might as well have tried to move the ice barrier itself. He had perceived that some one outside was talking to me, and in his frenzy he was imploring that some one should let him out.

While still endeavoring to move the man, I was seized by the arm, and turning, beheld the pallid face of the shoemaker. They had let him down so that he reached the floor. He tried to fall on his knees before me, but the rope was so short that he was able to go only part of the way down, and presented a most ludicrous appearance, with his toes scraping the icy floor and his arms thrown out as if he were paddling like a tadpole. "Oh, have mercy upon me, sir," he said, "and help me get out of this dreadful place. If you go to the hole and call up it's you, they will pull me up; but if they get you out first they will never think of me. I am a poor pauper, sir, but I never did nothin' to be packed in ice before I am dead."

Noticing that the Italian had left the end of the aperture in the block of ice, and that he was now shouting up the open shaft, I ran to the channel of communication which my Agnes had opened for me, and called through it; but the dear girl had gone.

The end of a ladder now appeared at the opening in the roof, and this was let down until it reached the floor. I started toward it, but before I had gone half the distance the frightened shoemaker and the maniac Italian sprang upon it, and, with shrieks and oaths, began a maddening fight for possession of the ladder. They might quickly have gone up one after the other, but each had no thought but to be first; and as one s,ized the rounds he was pulled away by the other, until I feared the ladder would be torn to pieces. The shoemaker finally pushed his way up a little distance, when the Italian sprang upon his back, endeavoring to climb over him; and so on they went up the shaft, fighting, swearing, kicking, scratching, shaking and wrenching the ladder, which had been tied to another one in order to increase its length, so that it was in danger of breaking, and tearing at each other in a fashion which made it wonderful that they did not both tumble headlong downward. They went on up, so completely filling the shaft with their struggling forms and their wild cries that I could not see or hear anything, and was afraid, in fact, to look up toward the outer air.

As I was afterward informed, the Italian, who had slipped into the hole by accident, ran away like a frightened hare the moment he got his feet on firm ground, and the shoemaker sat down and swooned. By this performance he obtained from a benovolent bystander a drink of whiskey, the first he had had since he was committed to the poorhouse.

But a voice soon came down the shaft calling to me. I recognized it as that of Tom Burton, and replied that I was safe, and that I was coming up the ladder. But in my attempt to climb, I found that I was unable to do so. Chilled and stiffened by the cold and weakened by fatigue and excitement, I believe I never should have been able to leave that ice chamber if my faithful friend had not come down the ladder and vigorously assisted me to reach the outer air.

Seated on the ground, my back against a great oak tree, I was quickly surrounded by a crowd of my neighbors, the workmen and the people who had been drawn to the spot by the news of the strange accident, to gaze at me as if I were some unknown being excavated from the bowels of the earth. I was sipping some brandy and water which Burton had handed me, when Aaron Boyce pushed himself in front of me.

"Well, sir," he said, "I am mighty glad you got out of that scrape. I'm bound to say I didn't expect you would. I have been sure all along that it wasn't right to meddle with things that go agin Nature, and I haven't any doubt that you'll see that for yourself and fill up all them tunnels and shafts you've made. The ice that comes on ponds and rivers was good enough for our forefathers, and it ought to be good enough for us. And as for this cold stuff you find in your gravel-pit, I don't believe it's ice at all; and if it is, like as not it's made of some sort of pizen stuff that freezes easier than water. For everybody knows that water don't freeze in a well, and if it don't do that, why should it do it in any kind of a hole in the ground? So perhaps it's just as well that you did git shut up there, sir, and find out for yourself what a dangerous thing it is to fool with

Nature and try to git ice from the bottom of the ground instead of the top of the water."

This speech made me angry, for I knew that old Boyce was a man who was always glad to get hold of anything which had gone wrong and try to make it worse; but I was too weak to answer him.

This, however, would not have been necessary, for Tom Burton turned upon him. "Idiot," said he, "if that is your way of thinking you might as well say that if a well caves in you should never again dig for water, or that nobody should have a cellar under his house for fear that the house should fall into it. There's no more danger of the ice beneath us ever giving way again than there is that this bluff should crumble under our feet. That break in the roof of the ice tunnel was caused by my digging away the face of the bluff very near that spot. The high temperature of the outer air weakened the ice, and it fell. But down here, under this ground and secure from the influences of the heat of the outer air, the mass of ice is more solid than rock. We will build a brick arch over the place where the accident happened, and then there will not be a safer mine on this continent than this ice-mine will be."

This was a wise and diplomatic speech from Burton, and it proved to be of great service to me; for the men who had been taking out ice had been a good deal frightened by the fall of the tunnel, and when it was proved that what Burton had said in regard to the cause of the weakening of the ice was entirely correct, they became willing to go to work again.

I now began to feel stronger and better, and, rising to my feet, I glanced here and there into the crowd, hoping to catch a sight of Agnes. But I was not very much surprised at not seeing her, because she would naturally shrink from forcing herself into the midst of this motley company; but I felt that I must go and look for her without the loss of a minute, for if she should return to her father's house I might not be able to see her again.

On the outskirts of the crowd I met Susan, who was almost overpowered with joy at seeing me safe again. I shook her by the hand, but, without replying to her warm-hearted protestations of thankfulness and delight, I asked her if she had seen Miss Havelot.

"Miss Agnes!" she exclaimed. "Why, no sir; I expect she's at home; and if she did come here with the rest of the neighbors I didn't see her; for when I found out what had happened, sir, I was so weak that I sat down in the kitchen all of a lump, and have just had strength enough to come out."

"Oh, I know she was here," I cried; "I am sure of that, and I do hope she's not gone home again."

"Know she was here!" exclaimed Susan. "Why, how on earth could you know that?"

I did not reply that it was not on the earth but under it, that I became aware of the fact, but hurried toward the Havelot house, hoping to overtake Agnes if she had gone that way. But I did not see her, and suddenly a startling idea struck me, and I turned and ran home as fast as I could go. When I reached my grounds I went directly to the mouth of the shaft. There was nobody there, for the crowd was collected into a solid mass on the top of the bluff, listening to a lecture from Tom Burton, who deemed it well to promote the growth of interest and healthy opinion in regard to his wonderful discovery and my valuable possession. I hurried down the shaft, and near the end of it, just before it joined the ice tunnel, I beheld Agnes sitting upon the wooden track. She was not unconscious, for as I approached she slightly turned her head. I sprang toward her; I kneeled beside her; I took her in my arms. "Oh, Agnes, dearest Agnes," I cried, "what is the matter? What has happened to you? Has a piece of ice fallen upon you? Have you slipped and hurt yourself?"

She turned her beautiful eyes up toward me and for a moment did not speak. Then she said: "And they got you out? And you are in your right mind?"

"Right mind!" I exclaimed. "I have never been out of my mind. What are you thinking of?"

"Oh, you must have been," she said, "when you screamed at me in that horrible way. I was so frightened that I fell back, and I must have fainted."

Tremulous as I was with love and anxiety, I could not help laughing. "Oh, my dear Agnes, I did not scream at you. That was a crazed Italian who fell through the hole that they dug." Then I told her what had happened.

She heaved a gentle sigh. "I am so glad to hear that," she said. "There was one thing that I was thinking about just before you came and which gave me a little bit of comfort; the words and yells I heard were dreadfully oniony, and somehow or other I could not connect that sort of thing with you."

It now struck me that during this conversation I had been holding my dear girl in my arms, and she had not shown the slightest sign of resistance or disapprobation. This made my heart beat high.

"Oh, Agnes," I said, "I truly believe you love me or you would not have been here, you would not have done for me all that you did. Why did you not answer me when I spoke to you through that wall of ice, through the hole your dear love had made in it? Why, when I was in such a terrible situation, not knowing whether I was to die or live, did you not comfort my heart with one sweet word?"

"Oh, Walter," she answered, "it wasn't at all

necessary for you to say all that you did say, for I had suspected it before, and as soon as you began to call me Agnes I knew, of course, how you felt about it. And, besides, it really was necessary that you should move about to keep yourself from freezing. But the great reason for my not encouraging you to go on talking in that way was that I was afraid people might come into the tunnel, and as, of course, you would not know that they were there, you would go on making love to me through my diploma case, and you know I should have perished with shame if I had had to stand there with that old Mr. Boyce, and I don't know who else, listening to your words, which were very sweet to me, Walter, but which would have sounded awfully funny to them."

When she said that my words had been sweet to her I dropped the consideration of all other subjects.

When, about ten minutes afterward, we came out of the shaft we were met by Susan.

"Bless my soul and body, Mr. Cuthbert!" she exclaimed. "Did you find that young lady down there in the centre of the earth? It seems to me as if everything that you want comes to you out of the ground. But I have been looking for you to tell you that Mr. Havelot has been here after his daughter, and I'm sure if he had known where she was, he would have been scared out of his wits."

"Father here!" exclaimed Agnes. "Where is he now?"

"I think he has gone home, miss. Indeed I'm sure of it; for my daughter Jennie, who was over here the same as all the other people in the county, I truly believe told him—and I was proud she had the spirit to speak up that way to him—that your heart was almost broke when you heard about Mr. Cuthbert being shut up in the ice, and that most likely you was in your own room a-cryin' your eyes out. When he heard that he stood lookin' all around the place, and he asked me if he might go in the house; and when I told him he was most welcome, he went in. I offered to show him about, which he said was no use, that he had been there often enough; and he went everywhere, I truly believe, except in the garret and the cellar. And after he got through with that he went out to the barn and then walked home."

"I must go to him immediately," said Agnes.

"But not alone," said I. And together we walked through the woods, over the little field and across the Havelot lawn to the house. We were told that the old gentleman was in his library, and together we entered the room. Mr. Havelot was sitting by a table on which were lying several open volumes of an encyclopedia. When he turned and saw us, he closed his book, pushed back his chair and took off his spectacles. "Upon my word, sir," he cried; "and so the first thing you do after they pull you out of the earth is to come here and break my commands."

"I came on the invitation of your daughter, sir."

"And what right has she to invite you, I'd like to know?"

"She has every right, for to her I owe my existence."

"What rabid nonsense!" exclaimed the old gentleman. "People don't owe their existence to the silly creatures they fall in love with."

"I assure you I am correct, sir." And then I related to him what his daughter had done, and how through her angelic agency my rescuers had found me a living being instead of a frozen corpse.

"Stuff!" said Mr. Havelot. "People can live in a temperature of thirty-two degrees above zero all winter. Out in Minnesota they think that's hot. And you gave him victuals and drink through your diploma case! Well, miss, I told you that if you tried to roast chestnuts in that diploma case the bottom would come out."

"But you see, father," said Agnes, earnestly, "the reason I did that was because when I roasted them in anything shallow they popped into the fire, but they could not jump out of the diploma case."

"Well, something else seems to have jumped out of it," said the old gentleman, "and something with which I am not satisfied. I have been looking over these books, sir, and have read the articles on ice, glaciers and caves, and I find no record of anything in the whole history of the world which in the least resembles the cock-and-bull story I am told about the butt-end of a glacier which tumbled into a cave in your ground, and has been lying there through all the geological ages, and the eras of formation, and periods of animate existence down to the days of Noah, and Moses, and Methuselah, and Rameses II, and Alexander the Great, and Martin Luther, and John Wesley, to this day, for you to dig out and sell to the Williamstown Ice Co."

"But that's what happened, sir," said I.

"And besides, father," added Agnes, "the gold and silver that people take out of mines may have been in the ground as long as that ice has been."

"Bosh!" said Mr. Havelot. "The cases are not at all similar. It is simply impossible that a piece of a glacier should have fallen into a cave and been preserved in that way. The temperature of caves is always above the freezing-point, and that ice would have melted a million years before you were born."

"But, father," said Agnes, "the temperature of caves filled with ice must be very much lower than that of common caves."

"And apart from that," I added, "the ice is still there, sir."

"That doesn't make the slightest difference," he replied. "It's against all reason and common-sense that such a thing could have happened. Even if there ever was a glacier in this part of the country and if the lower portion of it did stick out over an immense hole in the ground, that protruding end would never have broken off and tumbled in. Glaciers are too thick and massive for that."

"But the glacier is there, sir," said I, "in spite of your own reasoning."

"And then again," continued the old gentleman, "if there had been a cave and a projecting spur the ice would have gradually melted and dripped into the cave, and we would have had a lake and not an ice-mine. It is an absurdity."

"But it's there, notwithstanding," said I.

"And you can not subvert facts, you know, father," added Agnes.

"Confound facts!" he cried. "I base my arguments on sober, cool-headed reason; and there's nothing that can withstand reason. The thing's impossible and, therefore, it has never happened. I went over to your place, sir, when I heard of the accident, for the misfortunes of my neighbors interest me, no matter what may be my opinion of them, and when I found that you had been extricated from your ridiculous predicament, I went through your house, and I was pleased to find it in as good or better condition than I had known it in the days of your respected father. I was glad to see the improvement in your circumstances; but when I am told, sir, that your apparent prosperity rests upon such an absurdity as a glacier in a gravel hill, I can but smile with contempt, sir."

I was getting a little tired of this. "But the glacier is there, sir," I said, "and I am taking out ice every day, and have reason to believe that I can continue to take it out for the rest of my life. With such facts as these before me, I am bound to say, sir, that I don't care in the least about reason."

"And I am here, father," said Agnes, coming close to me, "and here I want to continue for the rest of my days."

The old gentleman looked at her. "And, I suppose," he said, "that you, too, don't in the least care about reason?"

"Not a bit," said Agnes.

"Well," said Mr. Havelot, rising, "I have done all I can to make you two listen to reason, and I can do no more. I despair of making sensible human beings of you, and so you might as well go on acting like a couple of ninny-hammers."

"Do ninny-hammers marry and settle on the property adjoining yours, sir?" I asked.

"Yes, I suppose they do," he said. "And when the aboriginal ice-house, or whatever the ridiculous thing is that they have discovered, gives out, I suppose that they can come to a reasonable man and ask him for a little money to buy bread and butter."

Two years have passed, and Agnes and the glacier are still mine; great blocks of ice now flow in almost a continuous stream from the mine to the railroad station, and in a smaller but quite as continuous stream an income flows in upon Agnes and me; and from one of the experimental excavations made by Tom Burton on the bluff comes a stream of ice-cold water running in a sparkling brook a-down my dell. On fine mornings before I am up, I am credibly informed that Aaron Boyce may generally be found, in season and out of season, endeavoring to catch the trout with which I am trying to stock that ice-cold stream. The diploma case, which I caused to be carefully removed from the ice-barrier which had imprisoned me, now hangs in my study and holds our marriage certificate.

Near the line-fence which separates his property from mine, Mr. Havelot has sunk a wide shaft. "If the glacier spur under your land was a quarter of a mile wide," he says to me, "it was probably at least a half a mile long; and if that were the case, the upper end of it extends into my place, and I may be able to strike it." He has a good deal of money, this worthy Mr. Havelot, but he would be very glad to increase his riches, whether they are based upon sound reason or ridiculous facts. As for Agnes and myself, no facts or any reason could make us happier than our ardent love and our frigid fortune.

# THE GOLD BUG

## BY E. A. POE

# THE GOLD BUG

BY E. A. POE

What ho! what ho! this fellow is dancing mad!
He hath been bitten by the Tarantula.
—*"All in the wrong"*

MANY years ago, I contracted an intimacy with a Mr. William Legrand. He was of an ancient Huguenot family, and had once been wealthy; but a series of misfortunes had reduced him to want. To avoid the mortification consequent upon his disasters, he left New Orleans, the city of his forefathers, and took up his residence at Sullivan's Island, near Charleston, South Carolina.

This Island is a very singular one. It consists of little else than the sea sand, and is about three miles long. Its breadth at no point exceeds a quarter of a mile. It is separated from the mainland by a scarcely perceptible creek, oozing its way through a wilderness of reeds and slime, a favorite resort of the marsh-hen. The vegetation, as might be supposed, is scant, or at least dwarfish. No trees of any magnitude are to be seen. Near the western extremity, where Fort Moultrie stands, and where are some miserable frame buildings, tenanted, during the summer, by the fugitives from Charleston dust and fever, may be found, indeed the bristly palmetto; but the whole island, with the exception of this western point, and a line of hard, white beach on the seacoast, is covered with a dense undergrowth of the sweet myrtle, so much prized by the horticulturists of England. The shrub here often attains the height of fifteen or twenty feet, and forms an almost impenetrable coppice, burthening the air with its fragrance.

In the inmost recesses of this coppice, not far from the eastern or more remote end of the island, Legrand had built himself a small hut, which he occupied when I first, by mere accident, made his acquaintance. This soon ripened into friendship—for there was much in the recluse to excite interest and esteem. I found him well educated, with unusual powers of mind, but infected with misanthropy, and subject to perverse moods of alternate enthusiasm and melancholy. He had with him many books, but rarely employed them. His chief amusements were gunning and fishing, or sauntering along the beach and through the myrtles, in quest of shells or entomological specimens;—his collection of the latter might have been envied by a Swammerdamn. In these excursions he was usually accompanied by an old negro, called Jupiter, who had been manumitted before the reverses of the family, but who could be induced, neither by threats nor by promises, to abandon what he considered his right of attendance upon the footsteps of his young "Massa

Will." It is not improbable that the relatives of
Legrand, conceiving him to be somewhat unsettled in intellect, had contrived to instill this
obstinacy into Jupiter, with a view to the super-
vision and guardianship of the wanderer.

The winters in the latitude of Sullivan's Island are seldom very severe, and in the fall of
the year it is a rare event indeed when a fire is
considered necessary. About the middle of Oc-
tober, 18—, there occurred, however, a day of
remarkable chilliness. Just before sunset I
scrambled my way through the evergreens to the
hut of my friend, whom I had not visited for
several weeks—my residence being, at that time,
in Charleston, a distance of nine miles from the
Island, while the facilities of passage and re-
passage were very far behind those of the present day. Upon reaching the hut I rapped, as
was my custom, and getting no reply, sought for
the key where I knew it was secreted, unlocked
the door and went in. A fine fire was blazing
upon the hearth. It was a novelty, and by no
means an ungrateful one. I threw off an overcoat, took an arm-chair by the crackling logs,
and awaited patiently the arrival of my hosts.

Soon after dark they arrived and gave me a
most cordial welcome. Jupiter, grinning from
ear to ear, bustled about to prepare some marsh-
hens for supper. Legrand was in one of his
fits—how else shall I term them?—of enthusiasm. He had found an unknown bivalve, form-

ing a new genus, and, more than this, he had
hunted down and secured, with Jupiter's assistance, a *scarabæus* which he believed to be totally
new, but in respect to which he wished to have
my opinion on the morrow.

"And why not to-night?" I asked, rubbing my
hands over the blaze' and wishing the whole tribe
of *scarabæi* at the devil.

"Ah, if I had only known you were here!"
said Legrand, "but it's so long since I saw you;
and how could I foresee that you would pay me
a visit this very night of all others? As I was
coming home I met Lieutenant G——, from the
fort, and, very foolishly, I lent him the bug; so
it will be impossible for you to see it until morning. Stay here to-night, and I will send Jup
down for it at sunrise. It is the loveliest thing
in creation!"

"What?—sunrise?"

"Nonsense! no!—the bug. It is of a brilliant
gold color—about the size of a large hickory-
nut—with two jet-black spots near one extremity of the back, and another, somewhat longer,
at the other. The *antennæ* are——"

"Dey ain't *no* tin in him' Massa Will, I keep
a tellin on you," here interrupted Jupiter; "de
bug is a goole bug, solid, ebery bit of him, inside and all, sep him wing—neber feel half so
hebby a bug in my life."

"Well, suppose it is, Jup," replied Legrand,
somewhat more earnestly, it seemed to me, than

the case demanded, "is that any reason for your letting the birds burn? The color"—here he turned to me—"is really almost enough to warrant Jupiter's idea. You never saw a more brilliant metallic lustre than the scales emit—but of this you cannot judge till to-morrow. In the meantime I can give you some idea of the shape." Saying this, he seated himself at a small table, on which were a pen and ink, but no paper. He looked for some in a drawer, but found none.

"Never mind," said he at length, "this will answer"; and he drew from his waistcoat pocket a scrap of what I took to be very dirty foolscap, and made upon it a rough drawing with the pen. While he did this, I retained my seat by the fire, for I was still chilly. When the design was complete, he handed it to me without rising. As I received it, a loud growl was heard succeeded by a scratching at the door. Jupiter opened it, and a large Newfoundland, belonging to Legrand, rushed in, leaped upon my shoulders, and loaded me with caresses; for I had shown him much attention during previous visits. When his gambols were over, I looked at the paper, and, to speak the truth, found myself not a little puzzled at what my friend had depicted.

"Well!" I said, after contemplating it for some minutes, "this *is* a strange *scarabæus*, I must confess: new to me: never saw anything like it before—unless it was a skull, or a death's-head—which it more nearly resembles than anything else that has come under *my* observation."

"A death's-head!" echoed Legrand—"Oh—yes—well, it has something of that appearance upon paper, no doubt. The two upper black spots look like eyes, eh? and the longer one at the bottom like a mouth—and then the shape of the whole is oval."

"Perhaps so," said I; "but, Legrand, I fear you are no artist. I must wait until I see the beetle itself, if I am to form any idea of its personal appearance."

"Well, I don't know," said he, a little nettled, "I draw tolerably—*should* do it at least—have had good masters, and flatter myself that I am not quite a blockhead."

"But, my dear fellow, you are joking then," said I, "this is a very passable *skull*—indeed, I may say that it is a very excellent skull, according to the vulgar notions about such specimens of physiology—and your *scarabæus* must be the queerest *scarabæus* in the world if it resembles it. Why, we may get up a very thrilling bit of superstition upon this hint. I presume you will call the bug *scarabæus caput hominis,* or something of that kind—there are many similar titles in the Natural Histories. But where are the *antennæ* you spoke of?"

"The *antennæ!*" said Legrand, who seemed to be getting unaccountably warm upon the subject; "I am sure you must see the *antennæ.* I made them as distinct as they are in the original insect, and I presume that is sufficient."

"Well, well," I said, "perhaps you have—still I don't see them;" and I handed him the paper without additional remark, not wishing to ruffle his temper; but I was much surprised at the turn affairs had taken; his ill humor puzzled me— and, as for the drawing of the beetle, there were positively *no antennæ* visible, and the whole *did* bear a very close resemblance to the ordinary cuts of a death's-head.

He received the paper very peevishly, and was about to crumple it, apparently to throw it in the fire, when a casual glance at the design seemed suddenly to rivet his attention. In an instant his face grew violently red—in another as excessively pale. For some minutes he continued to scrutinize the drawing minutely where he sat. At length he arose, took a candle from the table and proceeded to seat himself upon a sea-chest in the farthest corner of the room. Here again he made an anxious examination of the paper; turning it in all directions. He said nothing, however, and his conduct greatly astonished me; yet I thought it prudent not to exacerbate the growing moodiness of his temper by any comment. Presently he took from his coat pocket a wallet, placed the paper carefully in it, and deposited both in a writing-desk, which he locked. He now grew more composed in his demeanor; but his original air of enthusiasm had quite disappeared. Yet he seemed not so much sulky as abstracted. As the evening wore away he became more and more absorbed in reverie, from which no sallies of mine could arouse him. It had been my intention to pass the night at the hut, as I had frequently done before, but, seeing my host in this mood, I deemed it proper to take leave. He did not press me to remain, but as I departed, he shook my hand with even more than his usual cordiality.

It was about a month after this (and during the interval I had seen nothing of Legrand) when I received a visit, at Charleston, from his man, Jupiter. I had never seen the good old negro look so dispirited, and I feared that some serious disaster had befallen my friend.

"Well, Jup," said I, "what is the matter now? —how is your master?"

"Why, to speak de troof, massa, him not so berry well as mought be."

"Not well! I am truly sorry to hear it. What does he complain of?"

"Dar! dat's it!—him neber plain of notin—but him berry sick for all dat."

"*Very* sick, Jupiter!—why didn't you say so at once? Is he confined to bed?"

"No, dat he ain't!—he ain't find nowhar—dat's just whar de shoe pinch—my mind is got to be berry hebby bout poor Massa Will."

"Jupiter, I should like to understand what it

is you are talking about. You say your master is sick. Hasn't he told you what ails him?"

"Why, massa, tain't worf while for to git mad bout de matter—Massa Will say noffin at all ain't de matter wid him—but den what make him go about looking dis here way, wid he head down and he soldiers up, and as white as a gose? And den he keep a syphon all de time——"

"Keeps a what, Jupiter?"

"Keeps a syphon wid de figgurs on de slate— de queerest figgurs I ebber did see. I'se gittin be skeered, I tell you. Hab for to keep mighty tight eye pon him noovers. Todder day he gib me slip fore de sun up and was gone de whole ob de blessed day. I had a big stick ready cut for to gib him d—d good beating when he did come—but I'se sich a fool dat I hadn't de heart arter all—he look so berry poorly."

"Eh?—what?—ah yes!—upon the whole I think you had better not be too severe with the poor fellow—don't flog him, Jupiter—he can't very well stand it—but can you form no idea of what has occasioned this illness, or rather this change of conduct? Has anything unpleasant happened since I saw you?"

"No, massa, dey ain't bin noffin onpleasant *since* den—'twas *fore* den I'm feared—'twas de berry day you was dare."

"How? what do you mean?"

"Why, massa, I mean de bug—dare now."

"The what?"

"De bug—I'm berry sartain dat Massa Will bin bit somewhere bout de head by dat goole bug."

"And what cause have you, Jupiter, for such a supposition?"

"Claws enuff, massa, and mouff too. I nebber did see sich a d—d bug—he kick and he bite ebery ting what cum near him. Massa Will cotch him fuss, but had for to let him go gin mighty quick, I tell you—den was de time he must ha got de bite. I didn't like de look ob de bug mouff, myself, no how, so I wouldn't take hold ob him wid my finger, but I cotch him wid a piece ob paper dat I found. I rap him up in de paper and stuff piece ob it in he mouff—dat was de way."

"And you think, then that your master was really bitten by the beetle, and that the bite made him sick?"

"I don't tink noffin about it—I nose it. What make him dream bout de goole so much, if tain't cause he bit by de goole bug? I'se heerd bout dem goole bugs fore dis."

"But how do you know he dreams about gold?"

"How I know? why cause he talk about it in he sleep—dat's how I nose."

"Well, Jup, perhaps you are right; but to what fortunate circumstance am I to attribute the honor of a visit from you to-day?"

"What de matter, massa?"

"Did you bring any message from Mr. Legrand?"

THE GOLD BUG

"No, massa, I bring dis here pissel"; and here Jupiter handed me a note which ran thus:

My Dear—

Why have I not seen you for so long a time? I hope you have not been so foolish as to take offense at any little *brusquerie* of mine; but no, that is improbable.

Since I saw you I have had great cause for anxiety. I have something to tell you, yet scarcely know how to tell it, or whether I should tell it at all.

I have not been quite well for some days past, and poor old Jup annoys me, almost beyond endurance, by his well-meant attentions. Would you believe it?—he had prepared a huge stick, the other day, with which to chastise me for giving him the slip, and spending the day, *solus*, among the hills on the main land. I verily believe that my ill looks alone saved me a flogging.

I have made no addition to my cabinet since we met.

If you can, in any way, make it convenient, come over with Jupiter. *Do* come. I wish to see you *to-night*, upon business of importance. I assure you that it is of the *highest* importance.

Ever yours,
William Legrand

There was something in the tone of this note which gave me great uneasiness. Its whole style differed materially from that of Legrand. What could he be dreaming of? What new crotchet possessed his excitable brain? What "business of the highest importance" could *he* possibly have to transact? Jupiter's account of him boded no good. I dreaded lest the continued pressure of

193

misfortune had, at length, fairly unsettled the reason of my friend. Without a moment's hesitation, therefore, I prepared to accompany the negro.

Upon reaching the wharf, I noticed a scythe and three spades, all apparently new, lying in the bottom of the boat in which we were to embark.

"What is the meaning of all this, Jup?" I inquired.

"Him syfe, massa, and spade."

"Very true; but what are they doing here?"

"Him de syfe and de spade what Massa Will sis pon my buying for him in de town, and de debbil's own lot of money I had to gib for 'em."

"But what, in the name of all that is mysterious, is your 'Massa Will' going to do with scythes and spades?"

"Dat's more dan *I* know, and debbil take me if I don't believe 'tis more dan he know too. But it's all cum ob de bug."

Finding that no satisfaction was to be obtained of Jupiter, whose whole intellect seemed to be absorbed by "de bug," I now stepped into the boat and made sail. With a fair and strong breeze we soon ran into the little cove to the northward of Fort Moultrie, and a walk of some two miles brought us to the hut. It was about three in the afternoon when we arrived. Legrand had been awaiting us in eager expectation. He grasped my hand with a nervous *empressement* which alarmed me and strengthened the suspicions already entertained. His countenance was pale even to ghastliness, and his deep-set eyes glared with unnatural lustre. After some inquiries respecting his health, I asked him, not knowing what better to say, if he had yet obtained the *scarabæus* from Lieutenant G——.

"Oh, yes," he replied, coloring violently, "I got it from him the next morning. Nothing should tempt me to part with that *scarabæus*. Do you know that Jupiter is quite right about it?"

"In what way?" I asked with a sad foreboding at heart.

"In supposing it to be a bug of *real gold*." He said this with an air of profound seriousness, and I felt inexpressibly shocked.

"This bug is to make my fortune," he continued, with a triumphant smile, "to reinstate me in my family possessions. Is it any wonder, then, that I prize it? Since Fortune has thought fit to bestow it upon me, I have only to use it properly and I shall arrive at the gold of which it is the index. Jupiter, bring me that *scarabæus!*"

"What! de bug, massa? I'd rudder not go fer trubble dat bug—you mus git him for your own self." Hereupon Legrand arose, with a grave and stately air, and brought me the beetle from a glass case in which it was enclosed. It was a beautiful *scarabæus,* and, at that time, unknown to naturalists—of course a great prize in a scientific point of view. There were two round, black spots near one extremity of the back, and a long one near the other. The scales were exceedingly hard and glossy, with all the appearance of burnished gold. The weight of the insect was very remarkable, and, taking all things into consideration, I could hardly blame Jupiter for his opinion respecting it; but what to make of Legrand's agreement with that opinion, I could not, for the life of me, tell.

"I sent for you," said he, in a grandiloquent tone, when I had completed my examination of the beetle, "I sent for you, that I might have your counsel and assistance in furthering the views of Fate and of the bug——"

"My dear Legrand," I cried, interrupting him, "you are certainly unwell, and had better use some little precautions. You shall go to bed, and I will remain with you a few days, until you get over this. You are feverish and——"

"Feel my pulse," said he.

I felt it, and, to say the truth, found not the slightest indication of fever.

"But you may be ill and yet have no fever. Allow me this once to prescribe for you. In the first place, go to bed. In the next——"

"You are mistaken," he interposed, "I am as well as I can expect to be under the excitement which I suffer. If you really wish me well, you will relieve this excitement."

"And how is this to be done?"

"Very easily. Jupiter and myself are going

upon an expedition into the hills, upon the main land, and, in this expedition, we shall need the aid of some person in whom we can confide. You are the only one we can trust. Whether we succeed or fail, the excitement which you now perceive in me will be equally allayed."

"I am anxious to oblige you in any way" I replied; "but do you mean to say that this infernal beetle has any connection with your expedition into the hills?"

"It has."

"Then, Legrand, I can become a party to no such absurd proceeding."

"I am sorry—very sorry—for we shall have to try it by ourselves."

"Try it by yourselves! The man is surely mad! —but stay!—how long do you propose to be absent?"

"Probably all night. We shall start immediately, and be back, at all events, by sunrise."

"And will you promise me, upon your honor, that when this freak of yours is over, and the bug business (good God!) settled to your satisfaction, you will then return home and follow my advice implicitly, as that of your physician?"

"Yes; I promise; and now let us be off, for we have no time to lose."

With a heavy heart I accompanied my friend. We started about four o'clock—Legrand, Jupiter, the dog and myself. Jupiter had with him the scythe and spades—the whole of which he insisted upon carrying—more through fear, it seemed to me, of trusting either of the implements within reach of his master, than from any excess of industry or complaisance. His demeanor was dogged in the extreme, and "dat d—d bug" were the sole words which escaped his lips during the journey. For my own part, I had charge of a couple of dark lanterns, while Legrand contented himself with the *scarabæus*, which he carried attached to the end of a bit of whip-cord; twirling it to and fro, with the air of a conjuror, as he went. When I observed this last, plain evidence of my friend's aberration of mind, I could scarcely refrain from tears. I thought it best, however, to humor his fancy, at least for the present, or until I could adopt some more energetic measures with a chance of success. In the mean time I endeavored, but all in vain, to sound him in regard to the object of the expedition. Having succeeded in inducing me to accompany him, he seemed unwilling to hold conversation upon any topic of minor importance, and to all my questions vouchsafed no other reply than "we shall see!"

We crossed the creek at the head of the island by means of a skiff, and, ascending the high grounds on the shore of the main land, proceeded in a northwesterly direction, through a tract of country excessively wild and desolate, where no trace of a human footstep was to be seen. Legrand led the way with decision; pausing only for an instant, here and there, to consult what appeared to be certain landmarks of his own contrivance upon a former occasion.

In this manner we journeyed for about two hours, and the sun was just setting when we entered a region infinitely more dreary than any yet seen. It was a species of table land, near the summit of an almost inaccessible hill, densely wooded from base to pinnacle, and interspersed with huge crags that appeared to lie loosely upon the soil, and in many cases were prevented from precipitating themselves into the valleys below, merely by the support of the trees against which they reclined. Deep ravines, in various directions, gave an air of still sterner solemnity to the scene.

The natural platform to which we had clambered was thickly overgrown with brambles, through which we soon discovered that it would have been impossible to force our way but for the scythe; and Jupiter, by direction of his master, proceeded to clear for us a path to the foot of an enormously tall tulip-tree, which stood, with some eight or ten oaks, upon the level, and far surpassed them all, and all other trees which I had then ever seen, in the beauty of its foliage and form, in the wide spread of its branches, and in the general majesty of its appearance. When we reached this tree, Legrand turned to Jupiter and asked him if he thought he could climb it. The old man seemed a little staggered by the question, and for some moments made no reply. At length he approached the huge trunk, walked slowly around it, and examined it with minute attention. When he had completed his scrutiny, he merely said,

"Yes, massa, Jup climb any tree he ebber see in he life."

"Then up with you as soon as possible, for it will soon be too dark to see what we are about."

"How far mus go up, massa?" inquired Jupiter.

"Get up the main trunk first, and then I will tell you which way to go—and here—stop! take this beetle with you."

"De bug, Massa Will!—de goole bug!" cried the negro, drawing back in dismay—"what for mus tote de bug way up de tree?—d—n if I do!"

"If you are afraid, Jup, a great big negro like you, to take hold of a harmless little dead beetle, why you can carry it up by this string—but, if you do not take it up with you in some way, I shall be under the necessity of breaking your head with this shovel."

"What de matter now, massa?" said Jup, evidently shamed into compliance; "always want for to raise fuss wid old nigger. Was only funnin any how. *Me* feered de bug! what I keer for de bug?" Here he took cautiously hold of the extreme end of the string, and, maintaining the insect as far from his person as circumstances would permit, prepared to ascend the tree.

# THE GOLD BUG

In youth, the tulip-tree, or *Liriodendron Tu-lipiferum,* the most magnificent of American for-esters, has a trunk peculiarly smooth, and often rises to a great height without lateral branches; but, in its riper age, the bark becomes gnarled and uneven, while many short limbs make their appearance on the stem. Thus the difficulty of ascension, in the present case, lay more in sem-blance than in reality. Embracing the huge cyl-inder, as closely as possible, with his arms and knees, seizing with his hands some projections, and resting his naked toes upon others, Jupiter, after one or two narrow escapes from falling, at length wriggled himself into the first great fork, and seemed to consider the whole business as vir-tually accomplished. The *risk* of the achievement was, in fact, now over, although the climber was some sixty or seventy feet from the ground.

"Which way mus go now, Massa Will?" he asked.

"Keep up the largest branch—the one on this side," said Legrand. The negro obeyed him promptly, and apparently with but little trouble; ascending higher and higher, until no glimpse of his squat figure could be obtained through the dense foliage which enveloped it. Presently his voice was heard in a sort of halloo.

"How much fudder is got for go?"

"How high up are you?" asked Legrand.

"Ebber so fur," replied the negro; "can see de sky fru de top ob de tree."

201

"Never mind the sky but attend to what I say. Look down the trunk and count the limbs below you on this side. How many limbs have you passed?"

"One, two, tree, four, fibe—I done pass fibe big limb, massa, pon dis side."

"Then go one limb higher."

In a few minutes the voice was heard again, announcing that the seventh limb was attained.

"Now, Jup," cried Legrand, evidently much excited, "I want you to work your way out upon that limb as far as you can. If you see anything strange, let me know."

By this time what little doubt I might have entertained of my poor friend's insanity, was put finally at rest. I had no alternative but to conclude him stricken with lunacy, and I became seriously anxious about getting him home. While I was pondering upon what was best to be done, Jupiter's voice was again heard.

"Mos feered for to ventur pon dis limb berry far—'tis dead limb putty much all de way."

"Did you say it was a *dead* limb, Jupiter?" cried Legrand in a quavering voice.

"Yes, massa, him dead as de door-nail—done up for sartain—done departed dis here life."

"What in the name of heaven shall I do?" asked Legrand, seemingly in the greatest distress.

"Do!" said I, glad of an opportunity to interpose a word, "why come home and go to bed.

Come now!—that's a fine fellow. It's getting late, and, besides, you remember your promise."

"Jupiter," cried he, without heeding me in the least, "do you hear me?"

"Yes, Massa Will, hear you ebber so plain."

"Try the wood well, then, with your knife, and see if you think it *very* rotten."

"Him rotten, massa, sure nuff," replied the negro in a few moments, "but not so berry rotten as mought be. Mought ventur out leetle way pon de limb by myself, dat's true."

"By yourself!—what do you mean?"

"Why I mean de bug. 'Tis *berry* hebby bug. Spose I drop him down fuss, and den de limb won't break wid just de weight ob one nigger."

"You infernal scoundrel!" cried Legrand, apparently much relieved, "what do you mean by telling me such nonsense as that? As sure as you let that beetle fall!—I'll break your neck. Look here, Jupiter! do you hear me?"

"Yes, massa, needn't hollo at poor nigger dat style."

"Well, now listen!—if you will venture out on the limb as far as you think safe, and not let go the beetle, I'll make you a present of a silver dollar as soon as you get down."

"I'm gwine, Massa Will—deed I is," replied the negro promptly—"mos out to the eend now."

"*Out to the end!*" here fairly screamed Legrand, "do you say you are out to the end of that limb?"

"Soon be to de eend, massa,—o-o-o-o-oh! Lor-gol-a-marcy! what *is* dis here pon de tree?"

"Well!" cried Legrand, highly delighted, "what is it?"

"Why tain't noffin but a skull—somebody bin lef him head up de tree, and de crows done gobble ebery bit ob de meat off."

"A skull, you say!—very well!—how is it fastened to the limb?—what holds it on?"

"Sure nuff, massa; mus look. Why dis berry curous sarcumstance, pon my word—dare's a great big nail in de skull, what fastens ob it on to de tree."

"Well now, Jupiter, do exactly as I tell you—do you hear?"

"Yes, massa."

"Pay attention, then!—find the left eye of the skull."

"Hum! hoo! dat's good! why dar ain't no eye lef at all."

"Curse your stupidity! do you know your right hand from your left?"

"Yes, I nose dat—nose all 'bout dat—'tis my left hand what I chops de wood wid."

"To be sure! you are left-handed; and your left eye is on the same side as your left hand. Now, I suppose, you can find the left eye of the skull, or the place where the left eye has been. Have you found it?"

Here was a long pause. At length the negro asked,

"Is de lef eye of de skull pon de same side as de lef hand of de skull, too?—cause de skull ain't got not a bit ob a hand at all—nebber mind! I got de lef eye now—here the lef eye! what mus do wid it?"

"Let the beetle drop through it, as far as the string will reach—but be careful and not let go your hold of the string."

"All dat done, Massa Will; mighty easy ting for to put de bug fru de hole—look out for him dar below!"

During this colloquy no portion of Jupiter's person could be seen; but the beetle, which he had suffered to descend, was now visible at the end of the string, and glistened, like a globe of burnished gold, in the last rays of the setting sun, some of which still faintly illumined the eminence upon which we stood. The *scarabæus* hung quite clear of any branches, and, if allowed to fall, would have fallen at our feet. Legrand immediately took the scythe, and cleared with it a circular space, three or four yards in diameter, just beneath the insect, and, having accomplished this, ordered Jupiter to let go the string and come down from the tree.

Driving a peg, with great nicety, into the ground, at the precise spot where the beetle fell, my friend now produced from his pocket a tape-measure. Fastening one end of this at that point of the trunk of the tree which was nearest the peg, he unrolled it till it reached the peg, and thence farther unrolled it, in the direction already established by the two points of the tree and the peg, for the distance of fifty feet—Jupiter clearing away the brambles with the scythe. At the spot thus attained a second peg was driven, and about this, as a centre, a rude circle, about four feet in diameter, described. Taking now a spade himself, and giving one to Jupiter and one to me, Legrand begged us to set about digging as quickly as possible.

To speak the truth, I had no especial relish for such amusement at any time, and, at that particular moment, would most willingly have declined it; for the night was coming on, and I felt much fatigued with the exercise already taken; but I saw no mode of escape, and was fearful of disturbing my poor friend's equanimity by a refusal. Could I have depended, indeed, upon Jupiter's aid, I would have had no hesitation in attempting to get the lunatic home by force; but I was too well assured of the old negro's disposition, to hope that he would assist me, under any circumstances, in a personal contest with his master. I made no doubt that the latter had been infected with some of the innumerable Southern superstitions about money buried, and that his phantasy had received confirmation by the finding of the *scarabæus,* or, perhaps, by Jupiter's obstinacy in maintaining it to be "a bug of real gold." A mind disposed to lunacy would readily be led away by such sug-

gestions—especially if chiming in with favorite
preconceived ideas—and then I called to mind
the poor fellow's speech about the beetle's
being "the index of his fortune." Upon the
whole, I was sadly vexed and puzzled, but, at
length, I concluded to make a virtue of necessity—to dig with a good will, and thus the
sooner to convince the visionary, by ocular demonstration, of the fallacy of the opinions he
entertained.

The lanterns having been lit, we all fell to
work with a zeal worthy a more rational cause;
and, as the glare fell upon our persons and implements, I could not help thinking how picturesque a group we composed, and how strange and
suspicious our labors must have appeared to any
interloper who, by chance, might have stumbled
upon our whereabouts.

We dug very steadily for two hours. Little
was said; and our chief embarrassment lay in
the yelpings of the dog, who took exceeding interest in our proceedings. He, at length, became
so obstreperous that we grew fearful of his giving the alarm to some stragglers in the vicinity;
—or, rather, this was the apprehension of Legrand;—for myself, I should have rejoiced at
any interruption which might have enabled me
to get the wanderer home. The noise was, at
length, very effectually silenced by Jupiter, who'
getting out of the hole with a dogged air of deliberation, tied the brute's mouth up with one of

his suspenders, and then returned, with a grave chuckle, to his task.

When the time mentioned had expired, we had reached a depth of five feet, and yet no signs of any treasure became manifest. A general pause ensued, and I began to hope that the farce was at an end. Legrand, however, although evidently much disconcerted, wiped his brow thoughtfully and recommenced. We had excavated the entire circle of four feet diameter, and now we slightly enlarged the limit, and went to the farther depth of two feet. Still nothing appeared. The goldseeker, whom I sincerely pitied, at length clambered from the pit, with the bitterest disappointment imprinted upon every feature, and proceeded, slowly and reluctantly, to put on his coat, which he had thrown off at the beginning of his labor. In the mean time I made no remark. Jupiter at a signal from his master, began to gather up his tools. This done, and the dog having been unmuzzled, we turned in profound silence towards home.

We had taken, perhaps, a dozen steps in this direction, when, with a loud oath, Legrand strode up to Jupiter, and seized him by the collar. The astonished negro opened his eyes and mouth to the fullest extent, let fall the spades and fell upon his knees.

"You scoundrel," said Legrand, hissing out the syllables from between his clenched teeth— "you infernal black villain;—speak, I tell you!

—answer me this instant, without prevarication!
—which—which is your left eye?"

"Oh, my golly, Massa Will, ain't dis here my
lef eye for sartin?" roared the terrified Jupiter,
placing his hand upon his *right* organ of vision,
and holding it there with a desperate pertinacity,
as if in immediate dread of his master's attempt
at a gouge.

"I thought so!—I knew it!—hurrah!" vocifer-
ated Legrand, letting the negro go, and execut-
ing a series of curvets and caracols, much to the
astonishment of his valet, who, arising from his
knees, looked, mutely, from his master to myself,
and then from myself to his master.

"Come! we must go back," said the latter, "the
game's not up yet"; and he again led the way to
the tulip-tree.

"Jupiter," said he, when we reached its foot,
"come here! was the skull nailed to the limb with
the face outward or with the face to the limb?"

"De face was out, massa, so dat de crows could
get at de eyes good, widout any trouble."

"Well, then, was it this eye or that through
which you let the beetle fall?"—here Legrand
touched each of Jupiter's eyes.

" 'Twas dis eye, massa—de lef eye—jis as you
tell me," and here it was his right eye that the
negro indicated.

"That will do—we must try again."

Here my friend, about whose madness I now
saw, or fancied that I saw, certain indications of

method, removed the peg which marked the spot where the beetle fell, to a spot about three inches to the west-ward of its former position. Taking, now, the tape-measure from the nearest point of the trunk to the peg, as before· and continuing the extension in a straight line to the distance of fifty feet, a spot was indicated, removed, by several yards, from the point at which we had been digging.

Around the new position a circle, somewhat larger than in the former instance, was now described, and we again set to work with the spades. I was dreadfully weary, but, scarcely understanding what had occasioned the change in my thoughts, I felt no longer any great aversion from the labor imposed. I had become most unaccountably interested—nay, even excited. Perhaps there was something, amid all the extravagant demeanor of Legrand—some air of forethought, or of deliberation, which impressed me. I dug eagerly, and now and then caught myself actually looking, with something that very much resembled expectation, for the fancied treasure, the vision of which had demented my unfortunate companion. At a period when such vagaries of thought most fully possessed me, and when we had been at work perhaps an hour and a half, we were again interrupted by the violent howlings of the dog. His uneasiness, in the first instance, had been, evidently, but the result of playfulness or caprice, but he now assumed a bitter and serious tone. Upon Jupiter's again attempting to muzzle him, he made furious resistance, and, leaping into the hole, tore up the mould frantically with his claws. In a few seconds he had uncovered a mass of human bones, forming two complete skeletons, intermingled with several buttons of metal, and what appeared to be the dust of decayed woollen. One or two strokes of a spade upturned the blade of a large Spanish knife, and, as we dug farther, several loose pieces of gold and silver coin came to light.

At sight of these the joy of Jupiter could scarcely be restrained, but the countenance of his master wore an air of extreme disappointment. He urged us, however, to continue our exertions, and the words were hardly uttered when I stumbled and fell forward, having caught the toe of my boot in a large ring of iron that lay half buried in the loose earth.

We now worked in earnest, and never did I pass ten minutes of more intense excitement. During this interval we had fairly unearthed an oblong chest of wood, which, from its perfect preservation, and wonderful hardness, had plainly been subjected to some mineralizing process—perhaps that of the Bi-chloride of Mercury. This box was three feet and a half long, three feet broad, and two and a half feet deep. It was firmly secured by bands of wrought iron, riveted, and forming a kind of trellis-work over the whole. On each side of the chest, near the top, were three rings of iron—six in all—by means of which a firm hold could be obtained by six persons. Our utmost united endeavors served only to disturb the coffer very slightly in its bed. We at once saw the impossibility of removing so great a weight. Luckily, the sole fastenings of the lid consisted of two sliding bolts. These we drew back—trembling and panting with anxiety. In an instant, a treasure of incalculable value lay gleaming before us. As the rays of the lanterns fell within the pit, there flashed upwards, from a confused heap of gold and of jewels, a glow and a glare that absolutely dazzled our eyes.

I shall not pretend to describe the feelings with which I gazed. Amazement was, of course, predominant. Legrand appeared exhausted with excitement, and spoke very few words. Jupiter's countenance wore, for some minutes, as deadly a pallor as it is possible, in the nature of things, for any negro's visage to assume. He seemed stupefied—thunderstricken. Presently he fell upon his knees in the pit, and, burying his naked arms up to the elbows in gold, let them there remain, as if enjoying the luxury of a bath. At length, with a deep sigh, he exclaimed, as if in a soliloquy,

"And dis all cum ob de goole bug! de putty goole bug! de poor little goole bug, what I boosed in dat sabage kind ob style! Ain't you shamed ob yourself, nigger?—answer me dat!"

# THE GOLD BUG

It became necessary, at last, that I should arouse both master and valet to the expediency of removing the treasure. It was growing late, and it behooved us to make exertion, that we might get every thing housed before daylight. It was difficult to say what should be done; and much time was spent in deliberation—so confused were the ideas of all. We, finally, lightened the box by removing two thirds of its contents, when we were enabled, with some trouble, to raise it from the hole. The articles taken out were deposited among the brambles, and the dog left to guard them, with strict orders from Jupiter neither, upon any pretence, to stir from the spot, nor to open his mouth until our return. We then hurriedly made for home with the chest; reaching the hut in safety, but after excessive toil, at one o'clock in the morning. Worn out as we were, it was not in human nature to do more just then. We rested until two, and had supper; starting for the hills immediately afterwards, armed with three stout sacks, which, by good luck, were upon the premises. A little before four we arrived at the pit, divided the remainder of the booty, as equally as might be, among us, and, leaving the holes unfilled, again set out for the hut, at which, for the second time, we deposited our golden burthens, just as the first streaks of the dawn gleamed from over the tree-tops in the East.

We were now thoroughly broken down; but

the intense excitement of the time denied us repose. After an unquiet slumber of some three or four hours' duration, we arose, as if by preconcert, to make examination of our treasure.

The chest had been full to the brim, and we spent the whole day, and the greater part of the next night, in a scrutiny of its contents. There had been nothing like order or arrangement. Everything had been heaped in promiscuously. Having assorted all with care, we found ourselves possessed of even vaster wealth than we had at first supposed. In coin there was rather more than four hundred and fifty thousand dollars—estimating the value of the pieces, as accurately as we could, by the tables of the period. There was not a particle of silver. All was gold of antique date and of great variety—French, Spanish, and German money, with a few English guineas, and some counters, of which we had never seen specimens before. There were several very large and heavy coins, so worn that we could make nothing of their inscriptions. There was no American money. The value of the jewels we found more difficulty in estimating. There were diamonds—some of them exceedingly large and fine—a hundred and ten in all, and not one of them small; eighteen rubies of remarkable brilliancy;—three hundred and ten emeralds, all very beautiful; and twenty-one sapphires, with an opal. These stones had all been broken from their settings and thrown loose in the chest. The settings themselves, which we picked out from among the other gold, appeared to have been beaten up with hammers, as if to prevent identification. Besides all this, there was a vast quantity of solid gold ornaments;—nearly two hundred massive finger and ear rings; — rich chains—thirty of these, if I remember;—eighty-three very large and heavy crucifixes;—five gold censers of great value;—a prodigious golden punchbowl, ornamented with richly chased vine-leaves and Bacchanalian figures; with two sword-handles exquisitely embossed, and many other smaller articles which I cannot recollect. The weight of these valuables exceeded three hundred and fifty pounds avoirdupois; and in this estimate I have not included one hundred and ninety-seven superb gold watches; three of the number being worth each five hundred dollars, if one. Many of them were very old, and as time keepers valueless; the works having suffered, more or less, from corrosion—but all were richly jewelled and in cases of great worth. We estimated the entire contents of the chest, that night, at a million and a half of dollars; and, upon the subsequent disposal of the trinkets and jewels (a few being retained for our own use), it was found that we had greatly undervalued the treasure.

When, at length, we had concluded our examination, and the intense excitement of the time had, in some measure subsided, Legrand, who saw that I was dying with impatience for a solution of this most extraordinary riddle, entered into a full detail of all the circumstances connected with it.

"You remember," said he, "the night when I handed you the rough sketch I had made of the *scarabæus*. You recollect also, that I became quite vexed at you for insisting that my drawing resembled a death's-head. When you first made this assertion I thought you were jesting; but afterwards I called to mind the peculiar spots on the back of the insect, and admitted to myself that your remark had some little foundation in fact. Still, the sneer at my graphic powers irritated me—for I am considered a good artist—and, therefore, when you handed me the scrap of parchment, I was about to crumble it up and throw it angrily into the fire."

"The scrap of paper, you mean," said I.

"No; it had much of the appearance of paper, and at first I supposed it to be such, but when I came to draw upon it, I discovered it, at once, to be a piece of very thin parchment. It was quite dirty, you remember. Well, as I was in the very act of crumpling it up, my glance fell upon the sketch at which you had been looking, and you may imagine my astonishment when I perceived, in fact, the figure of a death's-head just where, it seemed to me I had made the drawing of the beetle. For a moment I was too much amazed to think with accuracy. I knew that my design was very different in detail from this—although there was a certain similarity in general outline. Presently I took a candle, and seating myself at the other end of the room, proceeded to scrutinize the parchment more closely. Upon turning it over, I saw my own sketch upon the reverse, just as I had made it. My first idea, now, was mere surprise at the really remarkable similarity of outline—at the singular coincidence involved in the fact, that unknown to me, there should have been a skull upon the other side of the parchment, immediately beneath my figure of the *scarabæus,* and that this skull, not only in outline, but in size, should so closely resemble my drawing. I say the singularity of this coincidence absolutely stupefied me for a time. This is the usual effect of such coincidences. The mind struggles to establish a connection—a sequence of cause and effect—and, being unable to do so, suffers a species of temporary paralysis. But, when I recovered from this stupor, there dawned upon me gradually a conviction which startled me even far more than the coincidence. I began distinctly, positively, to remember that there had been *no* drawing on the parchment when I made my sketch of the *scarabæus.* I became perfectly certain of this; for I recollected turning up first one side and then the other, in search of the cleanest spot. Had the skull been then there, of course I could not have failed to notice it. Here was indeed a mystery which I felt it impossible to explain; but, even at that early moment, there seemed to glimmer, faintly, within the most remote and secret chambers of my intellect a glow-worm-like conception of that truth which last night's adventure brought to so magnificent a demonstration. I arose at once, and putting the parchment securely away, dismissed all farther reflection until I should be alone.

"When you had gone, and when Jupiter was fast asleep, I betook myself to a more methodical investigation of the affair. In the first place I considered the manner in which the parchment had come into my possession. The spot where we discovered the *scarabæus* was on the coast of the main land, about a mile eastward of the island, and but a short distance above high water mark. Upon my taking hold of it, it gave me a sharp bite, which caused me to let it drop. Jupiter, with his accustomed caution, before seizing the insect, which had flown towards him, looked about him for a leaf, or something of that nature, by which to take hold of it. It was at this moment that his eyes, and mine also fell upon the scrap of parchment, which I then supposed to be paper. It was lying half buried in the sand, a corner sticking up. Near the spot where we found it, I observed the remnants of the hull of what appeared to have been a ship's long boat. The wreck seemed to have been there for a very great while; for the resemblance to boat timbers could scarcely be traced.

"Well, Jupiter picked up the parchment,

wrapped the beetle in it, and gave it to me. Soon afterwards we turned to go home, and on the way met Lieutenant G——. I showed him the insect, and he begged me to let him take it to the fort. On my consenting, he thrust it forthwith into his waistcoat pocket, without the parchment in which it had been wrapped, and which I had continued to hold in my hand during his inspection. Perhaps he dreaded my changing my mind, and thought it best to make sure of the prize at once—you know how enthusiastic he is on all subjects connected with Natural History. At the same time, without being conscious of it, I must have deposited the parchment in my own pocket.

"You remember that when I went to the table, for the purpose of making a sketch of the beetle, I found no paper where it was usually kept. I looked in the drawer, and found none there. I searched my pockets, hoping to find an old letter —and then my hand fell upon the parchment. I thus detail the precise mode in which it came into my possession; for the circumstances impressed me with peculiar force.

"No doubt you will think me fanciful—but I had already established a kind of *connection*. I had put together two links of a great chain. There was a boat lying on a sea-coast, and not far from the boat was a parchment—*not a paper* —with a skull depicted on it. You will, of course, ask 'where is the connection?' I reply that the skull, or death's-head, is the well-known emblem of the pirate. The flag of the death's-head is hoisted in all engagements.

"I have said that the scrap was parchment, and not paper. Parchment is durable—almost imperishable. Matters of little moment are rarely consigned to parchment; since, for the mere ordinary purposes of drawing or writing, it is not nearly so well adapted as paper. This reflection suggested some meaning—some relevancy—in the death's-head. I did not fail to observe also, the *form* of the parchment. Although one of its corners had been, by some accident, destroyed, it could be seen that the original form was oblong. It was just such a slip, indeed, as might have been chosen for a memorandum—for a record of something to be long remembered and carefully preserved."

"But," I interposed, "you say that the skull was *not* upon the parchment when you made the drawing of the beetle. How then do you trace any connection between the boat and the skull —since this latter, according to your own admission, must have been designed (God only knows how or by whom) at some period subsequent to your sketching the *scarabæus?*"

"Ah, hereupon turns the whole mystery; although the secret, at this point, I had comparatively little difficulty in solving. My steps were sure, and could afford but a single result. I reasoned, for example, thus: When I drew the *scarabæus,* there was no skull apparent on the parchment. When I had completed the drawing, I gave it to you and observed you narrowly until you returned it. *You,* therefore, did not design the skull, and no one else was present to do it. Then it was not done by human agency. And nevertheless it was done.

"At this stage of my reflections I endeavored to remember, and *did* remember, with entire distinctness, every incident which occurred about the period in question. The weather was chilly (oh rare and happy accident!), and a fire was blazing on the hearth. I was heated with exercise and sat near the table. You, however, had drawn a chair close to the chimney. Just as I placed the parchment in your hand, and as you were in the act of inspecting it, Wolf, the Newfoundland, entered, and leaped upon your shoulders. With your left hand you caressed him and kept him off, while your right, holding the parchment, was permitted to fall listlessly between your knees, and in close proximity to the fire. At one moment I thought the blaze had caught it, and was about to caution you, but, before I could speak, you had withdrawn it, and were engaged in its examination. When I considered all these particulars, I doubted not for a moment that *heat* had been the agent in bringing to light, on the parchment, the skull which I saw designed on it. You are well aware that chemical preparations exist, and have existed time out of mind, by means of which it is possible to write on either paper or vellum, so that the characters shall become visible only when subjected to the action of fire. Zaffre, digested in *aqua regia,* and diluted with four times its weight of water, is sometimes employed; a green tint results. The regulus of cobalt, dissolved in spirit of nitre, gives a red. These colors disappear at longer or shorter intervals after the material written on cools, but again become apparent upon the reapplication of heat.

"I now scrutinized the death's-head with care. Its outer edges—the edges of the drawing nearest the edge of the vellum—were far more *distinct* than the others. It was clear that the action of the caloric had been imperfect or unequal. I immediately kindled a fire, and subjected every portion of the parchment to a glowing heat. At first, the only effect was the strengthening of the faint lines in the skull; but, on persevering in the experiment, there became visible, at the corner of the slip, diagonally opposite to the spot in which the death's-head was delineated, the figure of what I at first supposed to be a goat. A closer scrutiny, however, satisfied me that it was intended for a kid."

"Ha! ha!" said I, "to be sure I have no right to laugh at you—a million and a half of money is too serious a matter for mirth—but you are not about to establish a third link in your chain —you will not find any especial connexion between your pirates and a goat—pirates, you

know, have nothing to do with goats; they apper-
tain to the farming interest."

"But I have just said that the figure was *not*
that of a goat."

"Well, a kid then—pretty much the same
thing."

"Pretty much, but not altogether," said Legrand. "You may have heard of one *Captain*
Kidd. I at once looked on the figure of the animal as a kind of punning or hieroglyphical signature. I say signature; because its position on the
vellum suggested this idea. The death's-head at
the corner diagonally opposite, had, in the same
manner, the air of a stamp, or seal. But I was
sorely put out by the absence of all else—of the
body to my imagined instrument—of the text for
my context."

"I presume you expected to find a letter between the stamp and the signature."

"Something of that kind. The fact is, I felt
irresistibly impressed with a presentiment of
some vast good fortune impending. I can
scarcely say why. Perhaps, after all, it was rather
a desire than an actual belief;—but do you know
that Jupiter's silly words, about the bug being
of solid gold, had a remarkable effect on my
fancy? And then the series of accidents and coincidences—these were so *very* extraordinary.
Do you observe how mere an accident it was that
these events should have occurred on the *sole* day
of all the year in which it has been, or may be,

sufficiently cool for fire, and that without the fire, or without the intervention of the dog at the precise moment in which he appeared, I should never have become aware of the death's-head, and so never the possessor of the treasure?"

"But proceed—I am all impatience."

"Well; you have heard, of course, the many stories current—the thousand vague rumors afloat about money buried somewhere on the Atlantic coast, by Kidd and his associates. These rumors must have had some foundation in fact. And that the rumors have existed so long and so continuously could have resulted, it appeared to me, only from the circumstance of the buried treasure still *remaining* entombed. Had Kidd concealed his plunder for a time, and afterwards reclaimed it, the rumors would scarcely have reached us in their present unvarying form. You will observe that the stories told are all about money-seekers, not about money-finders. Had the pirate recovered his money, there the affair would have dropped. It seemed to me that some accident—say the loss of a memorandum indicating its locality—had deprived him of the means of recovering it, and that this accident had become known to his followers, who otherwise might never have heard that treasure had been concealed at all, and who, busying themselves in vain, because unguided attempts, to regain it, had given first birth, and then universal currency, to the reports which are now so common.

# THE GOLD BUG

Have you ever heard of any important treasure being unearthed along the coast?"

"Never."

"But that Kidd's accumulations were immense, is well known. I took it for granted therefore, that the earth still held them; and you will scarcely be surprised when I tell you that I felt a hope, nearly amounting to certainty, that the parchment so strangely found, involved a lost record of the place of deposit."

"But how did you proceed?"

"I held the vellum again to the fire, after increasing the heat; but nothing appeared. I now thought it possible that the coating of dirt might have something to do with the failure; so I carefully rinsed the parchment by pouring warm water over it, and, having done this, I placed it in a tin pan, with the skull downwards, and put the pan upon a furnace of lighted charcoal. In a few minutes, the pan having become thoroughly heated, I removed the slip, and, to my inexpressible joy, found it spotted, in several places, with what appeared to be figures arranged in lines. Again I placed it in the pan, and suffered it to remain another minute. On taking it off, the whole was just as you see it now."

Here Legrand, having re-heated the parchment, submitted it to my inspection. The following characters were rudely traced, in a red tint, between the death's-head and the goat:

225

53‡‡†305))6*;4826)4‡.)4‡);806*;48†8¶60))
85;]3*;:‡*8†83 (88) 5*†;46 (;88*96*?;8) *‡(;
485);5*†2:*‡ (;4956*2(5*—4)8¶8*; 4069285);
)6†8) 4‡‡;1(‡9;48081;8:8‡1;48†85;4) 485†528
806*81(‡9;48;(88;4(‡?34;48)4‡;161;:188;‡?;

"But, said I, returning him the slip, "I am as
much in the dark as ever. Were all the jewels of
Golconda awaiting me on my solution of this
enigma, I am sure that I could not earn them."

"And yet," said Legrand, "the solution is by
no means so difficult as you might be led to imagine from the first hasty inspection of the characters. These characters, as any one might
readily guess, form a cipher—that is to say, they
convey a meaning; but then, from what is known
of Kidd, I could not suppose him capable of con-
structing any of the more abstruse cryptographs.
I made up my mind, at once, that this was of a
simple species—such, however, as would appear.
to the crude intellect of the sailor, absolutely in-
soluble without the key."

"And you really solved it?"

"Readily; I have solved others of an abstruse-
ness ten thousand times greater. Circumstances,
and a certain bias of mind, have led me to take
interest in such riddles, and it may well be
doubted whether human ingenuity can construct
an enigma of the kind which human ingenuity
may not, by proper application, resolve. In fact,
having once established connected and legible

characters, I scarcely gave a thought to the mere difficulty of developing their import.

"In the present case—indeed in all cases of secret writing—the first question regards the *language* of the cipher; for the principles of solution, so far, especially, as the more simple ciphers are concerned, depend on, and are varied by, the genius of the particular idiom. In general, there is no alternative but experiment (directed by probabilities) of every tongue known to him who attempts the solution, until the true one be attained. But, with the cipher now before us, all difficulty is removed by the signature. The pun on the word 'Kidd' is appreciable in no other language than the English. But for this consideration I should have begun my attempts with the Spanish and French, as the tongues in which a secret of this kind would naturally have been written by a pirate of the Spanish main. As it was, I assumed the cryptograph to be English.

"You observe there are no divisions between the words. Had there been divisions, the task would have been comparatively easy. In such case I should have commenced with a collation and analysis of the shorter words, and, had a word of a single letter occurred as is most likely, (*a* or *I*, for example,) I should have considered the solution as assured. But, there being no division, my first step was to ascertain the predominant letters, as well as the least frequent. Counting all, I constructed a table, thus:

Of the character 8 there are 33.

| | | |
|---|---|---|
| ; | " | 26. |
| 4 | " | 19. |
| ‡ ) | " | 16. |
| * | " | 13. |
| 5 | " | 12. |
| 6 | " | 11. |
| † 1 | " | 8. |
| 0 | " | 6. |
| 9 2 | " | 5. |
| : 3 | " | 4. |
| ? | " | 3. |
| ¶ | " | 2. |
| ] — . | " | 1. |

"Now, in English, the letter which most frequently occurs is *e*. Afterwards, the succession runs thus: *a o i d h n r s t u y c f g l m w b k p q x z*. E however predominates so remarkably that an individual sentence of any length is rarely seen, in which it is not the prevailing character.

"Here, then, we have, in the very beginning, the ground-work for something more than a mere guess. The general use which may be made of the table is obvious—but, in this particular cipher, we shall only very partially require its aid. As our predominant character is 8, we will commence by assuming it as the *e* of the natural alphabet. To verify the supposition, let us observe if the 8 be seen often in couples—for *e* is doubled with great frequency in English—in such words, for example, as 'meet,' 'fleet,' 'speed,' 'seen,' 'been,' 'agree,' &c. In the present instance we see it doubled no less than five times.

"Let us assume 8, then, as *e*. Now, of all *words* in the language, 'the' is most usual; let us see therefore, whether there are not repetitions of any three characters, in the same order of collocation, the last of them being 8. If we discover repetitions of such letters, so arranged, they will most probably represent the word 'the.' On inspection we find no less than seven such arrangements, the characters being ;48. We may, therefore, assume that the semicolon represents *t,* that 4 represents *h,* and that 8 represents *e*— the last being now well confirmed. Thus a great step has been taken.

"But, having established a single word, we are enabled to establish a vastly important point; that is to say, several commencements and terminations of other words. Let us refer, for example, to the last instance but one, in which the combination ;48 occurs—not far from the end of the cipher. We know that the semicolon immediately ensuing is the commencement of a word, and, of the six characters succeeding this 'the,' we are cognizant of no less than five. Let us set these characters down, thus, by the letters we know them to represent, leaving a space for the unknown—

t eeth.

"Here we are enabled, at once, to discard the *'th,'* as forming no portion of the word commencing with the first *t;* since, by experiment of the entire alphabet for a letter adapted to the vacancy we perceive that no word can be formed of which this *th* can be a part. We are thus narrowed into

t ee,

and, going through the alphabet, if necessary, as before, we arrive at the word 'tree,' as the sole possible reading. We thus gain another letter, *r,* represented by (, with the words 'the tree' in juxtaposition.

"Looking beyond these words, for a short distance, we again see the combination of ;48, and employ it by way of *termination* to what immediately precedes. We have thus this arrangement:

the tree;4 ( ‡ ?34 the,

or, substituting the natural letters, where known, it reads thus:

the tree thr‡ ?3h the.

"Now, if, in place of the unknown characters, we leave blank spaces, or substitute dots, we read thus:

the tree thr . . . h the,

when the word *'through'* makes itself evident at once. But this discovery gives us three new letters, *o, u* and *g,* represented by ‡? and 3.

"Looking now, narrowly, through the cipher for combinations of known characters, we find, not very far from the beginning, this arrangement,

83 (88, or egree,

which, plainly, is the conclusion of the word 'degree,' and gives us another letter, *d*, represented by †.

"Four letters beyond the word 'degree,' we perceive the combination

;46(;88*.

"Translating the known characters, and representing the unknown by dots, as before, we read thus:

th.rtee.

an arrangement immediately suggestive of the word 'thirteen,' and again furnishing us with two new characters, *i*, and *n*, represented by 6 and*.

"Referring, now, to the beginning of the cryptograph, we find the combination,

53‡‡†.

"Translating as before, we obtain

.good,

which assures us that the first letter is *A,* and that the first two words are 'A good.'

"To avoid confusion, it is now time that we arrange our key, as far as discovered, in a tabular form. It will stand thus:

| 5 | represents | a | | 6 | " | i |
|---|---|---|---|---|---|---|
| † | " | d | | * | " | n |
| 8 | " | e | | ‡ | " | o |
| 3 | " | g | | ( | " | r |
| 4 | " | h | | ; | " | t |

"We have, therefore, no less than ten of the most important letters represented, and it will be unnecessary to proceed with the details of the solution. I have said enough to convince you that ciphers of this nature are readily soluble, and to give you some insight into the *rationale* of their development. But be assured that the specimen before us appertains to the very simplest species of cryptograph. It now only remains to give you the full translation of the characters upon the parchment, as unriddled. Here it is:

"*'A good glass in the bishop's hostel in the devil's seat twenty-one degrees and thirteen minutes northeast and by north main branch seventh limb east side shoot from the left eye of the death's-head a bee line from the tree through the shot fifty feet out.'*"

"But" said I, "the enigma seems still in as bad a condition as ever. How is it possible to extort meaning from all this jargon about 'devil's seats,' 'death's-heads,' and 'bishop's hotels?'"

"I confess, replied Legrand, "that the matter still wears a serious aspect, when regarded with a casual glance. My first endeavor was to divide the sentence into the natural division intended by the cryptographist."

"You mean, to punctuate it?"

"Something of that kind."

"But how was it possible to effect this?"

"I reflected that it had been a *point* with the writer to run his words together without division, so as to increase the difficulty of solution. Now, a not over-acute man, in pursuing such an object, would be nearly certain to overdo the matter.

When, in the course of his composition, he arrived at a break in his subject which would naturally require a pause, or a point, he would be exceedingly apt to run his characters, at this place, more than usually close together. If you will observe the MS., in this instance, you will detect five cases of unusual crowding. Acting on this hint, I made the division thus:

"'*A good glass in the Bishop's hostel in the Devil's seat—twenty-one degrees and thirteen minutes—northeast and by north—main branch seventh limb east side—shoot from the left eye of the death's-head—a bee line from the tree through the shot fifty feet out.*'"

"Even this division leaves me still in the dark."

"It left me also in the dark," replied Legrand, "for a few days; during which I made diligent inquiry, in the neighborhood of Sullivan's Island, for any building which went by the name of the 'Bishop's Hotel'; for, of course, I dropped the obsolete word 'hostel.' Gaining no information on the subject, I was on the point of extending my sphere of search, and proceeding in a more systematic manner, when, one morning, it entered into my head, quite suddenly, that this 'Bishop's Hostel' might have some reference to an old family, of the name of Bessop, which, time out of mind, had held possession of an ancient manor-house, about four miles to the northward of the Island. I accordingly went over to the plantation, and re-instituted my inquiries among the older negroes of the place. At length one of the most aged of the women said she had heard of such a place as *Bessop's Castle,* and thought that she could guide me to it, but that it was not a castle, nor a tavern, but a high rock.

"I offered to pay her well for her trouble, and, after some demur, she consented to accompany me to the spot. We found it without much difficulty, when, dismissing her, I proceeded to examine the place. The 'castle' consisted of an irregular assemblage of cliffs and rocks—one of the latter being quite remarkable for its height as well as for its insulated and artificial appearance. I clambered to its apex, and then felt much at a loss as to what should be next done.

"While I was busied in reflection, my eyes fell upon a narrow ledge in the eastern face of the rock, perhaps a yard below the summit on which I stood. This ledge projected about eighteen inches, and was not more than a foot wide, while a niche in the cliff just above it, gave it a rude resemblance to one of the hollow-backed chairs used by our ancestors. I made no doubt that here was the 'devil's-seat' alluded to in the MS., and now I seemed to grasp the full secret of the riddle.

"The 'good glass,' I knew, could have reference to nothing but a telescope; for the word 'glass' is rarely employed in any other sense by seamen. Now here, I at once saw, was a telescope to be used, and a definite point of view *admitting no variation,* from which to use it. Nor did I hesitate to believe that the phrases, 'twenty-one degrees and thirteen minutes,' and 'northeast and by north,' were intended as directions for the levelling of the glass. Greatly excited by these discoveries, I hurried home, procured a telescope, and returned to the rock.

"I let myself down to the ledge, and found that it was impossible to retain a seat on it unless in one particular position. This fact confirmed my pre-conceived idea. I proceeded to use the glass. Of course, the 'twenty-one degrees and thirteen minutes' could allude to nothing but elevation above the visible horizon, since the horizontal direction was clearly indicated by the words, 'northeast and by north.' This latter direction I at once established by means of a pocket-compass; then, pointing the glass as nearly at an angle of twenty-one degrees of elevation as I could do it by guess, I moved it cautiously up or down, until my attention was arrested by a circular rift or opening in the foliage of a large tree that overtopped its fellows in the distance. In the centre of this rift I perceived a white spot, but could not, at first, see what it was. Adjusting the telescope, I again looked, and now made it out to be a human skull.

"On this discovery I was so sanguine as to consider the enigma solved for the phrase 'main branch, seventh limb, east side,' could refer only to the position of the skull on the tree, while 'shot from the left eye of the death's-head' admitted, also, of but one interpretation, in regard to a search for buried treasure. I perceived that the design was to drop a bullet from the left eye of the skull, and that a bee line, or, in other words, a straight line, drawn from the nearest point of the trunk through 'the shot' (or the spot where the bullet fell) and thence extended to a distance of fifty feet, would indicate a definite point—and beneath this point I thought it at least possible that a deposit of value lay concealed."

"All this," I said, "is exceedingly clear, and, although ingenious, still simple and explicit. When you left the Bishop's Hotel, what then?"

"Why, having carefully taken the bearings of the tree, I turned homewards. The instant that I left 'the devil's-seat,' however, the circular rift vanished; nor could I get a glimpse of it afterwards, turn as I would. What seems to me the chief ingenuity in this whole business, is the fact (for repeated experiment has convinced me it *is* a fact) that the circular opening is visible from no other attainable point of view than that afforded by the narrow ledge on the face of the rock.

"In this expedition to the 'Bishop's Hotel' I had been attended by Jupiter, who had, no doubt, observed, for some weeks past, the abstraction of my demeanor and took especial care not to leave me alone. But, on the next day, getting up very early, I contrived to give him the slip, and went into the hills in search of the tree. After much toil I found it. When I came home at night my valet proposed to give me a flogging. With the rest of the adventure you are well acquainted.

"I suppose," said I, "you missed the spot, in the first attempt at digging, through Jupiter's stupidity in letting the bug fall through the right instead of through the left eye of the skull."

"Precisely. This mistake made a difference of about two inches and a half in the 'shot'—that is to say, in the position of the peg nearest the tree; and had the treasure been *beneath* the 'shot,' the error would have been of little moment; but 'the shot,' together with the nearest point of the tree, were merely two points for the establishment of a line of direction; of course the error, however trivial in the beginning, increased as we proceeded with the line, and by the time we had gone fifty feet, threw us quite off the scent. But for my deep-seated convictions that treasure was here somewhere actually buried, we might have had all our labor in vain."

"I presume the fancy of *the skull,* of letting fall a bullet through the skull's eye—was suggested to Kidd by the piratical flag. No doubt he felt a kind of poetical consistency in recovering his money through this ominous insignium."

"Perhaps so; still I cannot help thinking that common-sense had quite as much to do with the matter as poetical consistency. To be visible from the devil's-seat, it was necessary that the object, if small, should be white; and there is nothing like your human skull for retaining and even increasing its whiteness under exposure to all vicissitudes of weather."

"But your grandiloquence, and your conduct in swinging the beetle—how excessively odd! I was sure you were mad. And why did you insist on letting fall the bug, instead of a bullet, from the skull?"

"Why, to be frank, I felt somewhat annoyed by your evident suspicions touching my sanity, and so resolved to punish you quietly, in my own way, by a little bit of sober mystification. For this reason I swung the beetle, and for this reason I let it fall from the tree. An observation of yours about its great weight suggested the idea."

"Yes, I perceive; and now there is only one point which puzzles me. What are we to make of the skeletons found in the hole?"

"That is a question I am no more able to answer than yourself. There seems, however, only one plausible way of accounting for them—and yet it is dreadful to believe in such atrocity as my suggestion would imply. It is clear that Kidd—if Kidd indeed secreted this treasure, which I doubt not—it is clear that he must have had assistance in the labor. But the worst of this labor concluded, he may have thought it expedient to remove all participants in his secret. Perhaps a couple of blows with a mattock were sufficient, while his coadjutors were busy in the pit; perhaps it required a dozen—who shall tell?"

# THE  DAMNED  THING

### BY AMBROSE BIERCE

# THE DAMNED THING

## I

BY THE light of a tallow candle, which had
been placed on one end of a rough table,
a man was reading something written in a
book. It was an old account book, greatly worn;
and the writing was not, apparently, very legible,
for the man sometimes held the page close to the
flame of the candle to get a stronger light upon it.
The shadow of the book would then throw into
obscurity a half of the room, darkening a number
of faces and figures; for besides the reader, eight
other men were present. Seven of them sat
against the rough log walls, silent and motionless,
and, the room being small, not very far from the
table. By extending an arm any one of them
could have touched the eighth man, who lay on
the table, face upward, partly covered by a sheet,
his arms at his sides. He was dead.

The man with the book was not reading aloud,
and no one spoke; all seemed to be waiting for
something to occur; the dead man only was without expectation. From the blank darkness outside came in, through the aperture that served for

Reprinted by permission. From "In the Midst of Life," copyright, 1898,
by G. P. Putnam's Sons.

a window, all the ever unfamiliar noises of night in the wilderness—the long, nameless note of a distant coyote; the stilly pulsing thrill of tireless insects in trees; strange cries of night birds, so different from those of the birds of day; the drone of great blundering beetles, and all that mysterious chorus of small sounds that seem always to have been but half heard when they have suddenly ceased, as if conscious of an indiscretion. But nothing of all this was noted in that company; its members were not overmuch addicted to idle interest in matters of no practical importance; that was obvious in every line of their rugged faces—obvious even in the dim light of the single candle. They were evidently men of the vicinity—farmers and woodmen.

The person reading was a trifle different; one would have said of him that he was of the world, worldly, albeit there was that in his attire which attested a certain fellowship with the organisms of his environment. His coat would hardly have passed muster in San Francisco: his footgear was not of urban origin, and the hat that lay by him on the floor (he was the only one uncovered) was such that if one had considered it as an article of mere personal adornment he would have missed its meaning. In countenance the man was rather prepossessing, with just a hint of sternness; though that he may have assumed or cultivated, as appropriate to one in authority. For he was a coroner. It was by virtue of his

242

office that he had possession of the book in which he was reading; it had been found among the dead man's effects—in his cabin, where the inquest was now taking place.

When the coroner had finished reading he put the book into his breast pocket. At that moment the door was pushed open and a young man entered. He, clearly, was not of mountain birth and breeding: he was clad as those who dwell in cities. His clothing was dusty, however, as from travel. He had, in fact, been riding hard to attend the inquest.

The coroner nodded; no one else greeted him.

"We have waited for you," said the coroner. "It is necessary to have done with this business to-night."

The young man smiled. "I am sorry to have kept you," he said. "I went away, not to evade your summons, but to post to my newspaper an account of what I suppose I am called back to relate."

The coroner smiled.

"The account that you posted to your newspaper," he said, "differs probably from that which you will give here under oath."

"That," replied the other, rather hotly and with a visible flush, "is as you choose. I used manifold paper and have a copy of what I sent. It was not written as news, for it is incredible, but as fiction. It may go as a part of my testimony under oath."

"But you say it is incredible."

'That is nothing to you, sir, if I also swear that it is true."

The coroner was apparently not greatly affected by the young man's manifest resentment. He was silent for some moments, his eyes upon the floor. The men about the sides of the cabin talked in whispers, but seldom withdrew their gaze from the face of the corpse. Presently the coroner lifted his eyes and said: "We will resume the inquest."

The men removed their hats. The witness was sworn.

"What is your name?" the coroner asked.

"William Harker."

"Age?"

"Twenty-seven."

"You knew the deceased, Hugh Morgan?"

"Yes."

"You were with him when he died?"

"Near him."

"How did that happen—your presence, I mean?"

"I was visiting him at this place to shoot and fish. A part of my purpose, however, was to study him, and his odd, solitary way of life. He seemed a good model for a character in fiction. I sometimes write stories."

"I sometimes read them."

"Thank you."

"Stories in general—not yours."

Some of the jurors laughed. Against a sombre background humor shows high lights. Soldiers in the intervals of battle laugh easily, and a jest in the death chamber conquers by surprise.

"Relate the circumstances of this man's death," said the coroner. "You may use any notes or memoranda that you please."

The witness understood. Pulling a manuscript from his breast pocket he held it near the candle, and turning the leaves until he found the passage that he wanted, began to read.

## II

" . . . The sun had hardly risen when we left the house. We were looking for quail, each with a shotgun, but we had only one dog. Morgan said that our best ground was beyond a certain ridge that he pointed out, and we crossed it by a trail through the *chaparral*. On the other side was comparatively level ground, thickly covered with wild oats. As we emerged from the *chaparral*, Morgan was but a few yards in advance. Suddenly, we heard, at a little distance to our right, and partly in front, a noise as of some animal thrashing about in the bushes, which we could see were violently agitated.

" 'We've started a deer,' I said. 'I wish we had brought a rifle.'

"Morgan, who had stopped and was intently

watching the agitated *chaparral,* said nothing, but had cocked both barrels of his gun, and was holding it in readiness to aim. I thought him a trifle excited, which surprised me, for he had a reputatior for exceptional coolness, even in moments of sudden and imminent peril.

" 'O, come!' I said. 'You are not going to fill up a deer with quail-shot, are you?'

"Still he did not reply; but, catching a sight of his face as he turned it slightly toward me, I was struck by the pallor of it. Then I understood that we had serious business on hand, and my first conjecture was that we had 'jumped' a grizzly. I advanced to Morgan's side, cocking my piece as I moved.

"The bushes were now quiet, and the sounds had ceased, but Morgan was as attentive to the place as before.

" 'What is it? What the devil is it?' I asked.

" 'That Damned Thing!' he replied, without turning his head. His voice was husky and unnatural. He trembled visibly.

"I was about to speak further, when I observed the wild oats near the place of the disturbance moving in the most inexplicable way. I can hardly describe it. It seemed as if stirred by a streak of wind, which not only bent it, but pressed it down—crushed it so that it did not rise, and this movement was slowly prolonging itself directly toward us.

# THE DAMNED THING

"Nothing that I had ever seen had affected me so strangely as this unfamiliar and unaccountable phenomenon, yet I am unable to recall any sense of fear. I remember—and tell it here because, singularly enough, I recollected it then—that once, in looking carelessly out of an open window, I momentarily mistook a small tree close at hand for one of a group of larger trees at a little distance away. It looked the same size as the others, but, being more distinctly and sharply defined in mass and detail, seemed out of harmony with them. It was a mere falsification of the law of aerial perspective, but it startled, almost terrified me. We so rely upon the orderly operation of familiar natural laws that any seeming suspension of them is noted as a menace to our safety, a warning of unthinkable calamity. So now the apparently causeless movement of the herbage, and the slow, undeviating approach of the line of disturbance were distinctly disquieting. My companion appeared actually frightened, and I could hardly credit my senses when I saw him suddenly throw his gun to his shoulders and fire both barrels at the agitated grass! Before the smoke of the discharge had cleared away I heard a loud savage cry—a scream like that of a wild animal—and, flinging his gun upon the ground, Morgan sprang away and ran swiftly from the spot. At the same instant I was thrown violently to the ground by the impact of something unseen in the smoke—some soft, heavy sub-

247

stance that seemed thrown against me with great force.

"Before I could get upon my feet and recover my gun, which seemed to have been struck from my hands, I heard Morgan crying out as if in mortal agony, and mingling with his cries were such hoarse savage sounds as one hears from fighting dogs. Inexpressibly terrified, I struggled to my feet and looked in the direction of Morgan's retreat; and may heaven in mercy spare me from another sight like that! At a distance of less than thirty yards was my friend, down upon one knee, his head thrown back at a frightful angle, hatless, his long hair in disorder and his whole body in violent movement from side to side, backward and forward. His right arm was lifted and seemed to lack the hand—at least, I could see none. The other arm was invisible. At times, as my memory now reports this extraordinary scene, I could discern but a part of his body; it was as if he had been partly blotted out—I can not otherwise express it—then a shifting of his position would bring it all into view again.

"All this must have occurred within a few seconds, yet in that time Morgan assumed all the postures of a determined wrestler vanquished by superior weight and strength. I saw nothing but him, and him not always distinctly. During the entire incident his shouts and curses were heard, as if through an enveloping uproar of such

sounds of rage and fury as I had never heard
from the throat of man or brute!

"For a moment only I stood irresolute, then,
throwing down my gun, I ran forward to my
friend's assistance. I had a vague belief that he
was suffering from a fit or some form of convul-
sion. Before I could reach his side he was down
and quiet. All sounds had ceased, but, with a
feeling of such terror as even these awful events
had not inspired, I now saw the same mysterious
movement of the wild oats prolonging itself from
the trampled area about the prostrate man toward
the edge of a wood. It was only when it had
reached the wood that I was able to withdraw
my eyes and look at my companion. He was
dead."

## III

The coroner rose from his seat and stood beside the dead man. Lifting an edge of the sheet
he pulled it away, exposing the entire body, altogether naked and showing in the candle light
a clay-like yellow. It had, however, broad macu-
lations of bluish-black, obviously caused by ex-
travasated blood from contusions. The chest and
sides looked as if they had been beaten with a
bludgeon. There were dreadful lacerations; the
skin was torn in strips and shreds.

The coroner moved round to the end of the
table and undid a silk handkerchief, which had

been passed under the chin and knotted on the top of the head. When the handkerchief was drawn away it exposed what had been the throat. Some of the jurors who had risen to get a better view repented their curiosity, and turned away their faces. Witness Harker went to the open window and leaned out across the sill, faint and sick. Dropping the handkerchief upon the dead man's neck, the coroner stepped to an angle of the room, and from a pile of clothing produced one garment after another, each of which he held up a moment for inspection. All were torn, and stiff with blood. The jurors did not make a closer inspection. They seemed rather uninterested. They had, in truth, seen all this before; the only thing that was new to them being Harker's testimony.

"Gentlemen," the coroner said, "we have no more evidence, I think. Your duty has been already explained to you; if there is nothing you wish to ask you may go outside and consider your verdict."

The foreman rose—a tall, bearded man of sixty, coarsely clad.

"I should like to ask one question, Mr. Coroner," he said. "What asylum did this yer last witness escape from?"

"Mr. Harker," said the coroner, gravely and tranquilly, "from what asylum did you last escape?"

Harker flushed crimson again, but said nothing, and the seven jurors rose and solemnly filed out of the cabin.

"If you have done insulting me, sir," said Harker, as soon as he and the officer were left alone with the dead man, "I suppose I am at liberty to go?"

"Yes."

Harker started to leave, but paused, with his hand on the door latch. The habit of his profession was strong in him—stronger than his sense of personal dignity. He turned about and said:

"The book that you have there—I recognize it as Morgan's diary. You seemed greatly interested in it; you read in it while I was testifying. May I see it? The public would like—"

"The book will cut no figure in this matter," replied the official, slipping it into his coat pocket; "all the entries in it were made before the writer's death."

As Harker passed out of the house the jury reentered and stood about the table on which the now covered corpse showed under the sheet with sharp definition. The foreman seated himself near the candle, produced from his breast pocket a pencil and scrap of paper, and wrote rather laboriously the following verdict, which with various degrees of effort all signed:

"We, the jury, do find that the remains come to their death at the hands of a mountain lion, but some of us thinks, all the same, they had fits."

## IV

In the diary of the late Hugh Morgan are certain interesting entries having, possibly, a scientific value as suggestions. At the inquest upon his body the book was not put in evidence; possibly the coroner thought it not worth while to confuse the jury. The date of the first of the entries mentioned can not be ascertained; the upper part of the leaf is torn away; the part of the entry remaining is as follows:

" . . . would run in a half circle, keeping his head turned always toward the centre and again he would stand still, barking furiously. At last he ran away into the brush as fast as he could go. I thought at first that he had gone mad, but on returning to the house found no other alteration in his manner than what was obviously due to fear of punishment.

"Can a dog see with his nose? Do odors impress some olfactory centre with images of the thing emitting them? . . .

"Sept. 2.—Looking at the stars last night as they rose above the crest of the ridge east of the house, I observed them successively disappear—from left to right. Each was eclipsed but an instant, and only a few at the same time, but along the entire length of the ridge all that were within a degree or two of the crest were blotted out. It was as if something had passed along between me and them; but I could not see it, and the stars

were not thick enough to define its outline. Ugh!
I don't like this. . . ."

Several weeks' entries are missing, three leaves
being torn from the book.

"Sept. 27.—It has been about here again—I
find evidences of its presence every day. I
watched again all of last night in the same cover,
gun in hand, double-charged with buckshot. In
the morning the fresh footprints were there, as
before. Yet I would have sworn that I did not
sleep—indeed, I hardly sleep at all. It is terrible,
insupportable! If these amazing experiences are
real I shall go mad; if they are fanciful I am mad
already.

"Oct. 3.—I shall not go—it shall not drive me
away. No, this is *my* house, *my* land. God
hates a coward. . . .

"Oct. 5.—I can stand it no longer; I have invited Harker to pass a few weeks with me—he
has a level head. I can judge from his manner
if he thinks me mad.

"Oct. 7.—I have the solution of the problem;
it came to me last night—suddenly, as by revelation. How simple—how terribly simple!

"There are sounds that we can not hear. At
either end of the scale are notes that stir no chord
of that imperfect instrument, the human ear.
They are too high or too grave. I have observed
a flock of blackbirds occupying an entire treetop
—the tops of several trees—and all in full song.
Suddenly—in a moment—at absolutely the same

instant—all spring into the air and fly away. How? They could not all see one another— whole treetops intervened. At no point could a leader have been visible to all. There must have been a signal of warning or command, high and shrill above the din, but by me unheard. I have observed, too, the same simultaneous flight when all were silent, among not only blackbirds, but other birds—quail, for example, widely separated by bushes—even on opposite sides of a hill.

"It is known to seamen that a school of whales basking or sporting on the surface of the ocean, miles apart, with the convexity of the earth between them, will sometimes dive at the same instant—all gone out of sight in a moment. The signal has been sounded—too grave for the ear of the sailor at the masthead and his comrades on the deck—who nevertheless feel its vibrations in the ship as the stones of a cathedral are stirred by the bass of the organ.

"As with sounds, so with colors. At each end of the solar spectrum the chemist can detect the presence of what are known as 'actinic' rays. They represent colors—integral colors in the composition of light—which we are unable to discern. The human eye is an imperfect instrument; its range is but a few octaves of the real 'chromatic scale.' I am not mad; there are colors that we can not see.

"And, God help me! the Damned Thing is of such a color!"

# THE LUCK OF ROARING CAMP

## BY FRANCIS BRET HARTE

# THE LUCK OF ROARING CAMP

BY FRANCIS BRET HARTE

THERE was commotion in Roaring Camp. It could not have been a fight, for in 1850 that was not novel enough to have called together the entire settlement. The ditches and claims were not only deserted, but "Tuttle's grocery" had contributed its gamblers, who, it will be remembered, calmly continued their game the day that French Pete and Kanaka Joe shot each other to death over the bar in the front room. The whole camp was collected before a rude cabin on the outer edge of the clearing. Conversation was carried on in a low tone, but the name of a woman was frequently repeated. It was a name familiar enough in the camp,—"Cherokee Sal."

Perhaps the less said of her the better. She was a coarse, and, it is to be feared, a very sinful woman. But at that time she was the only woman in Roaring Camp, and was just then lying in sore extremity, when she most needed the ministration of her own sex. Dissolute, abandoned, and irreclaimable, she was yet suffering a martyrdom hard enough to bear even when veiled by sympathizing womanhood, but now terrible in her loneliness. The primal curse had

257

come to her in that original isolation which must have made the punishment of the first transgression so dreadful. It was, perhaps, part of the expiation of her sin, that, at a moment when she most lacked her sex's intuitive tenderness and care, she met only the half-contemptuous faces of her masculine associates. Yet a few of the spectators were, I think, touched by her sufferings. Sandy Tipton thought it was "rough on Sal," and, in the contemplation of her condition, for a moment rose superior to the fact that he had an ace and two bowers in his sleeve.

It will be seen, also, that the situation was novel. Deaths were by no means uncommon in Roaring Camp, but a birth was a new thing. People had been dismissed the camp effectively, finally, and with no possibility of return; but this was the first time that anybody had been introduced *ab initio*. Hence the excitement.

"You go in there, Stumpy," said a prominent citizen known as "Kentuck," addressing one of the loungers. "Go in there, and see what you kin do. You've had experience in them things."

Perhaps there was a fitness in the selection. Stumpy, in other climes, had been the putative head of two families; in fact, it was owing to some legal informality in these proceedings that Roaring Camp—a city of refuge—was indebted to his company. The crowd approved the choice, and Stumpy was wise enough to bow to the majority. The door closed on the extempore surgeon and midwife, and Roaring Camp sat down outside, smoked its pipe, and awaited the issue.

The assemblage numbered about a hundred men. One or two of these were actual fugitives from justice, some were criminal, and all were reckless. Physically, they exhibited no indication of their past lives and character. The greatest scamp had a Raphael face, with a profusion of blond hair; Oakhurst, a gambler, had the melancholy air and intellectual abstraction of a Hamlet; the coolest and most courageous man was scarcely over five feet in height, with a soft voice and an embarrassed, timid manner. The term "roughs" applied to them was a distinction rather than a definition. Perhaps in the minor details of fingers, toes, ears, etc., the camp may have been deficient, but these slight omissions did not detract from their aggregate force. The strongest man had but three fingers on his right hand; the best shot had but one eye.

Such was the physical aspect of the men that were dispersed around the cabin. The camp lay in a triangular valley, between two hills and a river. The only outlet was a steep trail over the summit of a hill that faced the cabin, now illuminated by the rising moon. The suffering woman might have seen it from the rude bunk whereon she lay,—seen it winding like a silver thread until it was lost in the stars above.

A fire of withered pine-boughs added sociability to the gathering. By degrees the natural levity of Roaring Camp returned. Bets were freely offered and taken regarding the result. Three to five that "Sal would get through with it"; even, that the child would survive; side bets as to the sex and complexion of the coming stranger. In the midst of an excited discussion an exclamation came from those nearest the door, and the camp stopped to listen. Above the swaying and moaning of the pines, the swift rush of the river, and the crackling of the fire, rose a sharp, querulous cry,—a cry unlike anything heard before in the camp. The pines stopped moaning, the river ceased to rush, and the fire to crackle. It seemed as if Nature had stopped to listen too.

The camp rose to its feet as one man! It was proposed to explode a barrel of gunpowder, but, in consideration of the situation of the mother, better counsels prevailed, and only a few revolvers were discharged; for, whether owing to the rude surgery of the camp, or some other reason, Cherokee Sal was sinking fast. Within an hour she had climbed, as it were, that rugged road that led to the stars, and so passed out of Roaring Camp, its sin and shame forever. I do not think that the announcement disturbed them much, except in speculation as to the fate of the child. "Can he live now?" was asked of Stumpy. The answer was doubtful. The only being of Cherokee Sal's sex and maternal condition in

the settlement was an ass. There was some conjecture as to fitness, but the experiment was
tried. It was less problematical than the ancient
treatment of Romulus and Remus, and apparently as successful.

When these details were completed, which exhausted another hour, the door was opened, and
the anxious crowd of men who had already
formed themselves into a queue, entered in single
file. Beside the low bunk or shelf, on which the
figure of the mother was starkly outlined below
the blankets stood a pine table. On this a candle-
box was placed, and within it, swathed in staring
red flannel, lay the last arrival at Roaring Camp.
Beside the candle-box was placed a hat. Its use
was soon indicated. "Gentlemen," said Stumpy,
with a singular mixture of authority and *ex officio*
complacency,—"Gentlemen will please pass in
at the front door, round the table, and out at
the back door. Them as wishes to contribute
anything toward the orphan will find a hat
handy." The first man entered with his hat on;
he uncovered, however, as he looked about him,
and so, unconsciously, set an example to the next.
In such communities good and bad actions are
catching. As the procession filed in, comments
were audible, — criticisms addressed, perhaps,
rather to Stump, in the character of showman,—
"Is that him?" "mighty small specimen"; "hasn't
mor'n got the color"; "ain't bigger nor a der-
ringer." The contributions were as character-

istic: A silver tobacco-box; a doubloon; a navy revolver, silver mounted; a gold specimen; a very beautifully embroidered lady's handkerchief (from Oakhurst the gambler); a diamond breast-pin; a diamond ring (suggested by the pin, with the remark from the giver that he "saw that pin and went two diamonds better"); a slug shot; a Bible (contributor not detected); a golden spur; a silver teaspoon (the initials, I regret to say, were not the giver's); a pair of surgeon's shears; a lancet; a Bank of England note for £5; and about $200 in loose gold and silver coin. During these proceedings Stumpy maintained a silence as impassive as the dead on his left, a gravity as inscrutable as that of the newly born on his right. Only one incident occurred to break the monotony of the curious procession. As Kentuck bent over the candle-box half curiously, the child turned, and, in a spasm of pain, caught at his groping finger, and held it fast for a moment. Kentuck looked foolish and embarrassed. Something like a blush tried to assert itself in his weather-beaten cheek. "The d—d little cuss!" he said, as he extricated his finger, with, perhaps, more tenderness and care than he might have been deemed capable of showing. He held that finger a little apart from its fellows as he went out, and examined it curiously. The examination provoked the same original remark in regard to the child. In fact, he seemed to enjoy repeating it. "He rastled with my finger," he remarked to Tipton, holding up the member, "the d—d little cuss!"

It was four o'clock before the camp sought repose. A light burnt in the cabin where the watchers sat, for Stumpy did not go to bed that night. Nor did Kentuck. He drank quite freely, and related with great gusto his experience, invariably ending with his characteristic condemnation of the new-comer. It seemed to relieve him of any unjust implication of sentiment, and Kentuck had the weaknesses of the nobler sex. When everybody else had gone to bed, he walked down to the river, and whistled reflectingly. Then he walked up the gulch, past the cabin, still whistling with demonstrative unconcern. At a large redwood tree he paused and retraced his steps, and again passed the cabin. Half-way down to the river's bank he again paused, and then returned and knocked at the door. It was opened by Stumpy. "How goes it?" said Kentuck, looking past Stumpy toward the candle-box. "All serene," replied Stumpy. "Anything up?" "Nothing." There was a pause—an embarrassing one—Stumpy still holding the door. Then Kentuck had recourse to his finger, which he held up to Stumpy. "Rastled with it,—the d—d little cuss," he said, and retired.

The next day Cherokee Sal had such rude sepulture as Roaring Camp afforded. After her body had been committed to the hillside, there was a formal meeting of the camp to discuss what should be done with her infant. A resolution to adopt it was unanimous and enthusiastic. But an animated discussion in regard to the manner and feasibility of providing for its wants at once sprung up. It was remarkable that the argument partook of none of those fierce personalities with which discussions were usually conducted at Roaring Camp. Tipton proposed that they should send the child to Red Dog,—a distance of forty miles,—where female attention could be procured. But the unlucky suggestion met with fierce and unanimous opposition. It was evident that no plan which entailed parting from their new acquisition would for a moment be entertained. "Besides," said Tom Ryder, "them fellows at Red Dog would swap it, and ring in somebody else on us." A disbelief in the honesty of other camps prevailed at Roaring Camp as in other places.

The introduction of a female nurse in the camp also met with objection. It was argued that no decent woman could be prevailed upon to accept Roaring Camp as her home, and the speaker urged that "they didn't want any more of the other kind." This unkind allusion to the defunct mother, harsh as it may seem, was the first spasm of propriety,—the first system of the camp's regeneration. Stumpy advanced nothing. Perhaps he felt a certain delicacy in interfering with the selection of a possible successor in office. But when questioned, he averred stoutly that he and

"Jinny"—the mammal before alluded to—could manage to rear the child. There was something original, independent, and heroic about the plan that pleased the camp. Stumpy was retained. Certain articles were sent for to Sacramento. "Mind," said the treasurer, as he pressed a bag of gold-dust into the expressman's hand, "the best that can be got,—lace, you know, and fili-gree-work and frills, d—n the cost!"

Strange to say, the child thrived. Perhaps the invigorating climate of the mountain camp was compensation for material deficiencies. Nature took the foundling to her broader breast. In that rare atmosphere of the Sierra foot-hills,—that air pungent with balsamic odor, that ethereal cordial at once bracing and exhilarating,—he may have found food and nourishment, or a subtle chemistry that transmuted asses' milk to lime and phosphorus. Stumpy inclined to the belief that it was the latter and good nursing. "Me and that ass," he would say, "has been father and mother to him! Don't you," he would add, apostrophizing the helpless bundle before him, "never go back on us."

By the time he was a month old, the necessity of giving him a name became apparent. He had generally been known as "the Kid," "Stumpy's boy," "the Cayote" (an allusion to his vocal power), and even by Kentuck's endear-ing diminutive of "the d—d little cuss." But these were felt to be vague and unsatisfactory, and were at last dismissed under another influence. Gamblers and adventurers are generally superstitious, and Oakhurst one day declared that the baby had brought "the luck" to Roaring Camp. It was certain that of late they had been successful. "Luck" was the name agreed upon, with the prefix of Tommy for greater convenience. No allusion was made to the mother, and the father was unknown. "It's better," said the philosophical Oakhurst, "to take a fresh deal all round. Call him Luck, and start him fair." A day was accordingly set apart for the christening. What was meant by this ceremony the reader may imagine, who has already gathered some idea of the reckless irreverence of Roaring Camp. The master of ceremonies was one "Boston," a noted wag, and the occasion seemed to promise the greatest facetiousness. This ingenious satirist had spent two days in preparing a burlesque of the church service, with pointed local allusions. The choir was properly trained, and Sandy Tipton was to stand godfather. But after the procession had marched to the grove with music and banners, and the child had been deposited before a mock altar, Stumpy stepped before the expectant crowd. "It ain't my style to spoil fun, boys," said the little man, stoutly, eying the faces around him, "but it strikes me that this thing ain't exactly on the squar. It's playing it pretty low down on this yer baby to ring in fun on him that he ain't going to understand. And ef there's

going to be any godfathers round, I'd like to
see who's got any better rights than me." A
silence followed Stumpy's speech. To the credit
of all humorists be it said, that the first man to
acknowledge its justice was the satirist, thus
stopped of his fun. "But," said Stumpy, quickly,
following up his advantage, "we're here for a
christening, and we'll have it. I proclaim you
Thomas Luck, according to the laws of the
United States and the State of California, so
help me God." It was the first time that the
name of the Deity had been uttered otherwise
than profanely in the camp. The form of christening was perhaps even more ludicrous than
the satirist had conceived; but, strangely enough,
nobody saw it and nobody laughed. "Tommy"
was christened as seriously as he would have
been under a Christian roof, and cried and was
comforted in as orthodox fashion.

And so the work of regeneration began in
Roaring Camp. Almost imperceptibly a change
came over the settlement. The cabin assigned to
"Tommy Luck"—or "The Luck," as he was
more frequently called—first showed signs of
improvement. It was kept scrupulously clean
and white-washed. Then it was boarded, clothed,
and papered. The rosewood cradle — packed
eighty miles by mule—had, in Stumpy's way of
putting it, "sorter killed the rest of the furniture." So the rehabilitation of the cabin became
a necessity. The men who were in the habit of

lounging in at Stumpy's to see "how The Luck
got on" seemed to appreciate the change, and,
in self-defense, the rival establishment of "Tuttle's grocery" bestirred itself, and imported a
carpet and mirrors. The reflections of the latter
on the appearance of Roaring Camp tended to
produce stricter habits of personal cleanliness.
Again, Stumpy imposed a kind of quarantine
upon those who aspired to the honor and privilege
of holding "The Luck." It was a cruel mortification to Kentuck—who, in the carelessness of a
large nature and the habits of frontier life, had
begun to regard all garments as second cuticle,
which, like a snake's, only sloughed off through
decay—to be debarred this privilege from certain
prudential reasons. Yet such was the subtle
influence of innovation that he thereafter appeared regularly every afternoon in a clean shirt,
and face still shining from his ablutions. Nor
were moral and social sanitary laws neglected.
"Tommy," who was supposed to spend his whole
existence in a persistent attempt to repose, must
not be disturbed by noise. The shouting and
yelling which had gained the camp its infelicitous
title was not permitted within hearing distance
of Stumpy's. The men conversed in whispers,
or smoked with Indian gravity. Profanity was
tacitly given up in these sacred precincts, and
throughout the camp a popular form of expletive,
known as "D—n the luck!" and "Curse the
luck!" was abandoned, as having a new personal

bearing. Vocal music was not interdicted, being supposed to have a soothing, tranquillizing quality, and one song, sung by "Man-o'-War Jack," an English sailor, from her Majesty's Australian colonies, was quite popular as a lullaby. It was a lugubrious recital of the exploits of "the Arethusa, Seventy-four," in a muffled minor, ending with a prolonged dying fall at the burden of each verse, "On b-o-o-o-ard of the Arethusa." It was a fine sight to see Jack holding The Luck, rocking from side to side as if with the motion of a ship, and crooning forth this naval ditty. Either through the peculiar rocking of Jack or the length of his song,—it contained ninety stanzas and was continued with conscientious deliberation to the bitter end,—the lullaby generally had the desired effect. At such times the men would lie at full length under the trees, in the soft summer twilight, smoking their pipes and drinking in the melodious utterances. An indistinct idea that this was pastoral happiness pervaded the camp. "This 'ere kind o' think," said the Cockney Simmons, meditatively reclining on his elbow, "is 'evingly." It reminded him of Greenwich.

On the long summer days The Luck was usually carried to the gulch, from whence the golden store of Roaring Camp was taken. There, on a blanket spread over pine-boughs, he would lie while the men were working in the ditches below. Latterly, there was a rude attempt to decorate this bower with flowers and sweet-smelling shrubs, and generally some one would bring him a cluster of wild honeysuckle, azaleas, or the painted blossoms of Las Mariposas. The men had suddenly awakened to the fact that there were beauty and significance in these trifles, which they had so long trodden carelessly beneath their feet. A flake of glittering mica, a fragment of variegated quartz, a bright pebble from the bed of the creek, became beautiful to eyes thus cleared and strengthened, and were invariably put aside for "The Luck." It was wonderful how many treasures the woods and hillsides yielded that "would do for Tommy." Surrounded by playthings such as never child out of fairy-land had before, it is to be hoped that Tommy was content. He appeared to be securely happy, albeit there was an infantine gravity about him, a contemplative light in his round gray eyes that sometimes worried Stumpy. He was always tractable and quiet, and it is recorded that once, having crept beyond his "corral,"—a hedge of tassellated pine-boughs, which surrounded his bed,—he dropped over the bank on his head in the soft earth, and remained with his mottled legs in the air in that position for at least five minutes with unflinching gravity. He was extricated without a murmur. I hesitate to record the many other instances of his sagacity, which rest, unfortunately, upon the statements of prejudiced friends. Some of them were not without a tinge of superstition. "I crep' up the bank just now," said Kentuck one day, in a breathless state of excitement, "and dern my skin if he wasn't a talking to a jay-bird as was sittin' on his lap. There they was, just as free and sociable as anything you please, a jawin' at each other just like two cherry-bums." Howbeit, whether creeping over the pine-boughs or lying lazily on his back blinking at the leaves above him, to him the birds sang, the squirrels chattered, and the flowers bloomed. Nature was his nurse and playfellow. For him she would let slip between the leaves golden shafts of sunlight that fell just within his grasp; she would send wandering breezes to visit him with the balm of bay and resinous gums; to him the tall red-woods nodded familiarly and sleepily, the bumble-bees buzzed, and the rooks cawed a slumbrous accompaniment.

Such was the golden summer of Roaring Camp. They were "flush times,"—and The Luck was with them. The claims had yielded enormously. The camp was jealous of its privileges and looked suspiciously on strangers. No encouragement was given to immigration, and, to make their seclusion more perfect, the land on either side of the mountain wall that surrounded the camp they duly pre-empted. This, and a reputation for singular proficiency with the revolver, kept the reserve of Roaring Camp inviolate. The expressman—their only connecting link with the surrounding world—sometimes told wonderful stories of the camp. He would say, "They've a street up there in 'Roaring,' that would lay over any street in Red Dog. They've got vines and flowers round their houses, and they wash themselves twice a day. But they're mighty rough on strangers, and they worship an Ingin baby."

With the prosperity of the camp came a desire for further improvement. It was proposed to build a hotel in the following spring, and to invite one or two decent families to reside there for the sake of "The Luck,"—who might perhaps profit by female companionship. The sacrifice that this concession to the sex cost these men, who were fiercely skeptical in regard to its general virtue and usefulness, can only be accounted for by their affection for Tommy. A few still held out. But the resolve could not be carried into effect for three months, and the minority meekly yielded in the hope that something might turn up to prevent it. And it did.

The winter of 1851 will long be remembered in the foot-hills. The snow lay deep on the Sierras, and every mountain creek became a river, and every river a lake. Each gorge and gulch was transformed into a tumultuous watercourse that descended the hillsides, tearing down giant trees and scattering its drift and débris along the plain. Red Dog had been twice under water, and Roaring Camp had been forewarned.

"Water put the gold into them gulches," said Stumpy. "It's been here once and will be here again!" And that night the North Fork suddenly leaped over its banks, and swept up the triangular valley of Roaring Camp.

In the confusion of rushing water, crushing trees, and crackling timber, and the darkness which seemed to flow with the water and blot out the fair valley, but little could be done to collect the scattered camp. When the morning broke, the cabin of Stumpy nearest the river-bank was gone. Higher up the gulch they found the body of its unlucky owner; but the pride, the hope, the joy, the Luck, of Roaring Camp had disappeared. They were returning with sad hearts, when a shout from the bank recalled them.

It was a relief boat from down the river. They had picked up, they said, a man and an infant, nearly exhausted, about two miles below. Did anybody know them, and did they belong here?

It needed but a glance to show them Kentuck lying there, cruelly crushed and bruised, but still holding the Luck of Roaring Camp in his arms. As they bent over the strangely assorted pair, they saw that the child was cold and pulseless. "He is dead," said one. Kentuck opened his eyes. "Dead?" he repeated feebly. "Yes, my man, and you are dying too." A smile lit the eyes of the expiring Kentuck. "Dying," he repeated, "he's a taking me with him,—tell the boys I've got the Luck with me now"; and the strong man, clinging to the frail babe as a drowning man is said to cling to a straw, drifted away into the shadowy river that flows forever to the unknown sea.

# MARJORIE DAW

## BY THOMAS BAILEY ALDRICH

# MARJORIE DAW

## BY THOMAS BAILEY ALDRICH

DR. DILLON TO EDWARD DELANEY, ESQ., AT
THE PINES, NEAR RYE, N. H.

AUGUST, 8, 187–.

MY DEAR SIR—I am happy to assure
you that your anxiety is without reason.
Flemming will be confined to the sofa
for three or four weeks, and will have to be careful at first how he uses his leg. A fracture of this
kind is always a tedious affair. Fortunately the
bone was very skilfully set by the surgeon who
chanced to be in the drug-store where Flemming
was brought after his fall, and I apprehend no
permanent inconvenience from the accident.
*Flemming is doing perfectly well physically;*
but I must confess that the irritable and morbid
state of mind into which he has fallen causes me
a great deal of uneasiness. He is the last man in
the world who ought to break his leg. You know
how impetuous our friend is ordinarily, what a
soul of restlessness and energy, never content
unless he is rushing at some object, like a spor-
tive bull at a red shawl; but amiable withal. He
is no longer amiable. His temper has become
something frightful. Miss Fanny Flemming

came up from Newport, where the family are staying for the summer, to nurse him; but he packed her off the next morning in tears. He has a complete set of Balzac's works, twenty-seven volumes, piled up by his sofa, to throw at Watkins whenever that exemplary serving-man appears with his meals. Yesterday I very innocently brought Flemming a small basket of lemons. You know it was a strip of lemon-peel on the curbstone that caused our friend's mischance. Well, he no sooner set his eyes upon these lemons then he fell into such a rage as I cannot describe adequately. This is only one of his moods, and the least distressing. At other times he sits with bowed head regarding his splintered limb, silent, sullen, despairing. When this fit is on him—and it sometimes lasts all day—nothing can distract his melancholy. He refuses to eat; does not even read the newspapers; books—except as projectiles for Watkins—have no charms for him. His state is truly pitiable.

Now, if he were a poor man, with a family dependent on his daily labor, this irritability and despondency would be natural enough. But in a young fellow of twenty-four, with plenty of money, and seemingly not a care in the world, the thing is monstrous. If he continues to give way to his vagaries in this manner, he will end by bringing on an inflammation of the fibula. It was the fibula he broke. I am at my wits' end to know what to prescribe for him. I have anaesthetics and lotions to make people sleep and to soothe pain; but I've no medicine that will make a man have a little common-sense. That is beyond my skill, but maybe it is not beyond yours. You are Flemming's intimate friend, his *fidus Achates*. Write to him, write to him frequently, distract his mind, cheer him up, and prevent him from becoming a confirmed case of melancholia. Perhaps he has some important plans disarranged by his present confinement. If he has you will know, and will know how to advise him judiciously. I trust your father finds the change beneficial? I am, my dear sir, with great respect, &c.

## II

### EDWARD DELANEY TO JOHN FLEMMING, WEST 38TH STREET, NEW YORK

AUGUST 9, ——.

MY DEAR JACK—I had a line from Dillon this morning, and was rejoiced to learn that your hurt is not so bad as reported. Like a certain personage you are not so black and blue as you are painted. Dillon will put you on your pins again in two or three weeks, if you will only have patience and follow his counsels. Did you get my note of last Wednesday? I was greatly troubled when I heard of the accident.

I can imagine how tranquil and saintly you are with your leg in a trough! It's deuced awkward, to be sure, just as we had promised ourselves a glorious month together at the seaside; but we must make the best of it. It is unfortunate, too, that my father's health renders it impossible for me to leave him. I think he has much improved; the sea air is his native element; but he still needs my arm to lean upon in his walks, and requires some one more careful than a servant to look after him. I cannot come to you, dear Jack, but I have hours of unemployed time on hand, and I will write you a whole post-office full of letters if that will divert you. Heaven knows, I haven't anything to write about. It isn't as if we were living at one of the beach houses; then I could do you some character studies, and fill your imagination with hosts of sea-goddesses, with their (or somebody else's) raven and blond manes hanging down their shoulders. You should have Aphrodite in morning wrapper, in evening costume, and in her prettiest bathing suit. But we are far from all that here. We have rooms in a farm-house, on a cross-road, two miles from the hotels, and lead the quietest of lives.

I wish I were a novelist. This old house, with its sanded floors and high wainscots, and its narrow windows looking out upon a cluster of pines that turn themselves into aeolian-harps every time the wind blows, would be the place in which to write a summer romance. It should be a story with the odors of the forest and the breath of the sea in it. It should be a novel like one of that Russian fellow's—what's his name?— Tourguénieff. Tourguenef, Toorguniff, Turgénjew; nobody knows how to spell him. (I think his own mother must be in some doubt about him.) Yet I wonder if even a Liza or an Alexandra Paulovna could stir the heart of a man who has constant twinges in his leg. I wonder if one of our own Yankee girls of the best type, haughty and *spirituelle,* would be of any comfort to you in your present deplorable condition. If I thought so, I would rush down to the Surf House and catch one for you; or, better still, I would find you one over the way.

Picture to yourself a large white house just across the road, nearly opposite our cottage. It is not a house, but a mansion, built perhaps in the colonial period, with rambling extensions, and gambrel roof, and a wide piazza on three sides—a self-possessed, high-bred piece of architecture, with its nose in the air. It stands back from the road, and has an obsequious retinue of fringed elms and oaks and weeping willows. Sometimes in the morning, and oftener in the afternoon, when the sun has withdrawn from that part of the mansion, a young woman appears on the piazza, with some mysterious Penelope web of embroidery in her hand, or a book. There is a hammock over there—of pine-apple fibre, it looks from here. A hammock is very becoming when one is eighteen, and has gold hair, and dark eyes, and a blue illusion dress looped up after the fashion of a Dresden china shepherdess, and is *chaussée* like a belle of the time of Louis Quatorze. All this splendor goes into that hammock, and sways there like a pond-lily in the golden afternoon. The window of my bedroom looks down on that piazza, and so do I.

But enough of this nonsense, which ill becomes a sedate young attorney taking his vacation with an invalid father. Drop me a line, dear Jack, and tell me how you really are. State your case. Write me a long quiet letter. If you are violent or abusive I'll take the law to you.

## III

### John Flemming to Edward Delaney

August 11, ——.

Your letter, dear Ned, was a god-send. Fancy what a fix I am in; I, who never had a day's sickness since I was born. My left leg weighs three tons. It is embalmed in spices, and smothered in layers of fine linen like a mummy. I can't move. I haven't moved for five thousand years. I'm of the time of Pharaoh.

I lie from morning till night on a lounge staring into the hot street. Everybody is out of town enjoying himself. The brownstone-front houses across the street resemble a row of particularly ugly coffins set up on end. A green

mould is settling on the names of the deceased,
carved on the silver door-plates. Sardonic spi-
ders have sewed up the key-holes. All this is
silence and dust and desolation.—I interrupt this
a moment to take a shy at Watkins with the
second volume of *César Birotteau*. Missed him!
I think I could bring him down with a copy of
*Sainte-Beuve*, or the *Dictionnaire Universel*, if
I had it. These small Balzac books somehow
don't quite fit my hand. But I shall fetch him
yet. I've an idea Watkins is tapping the old
gentleman's Chateau Yquem. Duplicate key of
the wine-cellar. Hibernian swarries in the front
basement. Young Cheops upstairs, snug in his
cerements. Watkins glides into my chamber
with that colorless, hypocritical face of his
drawn out long like an accordion; but I know
he grins all the way downstairs, and is glad I
have broken my leg. Was not my evil star in
the very zenith when I ran up to town to attend
that dinner at Delmonico's? I didn't come up
altogether for that. It was partly to buy Frank
Livingston's roan mare Margot. And now I
shall not be able to sit in the saddle these two
months. I'll send the mare down to you at The
Pines; is that the name of the place?

Old Dillon fancies that I have something on
my mind. He drives me wild with lemons. Lemons for a mind diseased. Nonsense, I am only as
restless as the devil under this confinement—a
thing I'm not used to. Take a man who has

never had so much as a headache or a toothache in his life, strap one of his legs in a section of water-spout, keep him in a room in the city for weeks, with the hot weather turned on, and then expect him to smile, and purr, and be happy! It is preposterous. I can't be cheerful or calm.

Your letter is the first consoling thing I have had since my disaster, a week ago. It really cheered me up for half an hour. Send me a screed, Ned, as often as you can, if you love me. Anything will do. Write me more about that little girl in the hammock. That was very pretty, all that about the Dresden china shepherdess and the pond-lily; the imagery a little mixed perhaps, but very pretty. I didn't suppose you had so much sentimental furniture in your upper story. It shows how one may be familiar for years with the reception-room of his neighbor, and never suspect what is directly under his mansard. I supposed your loft stuffed with dry legal parchments, mortgages, and affidavits; you take down a package of manuscript, and lo! there are lyrics, and sonnets, and canzonettas. You really have a graphic descriptive touch, Edward Delaney, and I suspect you of short love-tales in the magazines.

I shall be a bear until I hear from you again. Tell me all about your pretty *inconnue* across the road. What is her name? Who is she? Who's her father? Where's her mother? Who's her lover? You cannot imagine how this will occupy

me. The more trifling the better. My imprison-
ment has weakened me intellectually to such a
degree that I find your epistolary gifts quite
considerable. I am passing into my second childhood. In a week or two I shall take to india-
rubber rings and prongs of coral. A silver cup
with an appropriate inscription would be a delicate attention on your part. In the meantime
write!

## IV

### EDWARD DELANEY TO JOHN FLEMMING

AUGUST 12, ——.

The sick pasha shall be amused. *Bismillah!* he
wills it so! If the story-teller becomes prolix and
tedious—the bow-string and the sack, and two
Nubians to drop him into the Piscataqua! But
truly, Jack, I have a hard task. There is literally
nothing here except the little girl over the way.
She is swinging in the hammock at this moment.
It is to me compensation for many of the ills of
life to see her now and then put out a small kid
boot, which fits like a glove, and set herself going. Who is she and what is her name? Her
name is Daw. Only daughter of Mr. Richard
W. Daw, ex-colonel and banker. Mother dead,
One brother at Harvard; elder brother killed at
the battle of Fair Oaks nine years ago. Old, rich
family the Daws. This is the homestead where
father and daughter pass eight months of the

twelve; the rest of the year in Baltimore and Washington. The New England winter too many for the old gentleman. The daughter is called Marjorie—Marjorie Daw. Sounds odd at first, doesn't it? But after you say it over to yourself half a dozen times you like it. There's a pleasing quaintness to it, something prim and violet-like. Must be a nice sort of girl to be called Marjorie Daw.

I had mine host of The Pines in the witness box last night, and drew the foregoing testimony from him. He has charge of Mr. Daw's vegetable garden, and has known the family these thirty years. Of course I shall make the acquaintance of my neighbors before many days. It will be next to impossible for me not to meet Mr. Daw or Miss Daw in some of my walks. The young lady has a favorite path to the seabeach. I shall intercept her some morning, and touch my hat to her. Then the princess will bend her fair head to me with courteous surprise, not unmixed with haughtiness. Will snub me, in fact. All this for thy sake, O Pasha of the Snapt Axle-tree! . . . How oddly things fall out! Ten minutes ago I was called down to the parlor— you know the kind of parlors in farmhouses on the coast; a sort of amphibious parlor, with seashells on the mantelpiece and spruce branches in the chimney-place—where I found my father and Mr. Daw doing the antique polite to each other. He had come to pay his respects to his new neighbors. Mr. Daw is a tall, slim gentleman of about fifty-five, with a florid face and snow-white mustache and side-whiskers. Looks like Mr. Dombey, or as Mr. Dombey would have looked if he had served a few years in the British army. Mr. Daw was a colonel in the late war, commanding the regiment in which his son was a lieutenant. Plucky old boy, backbone of New Hampshire granite. Before taking his leave the colonel delivered himself of an invitation, as if he were issuing a general order. Miss Daw has a few friends coming at 4 P. M., to play croquet on the lawn (parade-ground), and have tea (cold rations) on the piazza. Will we honor them with our company (or be sent to the guard-house)? My father declines on the plea of ill-health. My father's son bows with as much suavity as he knows, and accepts.

In my next I shall have something to tell you. I shall have seen the little beauty face to face. I have a presentiment, Jack, that this Daw is a *rara avis!* Keep up your spirits, my boy, until I write you another letter; and send me along word how's your leg.

## V

EDWARD DELANEY TO JOHN FLEMMING

AUGUST 13, ——.

The party, my dear Jack, was as dreary as possible. A lieutenant of the navy, the rector of the Episcopal church at Stillwater, and a society swell from Nahant. The lieutenant looked as if he had swallowed a couple of his buttons and found the bullion rather indigestible; the rector was a pensive youth of the daffydowndilly sort; and the swell from Nahant was a very weak tidal wave indeed. The women were much better, as they always are; the two Miss Kingsburys of Philadelphia, staying at the Sea-shell House, two bright and engaging girls. But Marjorie Daw!

The company broke up soon after tea, and I remained to smoke a cigar with the colonel on the piazza. It was like seeing a picture to see Miss Marjorie hovering around the old soldier and doing a hundred gracious little things for him. She brought the cigars and lighted the tapers with her own delicate fingers in the most enchanting fashion. As we sat there she came and went in the summer twilight, and seemed, with her white dress and pale gold hair, like some lovely phantom that had sprung into existence out of the smoke-wreaths. If she had melted into air, like the statue of the lady in the play, I should have been more sorry than surprised.

It was easy to perceive that the old colonel worshipped her, and she him. I think the relation between an elderly father and a daughter just blooming into womanhood the most beautiful possible. There is in it a subtle sentiment that cannot exist in the case of mother and daughter, or that of son and mother. But this is getting into deep water.

I sat with the Daws until half-past ten and saw the moon rise on the sea. The ocean, that had stretched motionless and black against the horizon, was changed by magic into a broken field of glittering ice. In the far distance the Isles of Shoals loomed up like a group of huge bergs drifting down on us. The polar regions in a June thaw! It was exceedingly fine. What did we talk about? We talked about the weather —and *you!* The weather has been disagreeable for several days past—and so have you. I glided from one topic to the other very naturally. I told my friends of your accident; how it had frustrated all our summer plans, and what our plans were. Then I described you; or, rather, I didn't. I spoke of your amiability; of your patience under this severe affliction; of your touching gratitude when Dillon brings you little presents of fruit; of your tenderness to your sister Fanny, whom you would not allow to stay in town to nurse you, and how you heroically sent her back to Newport, preferring to remain alone with Mary the cook and your man Watkins, to whom, by the way, you were devotedly attached. If you had been there, Jack, you wouldn't have known yourself. I should have excelled as a criminal lawyer if I had not turned my attention to a different branch of jurisprudence.

Miss Marjorie asked all manner of leading questions concerning you. It did not occur to me then, but it struck me forcibly afterwards that she evinced a singular interest in the conversation. When I got back to my room I recalled how eagerly she leaned forward, with her full, snowy throat in strong moonlight, listening to what I said. Positively, I think I made her like you!

Miss Daw is a girl whom you would like immensely, I can tell you that. A beauty without affectation; a high and tender nature, if one can read the soul in the face. And the old colonel is a noble character too.

I am glad the Daws are such pleasant people. The Pines is an isolated place and my resources are few. I fear I should have found life here rather monotonous before long with no other society than that of my excellent sire. It is true I might have made a target of the defenseless invalid; but I haven't a taste for artillery, *moi*.

## IV

John Flemming to Edward Delaney

August 17, ——.

For a man who hasn't a taste for artillery it occurs to me, my friend, you are keeping up a pretty lively fire on my inner works. But go on. Cynicism is a small brass field-piece that eventually bursts and kills the artillery man.

# MARJORIE DAW

You may abuse me as much as you like, and I'll not complain; for I don't know what I should do without your letters. They are curing me. I haven't hurled anything at Watkins since last Sunday, partly because I have grown more amiable under your teaching, and partly because Watkins captured my ammunition one night and carried it off to the library. He is rapidly losing the habit he had acquired of dodging whenever I rub my ear, or make any slight motion with my right arm. He is still suggestive of the wine cellar, however. You may break, you may shatter Watkins if you will, but the scent of the Roederer will hang around him still.

Ned, that Miss Daw must be a charming person. I should certainly like her. I like her already. When you spoke in your first letter of seeing a young girl swinging in a hammock under your chamber window I was somehow strangely drawn to her. I cannot account for it in the least. What you have subsequently written describing a woman I have known in some previous state of existence, or dreamed of in this. Upon my word, if you were to send me her photograph I believe I should recognize her at a glance. Her manner, that listening attitude, her traits of character, as you indicate them, the light hair and the dark eyes, they are all familiar things to me. Asked a lot of questions, did she? Curious about me? That is strange.

You would laugh in your sleeve, you wretched old cynic, if you knew how I lie awake nights, with my gas turned down to a star, thinking of The Pines and the house across the road. How cool it must be down there! I long for the salt smell in the air. I picture the colonel smoking his cheroot on the piazza. I send you and Miss Daw off on afternoon rambles along the beach. Sometimes I let you stroll with her under the elms in the moonlight, for you are great friends by this time, I take it, and see each other every day. I know your ways and your manners! Then I fall into a truculent mood and would like to destroy somebody. Have you noticed anything in the shape of a lover hanging around the colonial Lares and Penates? Does that lieutenant of the horse-marines or that young Stillwater parson visit the house much? Not that I am pining for news of them, but any gossip of the kind would be in order. I wonder, Ned, you don't fall in love with Miss Daw. I am ripe to do it myself. Speaking of photographs, couldn't you manage to slip one of her *cartes-de-visite* from her album—she must have an album, you know—and send it to me? I will return it before it could be missed. That's a good fellow! Did the mare arrive safe and sound? It will be a capital animal this autumn for Central Park.

Oh—my leg? I forgot about my leg. It's better.

## VII

### EDWARD DELANEY TO JOHN FLEMMING

AUGUST 20, ——.

You are correct in your surmises. I am on the
most friendly terms with our neighbors. The
colonel and my father smoke their afternoon
cigar together in our sitting-room, or on the
piazza opposite, and I pass an hour or two of
the day or the evening with the daughter. I am
more and more struck by the beauty, modesty,
and intelligence of Miss Daw.

You ask me why I do not fall in love with
her. I will be frank, Jack; I have thought of
that. She is young, rich, accomplished, uniting in
herself more attractions, mental and personal,
than I can recall in any girl of my acquaintance;
but she lacks the something that would be necessary to inspire in me that kind of interest. Possessing this unknown quantity, a woman neither
beautiful, not wealthy, nor very young could
bring me to her feet. But not Miss Daw. If we
were shipwrecked together on an uninhabited
island—let me suggest a tropical island, for it
costs no more to be picturesque—I would build
her a bamboo hut, I would fetch her bread-fruit
and cocoa-nuts, I would fry yams for her, I
would lure the ingenuous turtle and make her
nourishing soups; but I wouldn't make love to
her—not under eighteen months. I would like
to have her for a sister, that I might shield her

and counsel her, and spend half my income on thread-laces and camel's-hair shawls. (We are off the island now.) If such were not my feeling there would still be an obstacle to my loving Miss Daw. A greater misfortune could scarcely befall me than to love her. Flemming, I am about to make a revelation that will astonish you. I may be all wrong in my premises, and consequently in my conclusions; but you shall judge.

That night when I returned to my room after the croquet party at the Daws', and was thinking over the trivial events of the evening, I was suddenly impressed by the air of eager attention with which Miss Daw had followed my account of your accident. I think I mentioned this to you. Well, the next morning as I went to mail my letter, I overtook Miss Daw on the road to Rye, where the post-office is, and accompanied her thither and back—an hour's walk. The conversation again turned on you, and again I remarked that inexplicable look of interest which had lighted up her face the previous evening. Since then I have seen Miss Daw perhaps ten times, perhaps oftener, and on each occasion I found that when I was not speaking of you, or your sister, or some person or place associated with you, I was not holding her attention. She would be absent-minded; her eyes would wander away from me to the sea, or to some distant object in the landscape, her fingers would play with the leaves of a book in a way that convinced me she was not listening. At these moments if I abruptly changed the theme—I did it several times an an experiment—and dropped some remark about my friend Flemming, then the somber blue eyes would come back to me instantly.

Now, is not this the oddest thing in the world? No, not the oddest. The effect which, you tell me, was produced on you by my casual mention of an unknown girl swinging in a hammock, is certainly as strange. You can conjecture how that passage in your letter of Friday startled me. Is it possible then, that two people who have never met, and who are hundreds of miles apart, can exert a magnetic influence on each other? I have read of such psychological phenomena, but never credited them. I leave the solution of the problem to you. As for myself, all other things being favorable, it would be impossible for me to fall in love with a woman who listens to me only when I am talking of my friend!

I am not aware that any one is paying marked attention to my fair neighbor. The lieutenant of the navy—he is stationed at Rivermouth—sometimes drops in of an evening, and sometimes the rector from Stillwater; the lieutenant the oftener. He was there last night. I should not be surprised if he had an eye to the heiress; but he is not formidable. Mistress Daw carries a neat little spear of irony, and the honest lieutenant seems to have a particular facility for impaling himself on the point of it. He is not dangerous,

I should say; though I have known a woman to satirize a man for years and marry him after all. Decidedly the lowly rector is not dangerous; yet, again, who has not seen cloth of frieze victorious in the lists where cloth of gold went down?

As to the photograph. There is an exquisite ivorytype of Marjorie in *passe-partout,* on the drawing-room mantelpiece. It would be missed at once if taken. I would do anything reasonable for you, Jack; but I've no burning desire to be hauled up before the local justice of the peace on a charge of petty larceny.

P. S.—Enclosed is a spray of mignonette, which I advise you treat tenderly. Yes, we talked of you again last night as usual. It is becoming a little dreary for me.

## VIII

### EDWARD DELANEY TO JOHN FLEMMING

AUGUST 22, ———.

Your letter in reply to my last has occupied my thoughts all the morning. I do not know what to think. Do you mean to say that you are seriously half in love with a woman whom you have never seen—with a shadow, a chimera? for what else can Miss Daw be to you? I do not understand it at all. I understand neither you nor her. You are a couple of ethereal beings moving in finer air than I can breathe with my commonplace lungs. Such delicacy of sentiment is something I admire without comprehending. I am bewildered. I am of the earth earthy; and I find myself in the incongruous position of having to do with mere souls, with natures so finely tempered that I run some risk of shattering them in my awkwardness. I am as Caliban among the spirits!

Reflecting on your letter I am not sure it is wise in me to continue this correspondence. But no, Jack; I do wrong to doubt the good sense that forms the basis of your character. You are deeply interested in Miss Daw; you feel that she is a person whom you may perhaps greatly admire when you know her: at the same time you bear in mind that the chances are ten to five, that, when you do come to know her, she will fall far short of your ideal, and you will not care for her in the least. Look at it in this sensible light, and I will hold back nothing from you.

Yesterday afternoon my father and myself rode over to Rivermouth with the Daws. A heavy rain in the morning had cooled the atmosphere and laid the dust. To Rivermouth is a drive of eight miles, along a winding road lined all the way with wild barberry bushes. I never saw anything more brilliant than these bushes, the green of the foliage and the red of the coral berries intensified by the rain. The colonel drove, with my father in front, Miss Daw and I on the back seat. I resolved that for the first five miles your name should not pass my lips. I was amused by the artful attempts she made, at the start, to break through my reticence. Then a silence fell upon her; and then she became suddenly gay. That keenness which I enjoyed so much when it was exercised on the lieutenant was not so satisfactory directed against myself. Miss Daw has great sweetness of disposition, but she can be disagreeable. She is like that young lady in the rhyme, with the curl on her forehead,

> When she is good,
> She is very, very good,
> And when she is bad, she is horrid!

I kept to my resolution, however; but on the return home I relented, and talked of your mare! Miss Daw is going to try a side-saddle on Margot some morning. The animal is a trifle too light for my weight. By the by, I nearly forgot to say Miss Daw sat for a picture yesterday to a Rivermouth artist. If the negative turns out well I am to have a copy. So our ends will be accomplished without crime. I wish, though, I could send you the ivorytype in the drawing-room; it is cleverly colored, and would give you an idea of her hair and eyes, which, of course, the other will not.

No, Jack, the spray of mignonette did not come from me. A man of twenty-eight doesn't enclose flowers in his letters—to another man. But don't attach too much significance to the circumstance. She gives sprays of mignonette to the rector, sprays to the lieutenant. She has even given a rose from her bosom to your slave. It is her jocund nature to scatter flowers, like spring.

If my letters sometimes read disjointedly you must understand that I never finish one at a sitting, but write at intervals, when the mood is on me.

The mood is not on me now.

## IX

### EDWARD DELANEY TO JOHN FLEMMING

I have just returned from the strangest interview with Marjorie. She has all but confessed to me her interest in you. But with what modesty and dignity! Her words elude my pen as I attempt to put them on paper; and, indeed, it was not so much what she said as her manner; and that I cannot reproduce. Perhaps it was of a piece with the strangeness of this whole business that she should tacitly acknowledge to a third party the love she feels for a man she has never beheld! But I have lost, through your aid, the faculty of being surprised. I accept things as people do in dreams. Now that I am again in my room it all appears like an illusion—the black masses of shadow under the trees, the fire-flies whirling in Pyrrhic dances among the shrubbery, the sea over there, Marjorie sitting in the hammock!

It is past midnight, and I am too sleepy to write more.

*Tuesday Morning*—My father has suddenly taken it into his head to spend a few days at the Shoals. In the meanwhile you will not hear from me. I see Marjorie walking in the garden with the colonel. I wish I could speak to her alone, but shall probably not have an opportunity before we leave.

## X

### EDWARD DELANEY TO JOHN FLEMMING

AUGUST 28, ——.

You were passing into your second childhood, were you? Your intellect was so reduced that my epistolary gifts seemed quite considerable to you, did they? I rise superior to the sarcasm in your favour of the 11th instant, when I notice that five days' silence on my part is sufficient to throw you into the depths of despondency.

We returned only this morning from Appledore, that enchanted island—at four dollars per day. I find on my desk three letters from you! Evidently there is no lingering doubt in *your* mind as to the pleasure I derive from your correspondence. These letters are undated, but in what I take to be the latest are two passages that require my consideration. You will pardon my candor, dear Flemming, but the conviction forces itself upon me that as your leg grows stronger your head becomes weaker. You ask my advice on a certain point. I will give it. In my opinion you could do nothing more unwise than to address a note to Miss Daw, thanking her for the flower. It would, I am sure, offend her delicacy beyond pardon. She knows you only through me; you are to her an abstraction, a figure in a dream—a dream from which the slightest shock would awaken her. Of course, if you enclose a note to me and insist on its delivery, I shall deliver it; but I advise you not to do so.

You say you are able, with the aid of a cane, to walk about your chamber, and that you purpose to come to The Pines the instant Dillon thinks you strong enough to stand the journey. Again I advise you not to. Do you not see that, every hour you remain away, Marjorie's glamor deepens and your influence over her increases? You will ruin everything by precipitancy. Wait until you are entirely recovered; in any case do not come without giving me warning. I fear the effect of your abrupt advent here—in the circumstances.

Miss Daw was evidently glad to see us back again, and gave me both hands in the frankest way. She stopped at the door for a moment this afternoon in the carriage; she had been over to Rivermouth for her pictures. Unluckily the photographer had spilt some acid on the plate and she was obliged to give him another sitting. I have an impression that something is troubling Marjorie. She had an abstracted air not usual with her. However, it may be only my fancy ... I end this, leaving several things unsaid, to accompany my father on one of those long walks which are now his chief medicine—and mine!

## XI

### EDWARD DELANEY TO JOHN FLEMMING

AUGUST 29, ——.

I write in great haste to tell you what has taken place here since my letter of last night. I am in the utmost perplexity. Only one thing is plain—*you* must not dream of coming to The Pines. Marjorie has told her father everything! I saw her for a few minutes, an hour ago, in the garden; and, as near as I could gather from her confused statement, the facts are these: Lieutenant Bradley—that's the naval officer stationed at Rivermouth—has been paying court to Miss Daw for some time past, but not so much to her liking as to that of the colonel, who it seems is an old friend of the young gentleman's father. Yesterday (I knew she was in some trouble when she drove up to our gate) the colonel spoke to Marjorie of Bradley—urged his suit, I infer. Marjorie expressed her dislike for

302

the lieutenant with characteristic frankness, and finally confessed to her father—well, I really do not know what she confessed. It must have been the vaguest of confessions, and must have sufficiently puzzled the colonel. At any rate, it exasperated him. I suppose I am implicated in the matter and that the colonel feels bitterly towards me. I do not see why: I have carried no messages between you and Miss Daw; I have behaved with the greatest discretion. I can find no flaw anywhere in my proceeding. I do not see that anybody has done anything—except the colonel himself.

It is probable, nevertheless, that the friendly relations between the two houses will be broken off. "A plague o' both your houses," say you. I will keep you informed, as well as I can, of what occurs over the way. We shall remain here until the second week in September. Stay where you are, or at all events, do not dream of joining me. . . . Colonel Daw is sitting on the piazza looking rather ferocious. I have not seen Marjorie since I parted with her in the garden.

## XII

EDWARD DELANEY TO THOMAS DILLON, M.D., MADISON SQUARE, N. Y.

AUGUST 30, ——.

MY DEAR DOCTOR—If you have any influence over Flemming, I beg of you to exert it to prevent his coming to this place at present. There are circumstances, which I will explain to you before long, that make it of the first importance that he should not come into this neighborhood. His appearance here, I speak advisedly, would be disastrous to him. In urging him to remain in New York, or to go to some inland resort, you will be doing him and me a real service. Of course you will not mention my name in this connection. You know me well enough, my dear doctor, to be assured that, in begging your secret co-operation, I have reasons that will meet your entire approval when they are made plain to you. My father, I am glad to state, has so greatly improved that he can no longer be regarded as an invalid. With great esteem, I am, &c. &c.

## XIII

### EDWARD DELANEY TO JOHN FLEMMING

AUGUST 30, ——.

Your letter announcing your mad determination to come here has just reached me. I beg of you to reflect a moment. The step would be fatal to your interests and hers. You would furnish just cause for irritation to R. W. D.; and, though he loves Marjorie tenderly, he is capable of going to any lengths if opposed. You would not like, I am convinced, to be the means of causing him to treat *her* with severity. That would be the result of your presence at The Pines at this juncture. Wait and see what happens. Moreover, I understand from Dillon that you are in no condition to take so long a journey. He thinks the air of the coast would be the worst thing possible for you; that you ought to go inland, if anywhere. Be advised by me. Be advised by Dillon.

## XIV

### TELEGRAMS

SEPTEMBER 1, ——.

#### 1. TO EDWARD DELANEY

*Letter received. Dillon be hanged. I think I ought to be on the ground.*                  J. F.

#### 2. TO JOHN FLEMMING

*Stay where you are. You would only complicate matters. Do not move until you hear from me.*                  E. D.

#### 3. TO EDWARD DELANEY

*My being at The Pines could be kept secret. I must see her.*                  J. F.

### 4. To John Flemming

*Do not think of it. It would be useless. R. W. D. has locked M. in her room. You would not be able to effect an interview.* **E. D.**

### 5. To Edward Delaney

*Locked in her room! That settles the question. I shall leave by the 12:15 express.* **J. F.**

On the 2nd of September, 187–, as the down express due at 3.40 left the station at Hampton, a young man, leaning on the shoulder of a servant whom he addressed as Watkins, stepped from the platform into a hack, and requested to be driven to The Pines. On arriving at the gate of a modest farmhouse, a few miles from the station, the young man descended with difficulty from the carriage, and, casting a hasty glance across the road, seemed much impressed by some peculiarity in the landscape. Again leaning on the shoulder of the person Watkins, he walked to the door of the farmhouse and inquired for Mr. Edward Delaney. He was informed by the aged man who answered his knock that Mr. Edward Delaney had gone to Boston the day before, but that Mr. Jonas Delaney was within. This information did not appear satisfactory to the stranger, who inquired if Mr. Edward Delaney had left any message for Mr. John Flemming. There *was* a letter for Mr. Flemming, if he were that person. After a brief absence the aged man reappeared with a letter.

## XV

EDWARD DELANEY TO JOHN FLEMMING

SEPTEMBER 1, ——.

I am horror-stricken at what I have done! When I began this correspondence I had no other purpose than to relieve the tedium of your sick-chamber. Dillon told me to cheer you up. I tried to. I thought you entered into the spirit of the thing. I had no idea, until within a few days, that you were taking matters *au sérieux*.

What can I say? I am in sackcloth and ashes. I am a Pariah, a dog of an outcast. I tried to make a little romance to interest you, something soothing, idyllic, and, by Jove! I have done it only too well! My father doesn't know a word of this, so don't jar the old gentleman any more than you can help. I fly from the wrath to come —when you arrive! For O, dear Jack, there isn't any colonial mansion on the other side of the road, there isn't any piazza, there isn't any hammock—there isn't any Marjorie Daw!!

# THEY BROUGHT THEIR WOMEN

## WOMEN

BY EDNA FERBER

# THEY BROUGHT THEIR WOMEN

## BY EDNA FERBER

MURIEL is a name you cannot trifle with. She herself was like that. Even her husband called her Muriel. It was queer about her. Her skin was so fair, her eyes so blue, her hair held such glints that unobservant strangers, dazzled by all that pink and white and gold, failed to notice her jaw line and the set of her thin red lips. They soon learned.

All the other youngish married women of her crowd were known by nicknames, or by cozy abbreviations—Bunny, Bee, Lil, Peg. Jeff Boyd's wife, Claire, actually was known to everyone as Hank Boyd, so that her own lovely name was almost forgotten. When first she had come, a bride, to Chicago's far South Side, Jeff had declaimed, "It's just a rag, a bone, and a hank of hair—a poor thing, but mine own." Hence Hank.

Then, as now, after nine years of marriage and two children, she was a skinny little thing; enormous brown eyes in a sallow pointed face; white teeth in a rare grin; a straight bob; a béret hung precariously over one ear; her fists jammed into

Copyright, 1932, by Edna Ferber. Published by Doubleday Doran & Co., Inc.

the shapeless pockets of a leather jacket against the stiff Lake Michigan winds. She was Hank Boyd to the whole crowd of steel-mill aristocracy living in the Chicago suburb that was a magic circle of green just within sight of the searing glare of the steel-mill chimneys—those stark chimneys bristling high above the slag-tortured Illinois prairie.

Muriel never called her Hank. She addressed her as Mrs. Boyd; or—somehow, it sounded even more formal —occasionally Claire. But Hank never called her anything but Mrs. Starrett. "It —it's the long $u$," she said once, in unconvincing explanation. "Funniest thing. I've struggled with it since childhood. I think I must have been marked, prenatally. I was sixteen before I could say funeral."

"Rilly!" said Muriel Starrett.

The two women, so nearly of an age, yet so unlike, probably never would have exchanged ten words had it not been for the friendship existing between their husbands. And that was strange, for the two men were as unlike as their wives. They had been classmates—Leonard Starrett the son of a South Chicago steel millionaire—Jeff Boyd, a pseudo-Socialist, working his way through the engineering course with the help of a scholarship.

Jeff was not one of your gloomy, portentous haranguers. Gay, red-headed, loud-voiced, free, he was possessed of a genius for friendship. He

talked too much, he made execrable puns, he
ramped and roared; and was fundamentally
sound as Marx himself, and ten times as charming.

The first thing that welded the friendship between the two men was an accidental look at a
portfolio of drawings he had idly come across
while waiting in Starrett's rooms at college.
Leonard Starrett, entering hurriedly, late and
apologetic, had found a red-faced and vociferous
Boyd charging about the room, the drawings
spread on every table, chair, cushion, and shelf.

"Listen. Whose are these?"

"They're mine."

"No, no, fathead! I mean, who did them! Who
drew 'em!"

"I did."

"The hell you did!"

"Why not?"

"Say! Gosh!" He was so moved that Starrett
was a little embarrassed.

They were drawings, in charcoal and in pencil,
of steel-mill workers and their girls and their
wives and their smoke-blackened dwellings.
H u n k i e s, Bohemians, Poles, Hungarians,
Czechs, Lithuanians, Negroes. There were men,
stripped to the thighs, feeding the furnaces. You
could see the muscles, like coiled pythons, writhing under the skin; smell the sweat; feel the strain
of the eye sockets.

There were puddlers and rollers, in their shoddy store clothes and their silk shirts, their yellow snub-nosed shoes and round haircuts, the Saturday-night cigar between their teeth, standing on the street corner watching the high-heeled girls switch by. The watchers' Slavic eyes were narrower still, their lips more sensually curled. Their shoulders threatened the seams of their ridiculous clothing. There were big-hipped women in shanty doorways, a child at the breast. Through the open door a glimpse of a man sprawled asleep on a cot, in his mill clothes, his mouth open, his limbs distorted in dreadful repose.

"Holy gosh!" said Jeff Boyd again, inadequately.

Leonard Starrett explained politely. "That one I call The Boarder. Couple of rooms, family of seven, then they take in a boarder or two. Half of them work on the night shift and sleep in the beds during the day; the other half works the day shift and they use the beds at night. Neat little arrangement, what?"

"Say, listen, Len. Len, listen——"

"I call this one The Open Hearth, which isn't very bright of me because that's what it is. The big furnace where the stuff flows out white-hot. It's called the open hearth. One splash and you're burned through to the bone. It's exactly like a Doré picture of hell. I love the name of it. So cozy and homelike."

"You mean to tell me you been doing those things and never said a—— Why, say, Starrett, you've got to exhibit these, see! Exhibition of original drawings by Leonard Starrett. *Boy,* won't Prexy sit up!"

"Don't be dumb. I can't do that."

"Why can't you?"

"Can't."

"Now, listen. I don't know what I like, but I know about drawing. And you know's well as I do that these things are so good they're god-awful, so don't simper. Why, they're—they'll bust something wide open. You wait."

"I'm not simpering." He was gathering up the drawings and stacking them neatly into the portfolio. "My old man would have a stroke."

"Let him." Suddenly Jeff Boyd's high-colored boyish face grew thoughtful and almost stern. "What're you doing here, engineering, and chemistry and slop, when you can draw like that, my God!"

"Oh, these are just—amuse myself."

"Amuse, hell! This is important stuff and you know it. What's the idea—Papa'll have a stroke."

Leonard Starrett hesitated a moment. Confidences came hard to him who had known a misunderstood childhood. He even looked a little sheepish.

"Uh—well, my father's a great guy but he's one of those from-the-ground-up boys. That's the way he began, and so that's the way he wanted me to start. Summers, since I was sixteen, I used to have one month in Europe and two months in the mills. Can you beat it! That's how I began to draw. When the time came for me to start here in the scientific end I got kind of desperate and blabbed I wanted to go abroad and study.

"I showed him and my mother some sketches—these, and some others. What a row! White hair in sorrow to the grave, and all that stuff. So I agreed to come here for four years, anyway, and learn to be a good little steel official. Mother took me aside and explained that if these things ever came to light they'd let Dad down the tobaggan. I guess they might, at that. He got in early, of course, and made his pile, but he isn't one of the big shots."

Jeff Boyd lowered his head pugnaciously. "I'll tell you what. When you get through here, if your father's got enough soaked away to live on—which you damn well know he will have—and you don't go on drawing and refuse to go into the mills if they won't let you exhibit, I'll never speak to you again, so help me, for a white-livered, sniveling this-and-that."

But Leonard Starrett did not exhibit, and Jeff broke his oath, though the portfolio of drawings lay dusty and neglected through the months, through the years. For along came the war, and then along came Muriel, and then along came Junior. The big steel mills became monster mills, breathing fire and sulphur and gas over the sand dunes, over the prairie, over the lake, so that steel might be made wherewith Len and Jeff might kill the Germans and the Germans might kill Len and Jeff.

But the two came back, miraculously, whole; Leonard to his father's steel mills and to Muriel —Muriel so strong, so enveloping, so misleadingly pink and white and gold, so terrible in her possessive love. And Jeff took a job there in the South Chicago mills, for there was the post-war disillusionment, and there was Hank. And Leonard Starrett went back and forth between the roar of the steel-mill offices and the quiet of his big house facing the lake. And the boy must have this and the boy must have that and the Whatnots are coming for dinner and bridge and oh darling what a lovely bracelet you shouldn't have done it.

Jeff Boyd was known as a brilliant engineer. but too quick on the trigger, and what's this about his palling around with the Bohunks? He sounds like a Red, or something. His name came up occasionally and uneasily at board meetings.

"There's nothing red about Jeff except his hair," Leonard Starrett would say, smiling. "You pay him less than men who are worth half as much to us as he is. He doesn't ask for a raise. The Youngstown people would grab him at double the salary if he'd go."

Muriel protested, too, the sharp edge of her dislike sheathed in the velvet of loving pretense.

"Darling, I don't know what you see in that Boyd."

"That's all right, Muriel. You needn't."

"But it is important, in a way, dear, because it's kind of embarrassing for me. If you're a friend of his, and ask him here, I have to invite his wife."

"Have to invite her! Why, everybody's crazy about her. She's a wonderful girl. Jeff says she"—he broke off—"and she runs that house with one maid, sees to the kids, and keeps her job at the Welfare Station three full days a week."

"I always say, welfare begins at home. I don't think those Boyd children look any too well cared for, if you ask me."

"They're not little Lord Fauntleroys, if that's what you mean." His tone was tinged with bitterness.

"Fauntleroy. You don't think I've made a Fauntleroy of Junior, do you?"

"You'll pin a lace collar and curls on him yet."

"You're not very kind, dear. But that's because you're not well. Goodness knows I'm not the sort of wife to come between her husband and his friends. But it does seem queer for you, whose father was one of the founders of the mills—they say the Boyds often have the Hunkies in, evenings, not for welfare work, but as friends—as social equals. They had four of the mill Negroes in to sing last week. Imagine!"

"Yeah, that's terrible. We met Robeson at Alice Longworth's in Washington last year."

"Oh, well, look at her father!"

"Yes. Low character he was."

"Darling, you hurt me very much when you talk like that, so bitterly. If you were really well you wouldn't do it. You couldn't."

It was a queer thing about Leonard's health. Muriel explained that he wasn't really ill. He was delicate. Not strong. The least thing upset him. That was why she never left him. When he traveled, she traveled with him. I've left Junior many a time when it almost broke my heart. But a wife's place is with her husband. Leonard comes first.

Jeff and Hank Boyd sometimes talked of it. "He was strong as an ox at college. Crew man, and out of training could drink beer like a Munich *Vereiner*."

"It's her," said Hank, earnest and ungrammatical. "She wants him to be sick so that she can have him all to herself."

"That," he agreed thoughtfully, "and not doing what he wants. He has hated the mills for— oh, almost twenty years, I suppose. I told you about the way he can draw—or could. Well, you take twenty years of frustration, and believe me you've got enough toxic poisoning in you to put you in a wheel chair."

"Can't we do something about her?"

"They hang you for murder in Illinois."

When the plan for the Mexican business trip first came up Muriel fought it like a tigress.

"Mexico! You simply can't go. I won't hear of

it. Let them send somebody else. Why do you have to go?"

"Because we need what they've got, and because I think I can get it, and because we can't afford to overlook any bets these days and because the steel business, along with a lot of others, is, if I may coin a phrase, Mrs. Starrett, shot to hell-and-gone."

"That Boyd. Why are we taking that Boyd?"

He ignored the plural pronoun. "I'm taking Jeff because he speaks Spanish and because he knows more about manganese than any white man in North America and because he's a swell person to travel with."

"He won't be with us all the time, will he?"

"Now listen, Muriel. This is a trip you can't possibly take with me."

"But I'm going."

"It's impossible. Takes four nights and three days to get there, on the crack train. You don't know Mexico. The altitude's seventy-five hundred feet. It's in the tropics. The air's cool and the sun knocks you flat. They say it's dirtier than Italy before Mussolini, the food is terrible, you can't eat a thing, you can't drink the water, the country's full of typhoid and malaria and dysentery and lice and disease."

When she set her jaw like that he knew it was no use. "I can stand it better than you can. I'm stronger. I come of pioneer stock. If my great-grandmother could cross the country from New

England to Illinois in a covered wagon, with Indians and drought and all sorts of hardship, and if *her* great-grandmother could come over the ocean from England . . ."

He had heard all this many times. So had everyone else. Muriel was very proud of her ancestry. Her family had been "old North Side." Her marriage to Leonard Starrett, which had brought her, perforce, to dwell on the despised South Side, amounted in itself to a pioneer pilgrimage. Muriel, fortunately, was all ignorant of the fact that, among the more ribald of the younger mill office set, she was known as The Covered Wagon.

Her overweening pride of ancestry had once caused even Hank Boyd to show a rare claw. It was at a dinner at the Starretts' and Muriel had been more queenly than usual. In evening clothes Muriel looked her best and Hank her worst. Hank was the cardigan type. Muriel was all creamy shoulders and snowy bosom and dimpled back and copper-gold wave and exquisite scent and lace over flesh-colored satin. Hank, in careless and unbecoming black, looked as if she had slipped the dress over her shoulders, run a comb through her hair, and called it a costume. Which she had.

Muriel's blue eyes were fixed on Hank. There were eight at dinner—four North Siders of cerulean corpuscles; the Boyds; Muriel and Leonard. "You can't know what it means to one like myself, whose ancestors — well, I'm afraid that sounds like boasting—but I mean, when I read of all these dreadful new vulgar people crowding in, getting their names on committees, trying to push the fine old families out of their rightful place!"

"Oh, but I do know," said Hank warmly. Her voice was clear and light. "At least, I can imagine how my ancestors must have felt."

"Your an——?"

"Yes indeedy. There they were, down at the dock to welcome the *Mayflower* girlies when they stepped off the boat onto Plymouth Rock."

Muriel allowed herself a cool smile as her contribution to the shout that went up. Then, slowly, that smile stiffened into something resembling a grimace of horror, as the possible import of Hank's words was realized. She stared, frozen, at the smiling impish face, the eyes so deeply brown as to seem black, the straight black hair, the dusky tint of the bosom above the crêpe of her gown.

"You don't—mean you've got Indian blood!"

"Only about one eighth, I'm afraid. My great-great-grandpappy, they tell me, was old Mud-in-Your-Eye, or approximately that."

It got round. Perhaps Starrett himself told it, or the jovial Jeff. For days it enlivened South Side bridge tables, dinner tables, golf games, office meetings. And then she kind of stiffened and said, "You don't mean you've got Indian blood!"

Hank was a little ashamed of herself—but not much.

Leonard Starrett quietly went ahead with his preparations for the Mexican trip. So, less quietly, did Muriel. He might have uttered, simply, the truth. I don't want you. I want to be alone. Remember the man in *The Moon and Sixpence*. He did say something like this, finally, when it was too late.

"The firm won't pay your expenses, Muriel. This isn't a pleasure jaunt."

"Then I'll pay my own—if you won't pay them."

"How do I know how long I'll have to be down there! It may be a week, it may be a month. How about Junior? Planning to take him along too, I suppose."

"Mother'll move right in for as long as we need her."

"Remember the last time, when we came home from Europe? She'd darned near ruined him. Now listen, Muriel. I want to make this trip alone. I've taken a drawing room for Jeff and me from here to St. Louis, and from St. Louis on the Sunshine straight through to Mexico City. Please understand that Mexico is no tourist country, no matter what the ads say."

"I know more about it than you do," Muriel retorted. "I've been reading Gruening and Stuart Chase and Beals and all of them. I wouldn't let you go down there alone for a million dollars, with your indigestion and your colds and your——"

"Stop making an invalid of me, will you!" he shouted.

"There! You're a bundle of nerves."

"Oh——"

"What kind of clothes, I wonder. They say it's cool, evenings, and in the shade. Knitted things, I imagine, for daytime."

Defeat.

Hank Boyd, when she heard of it, flushed in deep rage—the slow, rare flush of the dark-skinned woman. "It's a rotten filthy shame, that's what it is."

"Oh, I won't let her bother me much."

"I wasn't thinking so much of you—you'll have an interesting time, no matter what. But poor Len."

"I wish you were going along, Hank."

"No, you don't, dolling. Thanks just the same. Though I've wanted all my life to see Mexico. Maybe, some day. Maybe it isn't as dazzling as they say it is. But Jeff, manganese or no manganese, find out all you can about the Indians; you know—if they're really as superb as I think they are, after the dirty deal Cortes gave them. Take a good look at the Riveras in Mexico City—and the ones at Cuernavaca, too. Find out if they pronounce Popocatepetl the way we were taught in school. Betcha dollar they don't. If you bring me home a serape I'll make you wear it to the office. Those things look terrible outside their native background. If there are any bandits or shooting, you run. I don't want no dead hero for a husband. I would relish one of those lumpy old gold Aztec necklaces, though I understand you have to tunnel a pyramid to get one. Don't touch water, except bottled . . ."

Hank and some of their friends came down to the train to bid Jeff good-bye. Two men and a girl. They were very cheerful. Muriel watched them from her drawing-room window, as at the last moment, they shouted to Jeff on the car platform.

"Good-bye dolling!" Hank called, above the noise of departure. "Remember, drink three Bacardis for me the minute you strike Mexican soil."

"Don't do anything I wouldn't do!" From one of the men. Then they all roared, as at something exquisitely witty. Then the four of them, arm in arm, began to execute a little tap dance there on the station platform, chanting meanwhile a doggerel which—Jeff explained, later—Hank had made up at the farewell cocktail party.

Tap-tap-tappity-tap.

> "If you would live a life of ease,
>   Go hunt the wary manganese,
>   The manganese so shy and eke so docile.
>   The manganese it aims to please,
>   The thing to do is just to seize
>   Upon it, be it fowl or fish or fossil.
>   The manganese . . ."

The train moved; the quartet began to recede from view. Muriel and Len, at their window, caught just a glimpse of Hank's face, the smile wiped from it. One of the men tucked his hand under Hank's arm. They turned to go. The train sped through Chicago's hideous outskirts.

"Well," said Muriel, taking off her topcoat. "She didn't seem to be very broken-hearted."

Jeff appeared in the drawing-room doorway. He had a lower in the same car. His face was wreathed in smiles.

"What a gal!" he said. "What a kid!"

"I was just saying to Leonard, you two don't seem to be much cut up at parting." Her voice was playful, her eyes cold.

"The smile that hides a br-r-reaking heart." He glanced at his wrist watch. "Well, I'm going in and feed the featyures before the stampede begins. You people coming in, or is it too early for you?"

"We had an early dinner before we left at six," Leonard said.

Muriel took off her hat, began to open a suitcase, rang the bell for the porter. She was the kind of woman who starts housekeeping instantly she sets foot on a train. "I don't eat any more meals on a diner than I can possibly help. Miserable indigestible stuff."

Jeff laughed good-naturedly. "Ever since I could afford it I've like to eat on a train. You'd think I'd be cured of it by now. I guess it comes of having watched the trains go by, when I was a kid on the farm in Ohio, with all the grand people eating at tables with flowers and lamps. I thought it must be heaven to be able to do that. I always order things you only get on trains. You know— dining-car stuff. Individual chicken pie and planked shad and those figs with cream that come in a bottle, and deep-dish blueberry tart and pork chops with candied yams. It's never as good as it sounds, but I just won't learn."

Leonard laughed. "That's the way to travel."

"Doesn't it make you sick?" Muriel asked primly.

"Sick as a dawg. That's part of traveling. You can be careful at home." He was off down the car aisle, humming.

"Where's that porter!" Muriel demanded. "If a drawing room can't get service I'd like to know what can."

By the time Jeff returned from the diner she evidently had got the porter, for the drawing room was swathed in sheets like a mortuary chamber. Shrouded coats, like angry ghosts, leaped out at you from hooks. Books were neatly stacked, bottles stood on shelves, an apple sat primly on a plate, flanked by a knife; an open suitcase over which Muriel was busy revealed almost geometric contents.

Jeff stood surveying this domestic scene. "Len, didn't you break the news to Muriel?"

She turned from her housewifely tasks. "News? What!"

Jeff grinned. "We get off this train, you know, Muriel, at St. Louis, and take another whole entirely different train for Mexico City."

"This is nothing," Len replied for her, rather wearily. "Muriel puts up sash curtains and a rubber plant when she's in a telephone booth."

Muriel bridled. "I can't help it. I'm a home woman. And I'm not ashamed of it."

"You'd have a fit at the way Hank and I travel. But boy! Do we see things!"

Muriel sniffed. "We'll see you in the morning, Jeff."

"Say, what do you mean—morning! It's only eight-thirty. Come on back in the buffet car, Len. I met a fellow in the diner name of Shields. Lives in Mexico City. Knows the whole works. He says Mateos is square enough, but the Monterey outfit is crooked as a dog's hind leg. He's with the Universal people at San Luis Potosí. Quite a guy! He wants to meet you. Good idea, too, I think. Come on back."

"Now, Leonard, dear, you're going to do nothing of the kind. Sitting there smoking and drinking till all hours. You need a good night's sleep after the week you've had. You look perfectly haggard."

During the days and nights of steady travel that followed the change of trains at St. Louis, Jeff Boyd was up and down the length of the train and in and out of it at every stop of more than thirty seconds. He talked to passengers, conductor, waiters, porters, brakemen, and loungers at railway stations. He spoke Spanish, English, and bad German, as occasion demanded.

Muriel read and sewed. The scene in the Starrett drawing room was very domestic. Muriel kept the shades down about halfway, and a sheet across the windows because of the Texas glare and dust. She read books on Mexico. The very first day out of St. Louis, she had looked up from her book with a little exclamation. Then, leaning toward Len, she had pointed a triumphant finger at a paragraph.

"Listen to this, Leonard! Listen to what Gruening says." She began to read aloud.

"The diversity between the two cultures south and north of the Rio Grande is sharply discernible in the respective status of their women. *The North American settlers brought their women.* The squaw-man was outcast. The exalted position of woman in the American ideology dates from the pioneer days of companionate hardship and effort . . . The Aztec female, on the other hand, played the part of hand-maiden to the warrior male."

She looked up, beaming. "There!"

Len looked about him, one eyebrow cocked a little, as when he was amused. "A drawing room on a limited train may be your idea of companionate hardship and effort——"

He went back to his book. It was not a book

on Mexico, but a slim little volume given him by Hank as a parting gift. Muriel had picked it up and looked at it. *Walden,* by David Henry Thoreau.

"Well, what in the world did she give you that for!"

He had wondered, too, at her choice of the plain chronicle of the man who had lived alone, in rigorous simplicity, at Walden Pond. He had opened the book, idly. He read a few pages. On page five he came to a line. Something shot straight to his heart, so that he jumped a little, as though he had been hit. Then he knew.

*The mass of men lead lives of quiet desperation.*

"You seem to be enjoying that book Mrs. Boyd gave you."

"Yes."

Every two or three hours Jeff charged in, bursting with facts valuable or fascinating or both. "That fat fellow with the fancy vest and one arm used to be the richest man in Mexico. They got him in the Revolution and did they take him for a ride! Burned down his hacienda, destroyed the crops, chopped up a couple of daughters, shot his right arm off. . . . Next time the conductor goes by get a load of him. He's Mex, named Cordoba, wears a wing collar and a plaid tie with an opal in it as big as your eye, and a gold cable watch chain from here to here with a sixteen-peso gold piece size of a dinner plate as a charm. . . . Say, Muriel, if you'll take down that Turkish harem drape at the window and look at what's going by you'll learn more about Mexico than from any book on Mexico—How to Tell the Flora from the Fauna."

At San Antonio they had had an hour and a half. The train drew in at eight. It would not leave until half-past nine.

"Come on, folks. Let's shake a leg. Get some of the train stiffness out of our bones. We can walk up into town, take a look around, and beat it back in plenty of time."

"Walk! At night! Through this district!"

Then it began in maddening futility. But what do you want to ride for, Muriel, when we've been riding for days? . . . Well, you two go and I'll just wait here. . . . No, I wouldn't do that . . . But I don't mind being here all alone at the station, really. I can just sit in the train . . . A walk will do you good . . . Jeff, you walk and Muriel and I will take a taxi . . . Good God, you can't see anything in a taxi. Besides, the idea is the walk . . . What is there to see? . . . Well, good gosh, let's not stand here arguing, or none of us will be able to go . . . Leonard, this porter says it's a good mile and a half to the main street . . . Well, what if it is? . . . Now listen, fifteen minutes wasted . . .

After the train passed the border at Laredo and they were in Mexico, Leonard put down his book to stare out of the window, denuded now of

Muriel's protecting sheet. She continued to read, placidly, while all the stark, cruel beauty of Mexico went by. The mesa; a cluster of adobe walls and huts, half-naked children, dogs, chickens, mules; cactus high as a man's head marching like an army of meager Indians across the desert; dusky women in pink petticoats and dark rebozos; swarthy men in dirty white pajamas, their unwashed powerful toes thrust into rope sandals; enormous straw sombreros, brilliant serapes flung across shoulders; white fences; crumbling Spanish churches, pale pink and white and misty gray—and always, against the sky, purple at dusk, rose at sunrise, the Sierras.

"God, it's beautiful! I didn't know Mexico was so beautiful."

"Look at them!" Jeff exclaimed. "Look, Len. Those are the peons Rivera's been painting. Some magnificent, what! Makes you realize how darn good he is, doesn't it?"

Leonard Starrett said nothing.

"My, they're dirty!" Muriel exclaimed. "That woman with the child slung in the rebozo and the jar balanced on her shoulder."

The hotel to which they went in Mexico City had been recommended because it was said to be clean and to have artesian well water. These turned out to be its only virtues. In all other respects it was like one of those fourth-rate little Paris hotels on the Left Bank in which the chambermaids run up and down the corridors on their heels, doors and windows slam, voices bellow or screech across the echoing court, and the mysterious custom of hurling what seems to be stove lids occurs every morning at five.

They could eat nothing there, though Muriel took her morning coffee and orange juice in her room. Len and Jeff breakfasted at Sanborn's, in the Avenida Madero. After three days of visiting other recommended restaurants, Muriel insisted on Sanborn's three times a day. In its American-Spanish patio hung with red velvet and bird cages she found, in all Mexico, the cleanliness, the familiar American language, and the creamed chicken, buttered beets, and apple pie to which she was accustomed.

"But this isn't Mexico," Len objected. "Might as well be eating at Childs. The other restaurants are full of people who seem healthy."

" 'When you're in Rome——' " quoted Jeff.

Muriel was adamant. "At least you're not getting malaria and typhoid. Those other places are impossible."

Jeff said she had pleasantly condensed two hackneyed sayings to the single When You Are in Rome Do As the Romans Do, and Die.

Jeff bounded off alone. He tried them all—native restaurants, open-front cafés, cantinas and pulquerias — while Len accompanied Muriel drearily to Sanborn's. Jeff took a good deal of bicarb but he ate all the fearful native dishes, the frijoles, the enchiladas, the tortillas. "Hot dog!

**333**

They burn the vitals to a cinder. Len, you got to taste *mole de guajolote*. Turkey cooked in twenty spices, any one of them guaranteed to eat a hole through asbestos." He even drank pulque. He insisted that they go with him for cocktails to a place he had discovered called Mac's Bar. He was enthusiastic about it. "Mac's an Irishman. He's lived in Mexico for forty years, without leaving it. He speaks of the United States as 'the old country.' Wait till you taste his Mac Special."

It turned out to be a dingy little vestibule of a place. Muriel said she certainly didn't think much of it. Jeff seemed a little chagrined and even bewildered. "I don't know. I guess I was wrong. I thought it was swell before. It doesn't seem like much. I guess it was just——"

They found time, during that first week, occupied though the two men were with their business, to make a short trip or two. They lunched well in the sundrenched patio of the Inn at San Ángel, once a monastery. They drifted down the Xochimilco canals and came home with armloads of violets and roses. They whirled down the dusty roads across the plains to the Pyramids at San Juan Teotihuacán.

Leonard Starrett, long silent as he looked out at the Mexican countryside unfolding before their eyes, said slowly, "It's more mysterious than Egypt."

"Egypt's finished and done. This thing's just

begun. You can feel the Indians boiling and seething underneath. Some day—bingo!"

Muriel looked about mildly. She was very careful to protect her fair skin from the straight rays of the Mexican sun. "Mysterious! Why, I was just thinking it looked a lot like the places outside of Los Angeles."

Muriel had a tiny camera, not more than four inches square. With it she took pictures of pyramids, mountains, rivers, cathedrals, and plazas. She had difficulty in pronouncing the Mexican names.

"Just call everything Ixcaxco," Jeff cheerfully advised her, "and let it go at that."

After a week Leonard came to her in some distress. "We're not getting anywhere. At least, we've just made a start. They don't do business here the way we do at home. They talk for hours. They only work about four hours a day. Jeff and I will have to be here a month, at least—maybe longer. I'd like to put you on the boat at Vera Cruz. They say it's a beautiful five-day trip. You'll land in New York, take the Century home, and we'll all be happier."

"I'm sorry my being here has made you and your friend unhappy."

"Oh, Muriel, for God's sake!"

"Please don't think I'm enjoying it. But I know what my duty is. And if you have to be here a month I'm going to look for an apartment."

"No!"

But for the next three days Jeff, stricken with dysentery, was wan and limp. That decided it. Muriel, with the aid of an agent, found an apartment in a good new building just off the magnificent Paseo de la Reforma. It was the apartment of some Americans named Sykes. He was a mining man. They were returning to the United States for three months. Mrs. Sykes showed Muriel all over the place. Very nicely furnished, and in good taste. A grand piano. There were even some good American antiques. A mahogany four-poster, a drop-leaf table, a fine old couch.

"These have been in the family for generations," Mrs. Sykes explained. "I'm very much attached to them. That's why I've never rented this apartment before, to strangers."

"I understand," Muriel said, with some hauteur. "I am a member and, in fact, an officer, of the Pioneer Daughters of Illinois."

"Oh, well, then," Mrs. Sykes said, reassured. She looked happily, pridefully, about her at her dear belongings. "You'd never know you were in Mexico, would you!"

Muriel repeated this to Leonard and to Jeff as she, in turn, showed them the apartment. You'd never know you were in Mexico.

"You certainly wouldn't," they both said; and roared with laughter.

"What's so funny about that?"

Mrs. Sykes had left her servants with Muriel. "They're very good," she had assured her. "As good as you can get—in Mexico. Jovita—the bigger one—she's rather handsome, don't you think?—is the cook. She's a—uh—I mean to say, she's a very good cook. She's used to having her own way. I wouldn't interfere with her if I were you." Then, as Muriel's eyebrows went up, "I mean, unless you're used to Indian ways—yes, she's Indian, and very proud of her ancestry— you might not understand. She does all the marketing."

"I always prefer to do my own marketing. It's the only way to get the freshest, the best. In Chicago——"

"But this isn't Chicago. Mexico is different. They wouldn't understand. Another thing. You'll find she sometimes has one or two of her children here for a day or so. They're very quiet. She has four."

"Oh, she's married!"

"No."

"Oh, I understood you to say four——"

"Jovita has four children, of four different fathers. She has never married. She does not believe in marriage. She is the finest cook in Mexico City. She used to pose for artists. She is highly respected. I wouldn't part with her for the world. I'd rather not let the apartment, really, if you——"

Muriel related this to Len and Jeff, expecting

from them masculine indignation. They seemed impressed, but not in the way she had expected. At their first dinner in the new apartment—Jeff dined with them—she saw the two men regarding Jovita, who assisted Lola in serving. The Indian girl, Jovita, bore herself magnificently. Her eyes were large and black; her skin a rich copper; her bosom deep, her shoulders superb, her hair straight, black, abundant.

"I really don't feel quite comfortable about Jovita," Muriel confided to the men, as they sat sipping their very good coffee, after dinner. "Having her here in the house, I mean."

"Well, I shouldn't think you would," Jeff agreed, with a great laugh. Muriel said, afterward, that she never realized how vulgar Jeff was, until the last two weeks. You really have to travel with people to know them.

Besides Jovita and Lola there was the Indian boy, Jesús. Muriel had objected to the name, but Mrs. Sykes had assured her that it was very common in Mexico among the Indians, and that he would be terribly offended if called by another name. The three servants were capable, quiet, and rather consistently dishonest about small things, according to American standards.

"Custom of the country," said Len. "Don't fuss about it. You're not going to live here. Take it as it comes."

"Jeff is always talking about how magnificent the Indians are, and how the race has survived in spite of everything, and how they'll rule some day. A lot he knows about it. If he can tell his precious Hank about her cousins the Indians I guess I can tell her a few things, myself."

Muriel was horrified to learn that Jovita usually slept on the floor of her little bedroom, rolled in her blanket, instead of on the very decent little cot bed provided for her. The boy, Jesús, had conceived an enormous and instant liking for Leonard. They discovered that he was in the habit of sleeping outside their bedroom door, like a faithful dog.

"I'd like to send them packing," said Muriel, again and again. "The whole dreadful kit of them. Oh, how wonderful it will be to get back to my own lovely clean house, and to Junior, and to Katy and Ellen, and a good thick steak and sweet butter and fresh cream and waffles and a big devil's food cake with fudge icing."

They had asked Jeff to share the apartment with them, but he had declined, a little embarrassment in his high-colored boyish face.

"It's mighty nice of you to want me. But I think I'll just stay on at the hotel. I kind of like to bum around the restaurants and cafés and streets. I like to see the way the people live, and talk to them. But if you'll ask me to dinner once in a while I'll certainly appreciate it."

Muriel, with her fine fair skin, her coils of copper-gold hair, her plump, firm figure, attracted attention when she went out alone. She was accustomed, at home, to walking. All her Chicago friends walked for the good of their figures. She found that she almost always was followed home by some amorous Mexican.

Her admirer used always the same tactics. He would pass and repass her. He would double on his tracks. He would appear at unexpected and impossible corners. She would think she had evaded him. She would jump hurriedly into one of the crazy little Ford taxis marked Libre. But when she reached her own flat there he would be, miraculously, lounging against the building in his bright blue suit, his feet, in their American tan shoes, negligently crossed, a cigarette between his slim brown fingers.

She complained to Leonard and Jeff about this. "Horrid creatures!"

"Hank would get a kick out of that," Jeff grinned.

"I suppose she would."

"They don't mean anything," Leonard assured her. "It's the Latin way of showing admiration."

"They frighten me, the nasty leering things."

"Try taking Jovita along as bodyguard."

"Oh, well, if that's all you care. I don't understand you lately, Leonard."

"It's the altitude," fliply.

The servants made her nervous. They were in and out of the room without a sound. She would look up from a letter she was writing to find Jovita standing there, silent, waiting.

"Goodness, how you startled me. What is it?"

Jovita spoke very little English, understood a little, thanks to the Sykeses.

Jeff came to dinner two or three times a week. He and Jovita would speak together in Spanish. Suddenly Jovita's dusky impassive face would grow vivid with a flashing smile.

Muriel didn't like it. "What are they talking about?" she demanded of Leonard.

"He's going down to Milpa Alta on business Thursday. She heard us talking and caught the name. She's telling him it's her native village, where two of her children are. She says it's very beautiful, and that there is a festival down there next week—an important festival when everyone dresses up and there are fireworks and dances and big doings. Let's all go."

"Don't be foolish, Leonard. Those festivals are childish and stupid; the sun blazes down; you can't eat the filthy food, nor drink the water. You know it as well as I do. It's a mercy Jeff has been able to take the necessary business trips into the other districts. I'm glad, now, that you brought him along. I'd never have let you take them. Never. You would have, though, if I hadn't been here. You're like a child. Really, sometimes I think you need as much looking after as Junior."

"Yes," Len said thoughtfully. "I would have taken all those trips into the country, by motor and by mule, with the hot sun beating down by day and the cold coming on at night; sleeping, perhaps, on straw mats on the floor of some pueblo hut—if it hadn't been for you."

"Well, then! And the way Jeff looked last time. Remember? Though you can't tell me that was only the hardship of the trip."

Jeff was off to Milpa Alta. If this trip proved successful they could leave at the end of the week; the last, then, of their six weeks' stay. Jeff would be gone four days.

Next morning Jovita was not there. She simply was not there. No word, no explanation. Lola and Jesús shook their heads, spread their palms in innocent denial.

"I'll tell you what I think," said Muriel, with the abrupt coarseness of the good woman. "She's gone there to be with Jeff, that's what I think."

"I hope so," said Leonard.

"What do you mean, Leonard Starrett!"

"I was just thinking."

"Thinking what?"

"I was just thinking how pleasant it would be to live for a year or two with Jovita in an old pink house, with a garden, in Cuernavaca, and paint pictures of the Indians, and of Jovita and her children, and sit in the sun, and in the evening, look at Popocatepetl and the Sleeping Woman against the sky."

"Leonard Starrett, have you gone crazy!"

"A little," said Leonard, "a little. But not enough."

# BIG BLONDE

## BY DOROTHY PARKER

# BIG BLONDE

BY DOROTHY PARKER

HAZEL MORSE was a large, fair woman of the type that incites some men when they use the word "blonde" to click their tongues and wag their heads roguishly. She prided herself upon her small feet and suffered for her vanity, boxing them in snub-toed, high-heeled slippers of the shortest bearable size. The curious things about her were her hands, strange terminations to the flabby white arms splattered with pale tan spots—long, quivering hands with deep and convex nails. She should not have disfigured them with little jewels.

She was not a woman given to recollections. At her middle thirties, her old days were a blurred and flickering sequence, an imperfect film, dealing with the actions of strangers.

In her twenties, after the deferred death of a hazy widowed mother, she had been employed as a model in a wholesale dress establishment—it was still the day of the big woman, and she was then prettily colored and erect and high-breasted. Her job was not onerous, and she met numbers of men and spent numbers of evenings with

From "Here Lies," copyright, 1930, 1933, and 1939. Used by permission of The Viking Press, Inc.

them, laughing at their jokes and telling them
she loved their neckties. Men liked her, and she
took it for granted that the liking of many men
was a desirable thing. Popularity seemed to her
to be worth all the work that had to be put into
its achievement. Men liked you because you were
fun, and when they liked you they took you out,
and there you were. So, and successfully, she
was fun. She was a good sport. Men like a
good sport.

No other form of diversion, simpler or more
complicated, drew her attention. She never pon-
dered if she might not be better occupied doing
something else. Her ideas, or, better, her accept-
ances, ran right along with those of the other
substantially built blondes in whom she found
her friends.

When she had been working in the dress establishment some years she met Herbie Morse. He
was thin, quick, attractive, with shifting lines
about his shiny, brown eyes and a habit of fiercely
biting at the skin around his finger nails. He
drank largely; she found that entertaining. Her
habitual greeting to him was an allusion to his
state of the previous night.

"Oh, what a peach you had," she used to say,
through her easy laugh. "I thought I'd die, the
way you kept asking the waiter to dance with
you."

She liked him immediately upon their meeting.
She was enormously amused at his fast, slurred

sentences, his interpolations of apt phrases from
vaudeville acts and comic strips; she thrilled at
the feel of his lean arm tucked firm beneath the
sleeve of her coat; she wanted to touch the wet,
flat surface of his hair. He was as promptly
drawn to her. They were married six weeks after
they had met.

She was delighted at the idea of being a bride;
coquetted with it, played upon it. Other offers
of marriage she had had, and not a few of them,
but it happened that they were all from stout,
serious men who had visited the dress establishment as buyers; men from Des Moines and
Houston and Chicago and, in her phrase, even
funnier places. They was always something immensely comic to her in the thought of living
elsewhere than New York. She could not regard
as serious proposals that she share a Western
residence.

She wanted to be married. She was nearing
thirty now, and she did not take the years well.
She spread and softened, and her darkening hair
turned her to inexpert dabblings with peroxide.
There were times when she had little flashes of
fear about her job. And she had had a couple of
thousand evenings of being a good sport among
her male acquaintances. She had come to be
more conscientious than spontaneous about it.

Herbie earned enough, and they took a little
apartment far uptown. There was a Mission-
furnished dining room and a hanging central

light globed in liver-colored glass; in the living room were an "overstuffed suite," a Boston fern, and a reproduction of the Henner *Magdalene* with the red hair and the blue draperies; the bedroom was in gray enamel and old rose, with Herbie's photograph on Hazel's dressing table and Hazel's likeness on Herbie's chest of drawers.

She cooked—and she was a good cook—and marketed and chatted with the delivery boys and the colored laundress. She loved the flat, she loved her life, she loved Herbie. In the first months of their marriage she gave him all the passion she was ever to know.

She had not realized how tired she was. It was a delight, a new game, a holiday, to give up being a good sport. If her head ached or her arches throbbed, she complained piteously, babyishly. If her mood was quiet, she did not talk. If tears came to her eyes, she let them fall.

She fell readily into the habit of tears during the first year of her marriage. Even in her good sport days she had been known to weep lavishly and disinterestedly on occasion. Her behavior at the theater was a standing joke. She could weep at anything in a play—tiny garments, love both unrequited and mutual, seduction, purity, faithful servitors, wedlock, the triangle.

"There goes Haze," her friends would say, watching her. "She's off again."

Wedded and relaxed, she poured tears freely.

To her who had laughed so much, crying was delicious. All sorrows became her sorrows; she was Tenderness. She would cry long and softly over newspaper accounts of kidnaped babies, deserted wives, unemployed men, strayed cats, heroic dogs. Even when the paper was no longer before her, her mind revolved upon these things and the drops slipped rhythmically over her plump cheeks.

"Honestly," she would say to Herbie, "all the sadness there is in the world when you stop to think about it!"

"Yeah," Herbie would say.

She missed nobody. The old crowd, the people who had brought her and Herbie together, dropped from their lives, lingeringly at first.

When she thought of this at all it was only to consider it fitting. This was marriage. This was peace.

But the thing was that Herbie was not amused.

For a time he had enjoyed being alone with her. He found the voluntary isolation novel and sweet. Then it palled with a ferocious suddenness. It was as if one night, sitting with her in the steam-heated living room, he would ask no more; and the next night he was through and done with the whole thing.

He became annoyed by her misty melancholies. At first, when he came home to find her softly tired and moody, he kissed her neck and patted her shoulder and begged her to tell her Herbie what was wrong. She loved that. But time slid by, and he found that there was never anything really, personally, the matter.

"Ah, for God's sake," he would say. "Crabbing again. All right, sit here and crab your head off. I'm going out."

And he would slam out of the flat and come back late and drunk.

She was completely bewildered by what happened to their marriage. First they were lovers; and then, it seemed without transition, they were enemies. She never understood it.

There were longer and longer intervals between his leaving his office and his arrival at the apartment. She went through agonies of picturing him run over and bleeding, dead and covered with a sheet. Then she lost her fears for his safety and grew sullen and wounded. When a person wanted to be with a person he came as soon as possible. She desperately wanted him to want to be with her; her own hours only marked the time till he would come. It was often nearly nine o'clock before he came home to dinner. Always he had had many drinks, and after their effect would die in him, leaving him loud and querulous and bristling for affronts.

He was too nervous, he said, to sit and do nothing for an evening. He boasted, probably not in all truth, that he had never read a book in his life.

"What am I expected to do—sit around this dump on my tail all night?" he would ask rhetorically. And again he would slam out.

She did not know what to do. She could not manage him. She could not meet him.

She fought him furiously. A terrific domesticity had come upon her, and she would bite and scratch to guard it. She wanted what she called "a nice home." She wanted a sober, tender husband, prompt at dinner, punctual at work. She wanted sweet, comforting evenings. The idea of intimacy with other men was terrible to her; the thought that Herbie might be seeking entertainment in other women set her frantic.

It seemed to her that almost everything she read—novels from the drugstore lending library, magazine stories, women's pages in the papers— dealt with wives who lost their husbands' love. She could bear those, at that, better than accounts of neat, companionable marriage and living happily ever after.

She was frightened. Several times when Herbie came home in the evening he found her determinedly dressed—she had had to alter those of her clothes that were not new, to make them fasten—and rouged.

"Let's go wild to-night, what do you say?" she would hail him. "A person's got lots time to hang around and do nothing when they're dead."

So they would go out, to chop houses and the less expensive cabarets. But it turned out badly. She could no longer find amusement in watching Herbie drink. She could not laugh at his whimsicalities, she was so tensely counting his indulgences. And she was unable to keep back her remonstrances—"Ah, come on, Herb, you've had enough, haven't you? You'll feel something terrible in the morning."

He would be immediately enraged. All right, crab; crab, crab, crab, that was all she ever did. What a lousy sport *she* was! There would be scenes, and one or the other of them would rise and stalk out in fury.

She could not recall the definite day that she started drinking herself. There was nothing separate about her days. Like drops upon a window-pane, they ran together and trickled away. She had been married six months; then a year; then three years.

She had never needed to drink, formerly. She could sit for most of a night at a table where the others were imbibing earnestly and never droop in looks or spirits, nor be bored by the doings of those about her. If she took a cocktail, it was so unusual as to cause twenty minutes or so of jocular comment. But now anguish was in her. Frequently, after a quarrel. Herbie would stay out for the night, and she could not learn from him where the time had been spent. Her heart felt tight and sore in her breast, and her mind turned like an electric fan.

She hated the taste of liquor. Gin, plain or in

mixtures, made her promptly sick. After experiment, she found that Scotch whisky was best for her. She took it without water, because that was the quickest way to its effect.

Herbie pressed it on her. He was glad to see her drink. They both felt it might restore her high spirits, and their good times together might again be possible.

"'Atta girl," he would approve her. "Let's see you get boiled, baby."

But it brought them no nearer. When she drank with him there would be a little while of gayety and then, strangely without beginning, they would be in a wild quarrel. They would wake in the morning not sure what it had all been about, foggy as to what had been said and done, but each deeply injured and bitterly resentful. There would be days of vengeful silence.

There had been a time when they had made up their quarrels, usually in bed. There would be kisses and little names and assurances of fresh starts . . . "Oh, it's going to be great now, Herb. We'll have swell times. I was a crab, I guess I might have been tired. But everything's going to be swell. You'll see."

Now there were no gentle reconciliations. They resumed friendly relations only in the brief magnanimity caused by liquor, before more liquor drew them into new battles. The scenes became more violent. There were shouted invectives and pushes, and sometimes sharp slaps.

Once she had a black eye. Herbie was horrified next day at sight of it. He did not go to work; he followed her about, suggesting remedies and heaping dark blame on himself. But after they had had a few drinks—"to pull themselves together"—she made so many wistful references to her bruise that he shouted at her, and rushed out, and was gone for two days.

Each time he left the place in rage he threatened never to come back. She did not believe him, nor did she consider separation. Somewhere in her head or her heart was the lazy, nebulous hope that things would change and she and Herbie settle suddenly into soothing married life. Here were her home, her furniture, her husband, her station. She summoned no alternatives.

She could no longer bustle and potter. She had no more vicarious tears; the hot drops she shed were for herself. She walked ceaselessly about the rooms, her thoughts running mechanically round and round Herbie. In those days began the hatred of being alone that she was never to overcome. You could be by yourself when things were all right, but when you were blue you got the howling horrors.

She commenced drinking alone, little, short drinks all through the day. It was only with Herbie that alcohol made her nervous and quick in offense. Alone, it blurred sharp things for her. She lived in a haze of it. Her life took on a dream-like quality. Nothing was astonishing.

A Mrs. Martin moved into the flat across the hall. She was a great blonde woman of forty, a promise in looks of what Mrs. Morse was to be. They made acquaintance, quickly became inseparable. Mrs. Morse spent her days in the opposite apartment. They drank together, to brace themselves after the drinks of the nights before.

She never confided her troubles about Herbie to Mrs. Martin. The subject was too bewildering to her to find comfort in talk. She let it be assumed that her husband's business kept him away. It was not regarded as important; husbands, as such, played but shadowy parts in Mrs. Martin's circle.

Mrs. Martin had no visible spouse; you were left to decide for yourself whether he was or was not dead. She had an admirer, Joe, who came to see her almost nightly. Often he brought several friends with him—"The Boys," they were called. The Boys were big, red, good-humored men, perhaps forty-five, perhaps fifty. Mrs. Morse was glad of invitations to join the parties—Herbie was scarcely ever home at night now. If he did come home, she did not visit Mrs. Martin. An evening with Herbie meant inevitably a quarrel, yet she would stay with him. There was always her thin and wordless idea, that, maybe, this night, things would begin to be all right.

The boys brought plenty of liquor along with them whenever they came to Mrs. Martin's. Drinking with them, Mrs. Morse became lively and good-natured and audacious. She was quickly popular. When she had drunk enough to cloud her most recent battle with Herbie, she was excited by their approbation. Crab, was she? Rotten sport, was she? Well, there were some that thought different.

Ed was one of The Boys. He lived in Utica—had "his own business" there, was the awed report—but he came to New York almost every week. He was married. He showed Mrs. Morse the then current photographs of Junior and Sister, and she praised them abundantly and sincerely. Soon it was accepted by the others that Ed was her particular friend.

He staked her when they all played poker; sat next her and occasionally rubbed his knee against hers during the game. She was rather lucky. Frequently she went home with a twenty-dollar bill or a ten-dollar bill or a handful of crumpled dollars. She was glad of them. Herbie was getting, in her words, something awful about money. To ask him for it brought an instant row.

"What the hell do you do with it?" he would say. "Shoot it all on Scotch?"

"I try to run this house halfway decent," she would retort. "Never thought of that, did you? Oh, no, his lordship couldn't be bothered with that."

Again, she could not find a definite day to fix the beginning of Ed's proprietorship. It became his custom to kiss her on the mouth when he

came in, as well as for farewell, and he gave her
little quick kisses of approval all through the
evening. She liked this rather more than she dis-
liked it. She never thought of his kisses when
she was not with him.

He would run his hand lingeringly over her
back and shoulders.

"Some dizzy blonde, eh?" he would say. "Some
doll."

One afternoon she came home from Mrs. Martin's to find Herbie in the bedroom. He had been
away for several nights, evidently on a prolonged drinking bout. His face was gray, his
hands jerked as if they were on wires. On the
bed were two old suitcases, packed high. Only
her photograph remained on his bureau, and
the wide doors of his closet disclosed nothing but
coat hangers.

"I'm blowing," he said. "I'm through with
the whole works. I got a job in Detroit."

She sat down on the edge of the bed. She had
drunk much the night before, and the four
Scotches she had had with Mrs. Martin had only
increased her fogginess.

"Good job?" she said.

"Oh, yeah," he said. "Looks all right."

He closed a suitcase with difficulty, swearing
at it in whispers.

"There's some dough in the bank," he said.
"The bank book's in your top drawer. You can
have the furniture and stuff."

He looked at her, and his forehead twitched.

"God damn it, I'm through, I'm telling you," he cried. "I'm through."

"All right, all right," she said. "I heard you, didn't I?"

She saw him as if he were at one end of an cañon and she at the other. Her head was beginning to ache bumpingly, and her voice had a dreary, tiresome tone. She could not have raised it.

"Like a drink before you go?" she asked.

Again he looked at her, and a corner of his mouth jerked up.

"Cockeyed again for a change, aren't you?" he said. "That's nice. Sure, get a couple of shots, will you?"

She went to the pantry, mixed him a stiff highball, poured herself a couple of inches of whisky, and drank it. Then she gave herself another portion and brought the glasses into the bedroom. He had strapped both suitcases and had put on his hat and overcoat.

He took his highball.

"Well," he said, and he gave a sudden, uncertain laugh. "Here's mud in your eye."

"Mud in your eye," she said.

They drank. He put down his glass and took up the heavy suitcase.

"Got to get a train around six," he said.

She followed him down the hall. There was a song, a song that Mrs. Martin played doggedly on the phonograph, running loudly through her mind. She had never liked the thing.

> Night and daytime,
> Always playtime.
> Ain't we got fun?

At the door he put down the bags and faced her.

"Well," he said. "Well, take care of yourself. You'll be all right, will you?"

"Oh, sure," she said.

He opened the door, then came back to her, holding out his hand.

" 'Bye, Haze," he said. "Good luck to you."

She took his hand and shook it.

"Pardon my wet glove," she said.

When the door had closed behind him she went back to the pantry.

She was flushed and lively when she went in to Mrs. Martin's that evening. The Boys were there, Ed among them. He was glad to be in town, frisky and loud and full of jokes. But she spoke quietly to him for a minute.

"Herbie blew to-day," she said. "Going to live out West."

"That so?" he said. He looked at her and played with the fountain pen clipped to his waistcoat pocket.

"Think he's gone for good, do you?" he asked.

"Yeah," she said. "I know he is. I know. Yeah."

"You going to live on across the hall just the same?" he said. "Know what you're going to do?"

"Gee, I don't know," she said. "I don't give much of a damn."

"Oh, come on, that's no way to talk," he told her. "What you need—you need a little snifter. How about it?"

"Yeah," she said. "Just straight."

She won forty-three dollars at poker. When the game broke up Ed took her back to her apartment.

"Got a little kiss for me?" he asked.

He wrapped her in his big arms and kissed her violently. She was entirely passive. He held her away and looked at her.

"Little tight, honey?" he asked anxiously. "Not going to be sick, are you?"

"Me?" she said. "I'm swell."

II

When Ed left in the morning he took her photograph with him. He said he wanted her picture to look at, up in Utica. "You can have that one on the bureau," she said.

She put Herbie's picture in a drawer, out of her sight. When she could look at it she meant to tear it up. She was fairly successful in keeping her mind from racing around him. Whisky slowed it for her. She was almost peaceful, in her mist.

# BIG BLONDE

She accepted her relationship with Ed without question or enthusiasm. When he was away she seldom thought definitely of him. He was good to her; he gave her frequent presents and a regular allowance. She was even able to save. She did not plan ahead of any day, but her wants were few, and you might as well put money in the bank as have it lying around.

When the lease of her apartment neared its end it was Ed who suggested moving. His friendship with Mrs. Martin and Joe had become strained over a dispute at poker; a feud was impending.

"Let's get the hell out of here," Ed said. "What I want you to have is a place near the Grand Central. Make it easier for me."

So she took a little flat in the Forties. A colored maid came in every day to clean and to make coffee for her—she was "through with that housekeeping stuff," she said, and Ed, twenty years married to a passionately domestic woman, admired this romantic uselessness and felt doubly a man of the world in abetting it.

The coffee was all she had until she went out to dinner, but alcohol kept her fat. Prohibition she regarded only as a basis for jokes. You could always get all you wanted. She was never noticeably drunk and seldom nearly sober. It required a larger daily allowance to keep her misty-minded. Too little, and she was achingly melancholy.

Ed brought her to Jimmy's. He was proud, with the pride of the transient who would be mistaken for a native, in his knowledge of small, recent restaurants occupying the lower floors of shabby brownstone houses; places where, upon mentioning the name of an habitué friend, might be obtained strange whisky and fresh gin in many of their ramifications. Jimmy's place was the favorite of his acquaintances.

There, through Ed, Mrs. Morse met many men and women, formed quick friendships. The men often took her out when Ed was in Utica. He was proud of her popularity.

She fell into the habit of going to Jimmy's alone when she had no engagement. She was certain to meet some people she knew, and join them. It was a club for her friends, both men and women.

The women at Jimmy's looked remarkably alike, and this was curious, for, through feuds, removals and opportunities of more profitable contracts, the personnel of the group changed constantly. Yet always the newcomers resembled those whom they replaced. They were all big women and stout, broad of shoulder and abundantly breasted, with faces thickly clothed in soft, high-colored flesh. They laughed loud and often, showing opaque and lusterless teeth like squares of crockery. There was about them the health of the big, yet a slight unwholesome suggestion of stubborn preservation. They might have been thirty-six or forty-five or anywhere between.

They composed their titles of their own first names with their husband's surnames—Mrs. Florence Miller, Mrs. Vera Riley, Mrs. Lilian Block. This gave at the same time the solidity of marriage and the glamour of freedom. Yet only one or two were actually divorced. Most of them never referred to their dimmed spouses; some, a shorter time separate, described them in terms of great biological interest. Several were mothers, each of an only child—a boy at school somewhere, or a girl being cared for by a grandmother. Often well on toward morning, there would be displays of kodak portraits and of tears.

They were comfortable women, cordial and friendly and irrepressibly matronly. Theirs was the quality of ease. Become fatalistic, especially about money matters, they were unworried. Whenever their funds dropped alarmingly, a new donor appeared; this had always happened. The aim of each was to have one man, permanently, to pay all her bills, in return for which she would have immediately given up other admirers and probably would have become exceedingly fond of him; for the affections of all of them were, by now, unexacting, tranquil, and easily arranged. This end, however, grew increasingly difficult yearly. Mrs. Morse was regarded as fortunate.

Ed had a good year, increased her allowance and gave her a sealskin coat. But she had to be careful of her moods with him. He insisted upon gayety. He would not listen to admissions of aches or weariness.

"Hey, listen," he would say, "I got worries of my own, and plenty. Nobody wants to hear other people's troubles, sweetie. What you got to do, you got to be a sport and forget it. See? Well, slip us a little smile, then, That's my girl."

She never had enough interest to quarrel with him as she had with Herbie, but she wanted the privilege of occasional sadness. It was strange. The other women she saw did not have to fight their moods. There was Mrs. Florence Miller who got regular crying jags, and the men sought only to cheer and comfort her. The others spent whole evenings in grieved recitals of worries, and ills; their escorts paid them deep sympathy. But she was instantly undesirable when she was low in spirits. Once, at Jimmy's when she could not make herself lively, Ed had walked out and left her.

"Why the hell don't you stay home and not go spoiling everybody's evening?" he had roared.

Even her slightest acquaintance seemd irritated if she were not conspicuously light-hearted.

"What's the matter with you, anyway?" they would say. "Be your age, why don't you? Have a little drink and snap out of it."

When her relationship with Ed had continued

nearly three years he moved to Florida to live.
He hated leaving her; he gave her a large check
and some shares of a sound stock, and his pale
eyes were wet when he said good-bye. She did
not miss him. He came to New York infre-
quently, perhaps two or three times a year, and
hurried directly from the train to see her. She
was always pleased to have him come and never
sorry to see him go.

Charley, an acquaintance of Ed's that she met
at Jimmy's had long admired her. He had always made opportunities of touching her and
leaning close to talk to her. He asked repeatedly
of all their friends if they had ever heard of such
a fine laugh as she had. After Ed left Charley
became the main figure in her life. She classified
him and spoke of him as "not so bad." There
was nearly a year of Charley; then she divided
her time between him and Sydney, another fre-
quenter of Jimmy's; then Charley slipped away
altogether.

Sydney was a little, brightly dressed, clever
Jew. She was perhaps nearest contentment with
him. He amused her always; her laughter was
not forced.

He admired her completely. Her softness and
size delighted him. And he thought she was
great, he often told her, because she kept gay and
lively when she was drunk.

"Once I had a gal," he said, "used to try to
throw herself out of the window every time

she got a can on. Jee-*zuss*," he added feelingly.

Then Sydney married a rich and watchful bride, and then there was Billy. No—after Sydney came Ferd, then Billy. In her haze she never recalled how men entered her life and left it. There were no surprises. She had no thrill at their advent nor woe at their departure. She seemed to be always able to attract men. There was never another as rich as Ed, but they were all generous to her, in their means.

Once she had news of Herbie. She met Mrs. Martin dining at Jimmy's, and the old friendship was vigorously renewed. The still admiring Joe, while on a business trip, had seen Herbie. He had settled in Chicago, he looked fine, he was living with some woman—seemed to be crazy about her. Mrs. Morse had been drinking vastly that day. She took the news with mild interest, as one hearing of the sex peccadilloes of some-body whose name is, after a moment's groping, familiar.

"Must be damn near seven years since I saw him," she commented. "Gee. Seven years."

More and more her days lost their individuality. She never knew dates, nor was sure of the day of the week.

"My God, was that a year ago!" she would exclaim, when an event was recalled in conversation.

She was tired so much of the time. Tired and blue. Almost everything could give her the blues.

Those old horses she saw on Sixth Avenue—
struggling and slipping along the car tracks, or
standing at the curb, their heads dropped level
with their worn knees. The tightly stored tears
would squeeze from her eyes as she teetered past
on her aching feet in the stubby, champagne-
colored slippers.

The thought of death came and stayed with
her and lent her a sort of drowsy cheer. It would
be nice, nice and restful, to be dead.

There was no settled, shocked moment when
she first thought of killing herself; it seemed to
her as if the idea had always been with her. She
pounced upon all the accounts of suicides in the
newspapers. There was an epidemic of self-kill-
ings—or maybe it was just that she searched for
the stories of them so eagerly that she found
many. To read of them roused reassurance in
her; she felt a cozy solidarity with the big company of the voluntary dead.

She slept, aided by whisky, till deep into the
afternoons, then lay abed, a bottle and glass at
her hand, until it was time to dress to go out for
dinner. She was beginning to feel toward alcohol
a little puzzled distrust, as toward an old friend
who has refused a simple favor. Whisky could
still soothe her for most of the time, but there
were sudden, inexplicable moments when the
cloud fell treacherously away from her, and she
was sawn by the sorrow and bewilderment and
nuisance of all living. She played voluptuously

with the thought of cool, sleepy retreat. She had never been troubled by religious belief, and no vision of an after-life intimidated her. She dreamed by day of never again putting on tight shoes, of never having to laugh and listen and admire, of never more being a good sport. Never.

But how would you do it? It made her sick to think of jumping from heights. She could not stand a gun. At the theater, if one of the actors drew a revolver, she crammed her fingers into her ears and could not even look at the stage until after the shot had been fired. There was no gas in her flat. She looked long at the bright blue veins in her slim wrists—a cut with a razor blade, and there you'd be. But it would hurt, hurt like hell, and there would be blood to see. Poison—something tasteless and quick and painless—was the thing. But they wouldn't sell it to you in the drug stores, because of the law.

She had few other thoughts.

There was a new man now—Art. He was short and fat and exacting and hard on her patience when he was drunk. But there had been only occasionals for some time before him, and she was glad of a little stability. Too, Art must be away for weeks at a stretch, selling silks, and that was restful. She was convincingly gay with him, though the effort shook her viciously.

"The best sport in the world," he would murmur, deep in her neck. "The best sport in the world."

One night, when he had taken her to Jimmy's, she went into the dressing room with Mrs. Florence Miller. There, while designing curly mouths on their faces with lip rouge, they compared experiences of insomnia.

"Honestly," Mrs. Morse said, "I wouldn't close an eye if I didn't go to bed full of Scotch. I lie there and toss and turn and toss and turn. Blue! Does a person get blue lying awake that way!"

"Say, listen, Hazel," Mrs. Miller said impressively, "I'm telling you I'd be awake for a year if I didn't take veronal. That stuff makes you sleep like a fool."

"Isn't it poison or something?" Mrs. Morse asked.

"Oh, you take too much and you're out for the count," said Mrs. Miller. "I just take five grains —they come in tablets. I'd be scared to fool around with it. But five grains and you cork off pretty."

"Can you get it anywhere?" Mrs. Morse felt superbly Machiavellian.

"Get all you want in Jersey," said Mrs. Miller. "They won't give it to you here without you have a doctor's prescription. Finished? We'd better go back and see what the boys are doing."

That night Art left Mrs. Morse at the door of her apartment; his mother was in town. Mrs. Morse was still sober, and it happened that there was no whisky left in her cupboard. She lay in bed, looking up at the black ceiling.

She rose early, for her, and went to New Jersey. She had never taken the tube, and did not understand it. So she went to the Pennsylvania Station and bought a railroad ticket to Newark. She thought of nothing in particular on the trip out. She looked at the uninspired hats of the women about her and gazed through the smeared window at the flat, gritty scene.

In Newark, in the first drug store she came to, she asked for a tin of talcum powder, a nail brush, and a box of veronal tablets. The powder and the brush were to make the hypnotic seem also a casual need. The clerk was entirely unconcerned. "We only keep them in bottles," he said, and wrapped up for her a little glass vial containing ten white tablets, stacked one on another.

She went to another drug store and bought a face cloth, an orangewood stick, and a bottle of veronal tablets. The clerk was also uninterested.

"Well, I guess I got enough to kill an ox," she thought, and went back to the station.

At home, she put the little vials in the drawer of her dressing table and stood looking at them with a dreamy tenderness.

"There they are, God bless them," she said, and she kissed her finger tip and touched each bottle.

# BIG BLONDE

The colored maid was busy in the living room.

"Hey, Nettie," Mrs. Morse called. "Be an angel, will you? Run around to Jimmy's and get me a quart of Scotch."

She hummed while she awaited the girl's return.

During the next few days, whisky ministered to her as tenderly as it had done when she first turned to its aid. Alone, she was soothed and vague, at Jimmy's she was the gayest of the groups. Art was delighted with her.

Then, one night, she had an appointment to meet Art at Jimmy's for an early dinner. He was to leave afterward on a business excursion, to be away for a week. Mrs. Morse had been drinking all the afternoon; while she dressed to go out she felt herself rising pleasurably from drowsiness to high spirits. But as she came out into the street the effects of the whisky deserted her completely, and she was filled with a slow, grinding wretchedness so horrible that she stood swaying on the pavement, unable for a moment to move forward. It was a gray night with spurts of mean, thin snow, and the streets shone with dark ice. As she slowly crossed Sixth Avenue consciously dragging one foot past the other, a big, scarred horse pulling a rickety express wagon crashed to his knees before her. The driver swore and screamed and lashed the beast insanely, bringing the whip back over his shoulder for every blow, while the horse struggled to get a footing on the slippery asphalt. A group gathered and watched with interest.

Art was waiting, when Mrs. Morse reached Jimmy's.

"What's the matter with you, for God's sake?" was his greeting to her.

"I saw a horse," she said. "Gee, I—a person feels sorry for horses. I—it isn't just horses. Everything's kind of terrible, isn't it? I can't help getting sunk."

"Ah, sunk, me eye," he said. "What's the idea of all the bellyaching? What have you got to be sunk about?"

"I can't help it," she said.

"Ah, help it, me eye," he said. "Pull yourself together, will you? Come on and sit down, and take that face off you."

She drank industriously and she tried hard, but she could not overcome her melancholy. Others joined them and commented on her gloom, and she could do no more for them than smile weakly. She made little dabs at her eyes with her handkerchief, trying to time her movements so they would be unnoticed, but several times Art caught her and scowled and shifted impatiently in his chair.

When it was time for him to go to his train she said she would leave, too, and go home.

"And not a bad idea, either," he said. "See if you can't sleep yourself out of it. I'll see you

Thursday. For God's sake, try and cheer up by then, will you?"

"Yeah," she said. "I will."

In her bedroom she undressed with a tense speed wholly unlike her usual slow uncertainty. She put on her nightgown, took off her hair net, and passed the comb quickly through her dry, varicolored hair. Then she took the two little vials from the drawer and carried them into the bathroom. The splintering misery had gone from her, and she felt the quick excitement of one who is about to receive an anticipated gift.

She uncorked the vials, filled a glass with water, and stood before the mirror, a tablet between her fingers. Suddenly she bowed graciously to her reflection and raised the glass to it.

"Well, here's mud in your eye," she said.

The tablets were unpleasant to take, dry and powdery and sticking obstinately halfway down her throat. It took her a long time to swallow all twenty of them. She stood watching her reflection with deep, impersonal interest, studying the movements of the gulping throat. Once more she spoke aloud to it.

"For God's sake, try and cheer up by Thursday, will you?" she said. "Well, you know what he can do. He and the whole lot of them."

She had no idea how quickly to expect effect from the veronal. When she had taken the last tablet she stood uncertainly, wondering, still with a courteous, vicarious interest, if death would strike her down then and there. She felt in no way strange, save for a slight stirring of sickness from the effort of swallowing the tablets, nor did her reflected face look at all different. It would not be immediate, then; it might even take an hour or so.

She stretched her arms high and gave a vast yawn.

"Guess I'll go to bed," she said. "Gee, I'm nearly dead."

That struck her as comic, and she turned out the bathroom light and went in and laid herself down in her bed, chuckling softly all the time.

"Gee. I'm nearly dead," she quoted. "That's a hot one!"

## III

Nettie, the colored maid, came in late the next afternoon to clean the apartment and found Mrs. Morse in her bed. But then, that was not unusual. Usually, though, the sounds of cleaning waked her, and she did not like to wake up. Nettie, an agreeable girl, had learned to move softly about her work.

But when she had done the living room and stolen in to tidy the little square bedroom, she could not avoid a tiny clatter as she arranged the objects on the dressing table. Instinctively she glanced over her shoulder at the sleeper, and without warning a sickly uneasiness crept over

374

her. She came to the bed and stared down at the woman lying there.

Mrs. Morse lay on her back, one flabby white arm flung up, the wrist against her forehead. Her stiff hair hung untenderly along her face. The bed covers were pushed down, exposing a deep square of soft neck and a pink nightgown, its fabric worn uneven by many launderings; her great breasts, freed from their tight confiner, sagged beneath her armpits. Now and then she made knotted, snoring sounds, and from the corner of her opened mouth to the blurred turn of her jaw ran a lane of crusted spittle.

"Mis' Morse," Nettie called. "Oh, Mis' Morse! It's terrible late."

Mrs. Morse made no move.

"Mis' Morse," said Nettie. "Look, Mis' Morse. How'm I goin' get this bed made?"

Panic sprang upon the girl. She shook the woman's hot shoulder.

"Ah, wake up, will yuh?" she whined. "Ah, please wake up."

Suddenly the girl turned and ran out in the hall to the elevator door, keeping her thumb firm on the black, shiny button until the elderly car and its Negro attendant stood before her. She poured a jumble of words over the boy and led him back to the apartment. He tiptoed creakingly in to the bedside; first gingerly, then so lustily that he left marks in the soft flesh, he prodded the unconscious woman.

"Hey, there!" he cried, and listened intently, as for an echo.

"Jeez. Out like a light," he commented.

At his interest in the spectacle, Nettie's panic left her. Importance was big in both of them. They talked in quick, unfinished whispers, and it was the boy's suggestion that he fetch the young doctor who lived on the ground floor. Nettie hurried along with him. They looked forward to the limelit moment of breaking their news of something untoward, something pleasurably unpleasant. Mrs. Morse had become the medium of drama. With no ill wish to her, they hoped that her state was serious, that she would not let them down by being awake and normal on their return. A little fear of this determined them to make the most, to the doctor, of her present condition. "Matter of life and death" returned to Nettie from her thin store of reading. She considered startling the doctor with the phrase.

The doctor was in and none too pleased at interruption. He wore a yellow and blue striped dressing gown, and he was lying on his sofa, laughing, with a dark girl, her face scaly with inexpensive powder, who perched on the arm. Half-emptied highball glasses stood beside them, and her coat and hat were neatly hung up with the comfortable implication of a long stay.

Always something, the doctor grumbled. Couldn't let anybody alone after a hard day. But he put some bottles and instruments into a case,

changed his dressing gown for his coat, and
started out with the Negroes.

"Snap it up there, big boy," the girl called
after him. "Don't be all night."

The doctor strode loudly into Mrs. Morse's
flat and on to the bedroom, Nettie and the boy
right behind him. Mrs. Morse had not moved;
her sleep was as deep, but soundless, now. The
doctor looked sharply at her, then plunged his
thumbs into the lidded pits above her eyeballs
and threw his weight upon them. A high, sick-
ened cry broke from Nettie.

"Look like he tryin' to push her right on
th'ough the bed," said the boy. He chuckled.

Mrs. Morse gave no sign under the pressure.
Abruptly the doctor abandoned it, and with one
quick movement swept the covers down to the
foot of the bed. With another he flung her nightgown back and lifted the thick, white legs, cross-
hatched with blocks of tiny, iris-colored veins.
He pinched them repeatedly, with long, cruel
nips, back of the knees. She did not awaken.

"What's she been drinking?" he asked Nettie,
over his shoulder.

With the certain celerity of one who knows
just where to lay hands on a thing, Nettie went
into the bathroom, bound for the cupboard where
Mrs. Morse kept her whisky. But she stopped
at the sight of the two vials, with their red and
white labels, lying before the mirror. She brought
them to the doctor.

"Oh, for the Lord Almighty's sweet sake!" he said. He dropped Mrs. Morse's limp legs and pushed them impatiently across the bed. "What did she want to go taking that tripe for? Rotten yellow trick, that's what a thing like that is. Now we'll have to pump her out, and all that stuff. Nuisance, a thing like that is; that's what it amounts to. Here, George, take me down in the elevator. You wait here, maid. She won't do anything."

"She won't die on me, will she?" cried Nettie.

"No," said the doctor. "God, no. You couldn't kill her with an ax."

## IV

After two days Mrs. Morse came back to consciousness, dazed at first, then with a comprehension that brought with it the slow, saturating wretchedness.

"Oh, Lord, oh, Lord," she moaned, and tears for herself and for life striped her cheeks.

Nettie came in at the sound. For two days she had done the ugly, incessant tasks in the nursing of the unconscious, for two nights she had caught broken bits of sleep on the living room couch. She looked coldly at the big, blown woman in the bed.

"What you been tryin' to do, Mis' Morse?" she said. "What kine o' work is that, takin' all that stuff?"

"Oh, Lord," moaned Mrs. Morse again, and she tried to cover her eyes with her arms. But the joints felt stiff and brittle, and she cried out at their ache.

"Tha's no way to ack, takin' them pills," said Nettie. "You can thank you' stars you heah at all. How you feel now?"

"Oh, I feel great," said Mrs. Morse. "Swell, I feel."

Her hot, painful tears fell as if they would never stop.

"Tha's no way to take on, cryin' like that," Nettie said. "After what you done. The doctor, he says he could have you arrested, doin' a thing like that. He was fit to be tied, here."

"Why couldn't he let me alone?" wailed Mrs. Morse. "Why the hell couldn't he have?"

"That's terr'ble, Mis' Morse, swearin' an' talkin' like that," said Nettie, "after what people done for you. Here I ain't had no sleep at all, an' I had to give up goin' out to my other ladies!"

"Oh, I'm sorry, Nettie," she said. "You're a peach. I'm sorry I've given you so much trouble. I couldn't help it. I just got sunk. Didn't you ever feel like doing it? When everything looks just lousy to you?"

"I wouldn't think o' no such thing," declared Nettie. "You got to cheer up. Tha's what you got to do. Everybody's got their troubles."

"Yeah," said Mrs. Morse. "I know."

"Come a pretty picture card for you," Nettie said. "Maybe that will cheer you up."

She handed Mrs. Morse a post card. Mrs. Morse had to cover one eye with her hand, in order to read the message; her eyes were not yet focusing correctly.

It was from Art. On the back of a view of the Detroit Athletic Club he had written:

Greetings and salutations. Hope you have lost that gloom. Cheer up and don't take any rubber nickels. See you on Thursday.

She dropped the card to the floor. Misery crushed her as if she were between great smooth stones. There passed before her a slow, slow pageant of days spent lying in her flat, of evenings at Jimmy's being a good sport, making herself laugh and coo at Art and other Arts; she saw a long parade of weary horses and shivering beggars and all beaten, driven, stumbling things. Her feet throbbed as if she had crammed them into the stubby champagne-colored slippers. Her heart seemed to swell and fester.

"Nettie," she cried, "for heaven's sake, pour me a drink, will you?"

The maid looked doubtful

"Now you know, Mis' Morse," she said, "you been near daid. I don' know if the doctor he let you drink nothin' yet."

"Oh, never mind him," she said. "You get me one and bring in the bottle. Take one yourself."

380

"Well," said Nettie.

She poured them each a drink, deferentially leaving hers in the bathroom to be taken in solitude, and brought Mrs. Morse's glass in to her.

Mrs. Morse looked into the liquor and shuddered back from its odor. Maybe it would help. Maybe, when you had been knocked cold for a few days, your very first drink would give you a lift. Maybe whisky would be her friend again. She prayed without addressing a God, without knowing a God. Oh, please, please, let her be able to get drunk, please keep her always drunk.

She lifted the glass.

"Thanks, Nettie," she said. "Here's mud in your eye."

The maid giggled. "Tha's the way, Mis' Morse," she said. "You cheer up, now."

"Yeah," said Mrs. Morse. "Sure."